D0043488

continued . . .

"Entertaining and well-written. The pace is very fast and the mystery is particularly rewarding." —*Roundtable Reviews*

"A fine turn-of-the-twentieth-century historical."
—*Library Journal*

MURDER ON MARBLE ROW

"Cleverly plotted . . . provides abundant fair play and plenty of convincing period detail. This light, quick read engages the readers' emotions." —*Publishers Weekly*

"Engaging characters . . . an enjoyable read."
—Margaret Frazer, author of *The Traitor's Tale*

"Victoria Thompson has a knack for putting the reader inside her character's heads, and her detailed descriptions of New York at the turn of the century bring the setting vividly to life." —Kate Kingsbury, author of *Slay Bells*

MURDER ON MULBERRY BEND

"An exciting intrigue of murder, deception, and bigotry. *Gangs of New York* eat your heart out—this book is the real thing." —*Mystery Scene*

"A thrilling, informative, challenging mystery."
—*The Drood Review of Mystery*

"There are few mysteries set back in history that I enjoy reading. This mystery series is one of those. The characters and settings are so real . . . I highly recommend this book and series." —*The Best Reviews*

Gaslight Mysteries by Victoria Thompson

MURDER IN LITTLE ITALY

A Gaslight Mystery

Victoria Thompson

BERKLEY PRIME CRIME, NEW YORK

THE BERKLEY PUBLISHING GROUP
Published by the Penguin Group
Penguin Group (USA) Inc.
375 Hudson Street, New York, New York 10014, USA

Penguin Group (Canada), 90 Eglinton Avenue East, Suite 700, Toronto, Ontario M4P 2Y3, Canada
(a division of Pearson Penguin Canada Inc.)
Penguin Books Ltd., 80 Strand, London WC2R 0RL, England
Penguin Group Ireland, 25 St. Stephen's Green, Dublin 2, Ireland (a division of Penguin Books Ltd.)
Penguin Group (Australia), 250 Camberwell Road, Camberwell, Victoria 3124, Australia
(a division of Pearson Australia Group Pty. Ltd.)
Penguin Books India Pvt. Ltd., 11 Community Centre, Panchsheel Park, New Delhi—110 017, India
Penguin Group (NZ), 67 Apollo Drive, Rosedale, North Shore 0745, Auckland, New Zealand
(a division of Pearson New Zealand Ltd.)
Penguin Books (South Africa) (Pty.) Ltd., 24 Sturdee Avenue, Rosebank, Johannesburg 2196,
South Africa

Penguin Books Ltd., Registered Offices: 80 Strand, London WC2R 0RL, England

This is a work of fiction. Names, characters, places, and incidents either are the product of the author's imagination or are used fictitiously, and any resemblance to actual persons, living or dead, business establishments, events, or locales is entirely coincidental. The publisher does not have any control over and does not assume any responsibility for author or third-party websites or their content.

MURDER IN LITTLE ITALY

A Berkley Prime Crime Book / published by arrangement with the author

PRINTING HISTORY
Berkley Prime Crime hardcover edition / June 2006
Berkley Prime Crime mass-market edition / June 2007

Copyright © 2006 by Victoria Thompson.
The Edgar® name is a registered service mark of the Mystery Writers of America, Inc.
Cover art by Karen Chandler.
Cover design by Rita Frangie.

ISBN: 978-0-425-21606-4

BERKLEY® PRIME CRIME
Berkley Prime Crime Books are published by The Berkley Publishing Group,
a division of Penguin Group (USA) Inc.,
375 Hudson Street, New York, New York 10014.
The name BERKLEY PRIME CRIME and the BERKLEY PRIME CRIME design
are trademarks belonging to Penguin Group (USA) Inc.

PRINTED IN THE UNITED STATES OF AMERICA

10 9 8 7 6 5 4 3 2 1

With love to all my Italian relatives,
living in this world and the next.
Thanks for giving me such an interesting and
delightful heritage!

I

Sarah Brandt was just clearing away the luncheon dishes when she heard someone ringing her front doorbell. She felt a small stab of disappointment, and when she looked down at the little girl helping her carry dishes to the sink, she saw that disappointment mirrored in her brown eyes. They'd both been looking forward to a quiet afternoon playing with baby dolls, but now a real baby's arrival was probably going to ruin those plans.

"Should I get it, Mrs. Brandt?" Maeve asked. Maeve worked as a nursemaid for the child Sarah had begun to think of as her daughter.

"No, I'll go. You two can finish up here," she said, taking off her apron. Sarah smiled down at little Aggie, who made a disgusted face. She knew a knock at the door most often meant Sarah had to go off to help deliver someone's baby.

Aggie didn't like it, but she also couldn't stop Sarah from going. Sarah had explained many times that it was how she earned her living and paid for their food and clothes and home.

Sarah dropped a kiss on Aggie's silken head and then hurried to answer the persistent ringing of the bell. As she'd suspected, a young man stood at the door, looking anxious.

"Mrs. Brandt, can you come? The baby, he's coming soon."

"Mr. Ruocco, isn't it?" Sarah asked, recognizing him as one of the three handsome brothers she remembered. "From Mama's Restaurant."

"Yes, that's right," he confirmed. Mama's was one of the most popular restaurants in Little Italy. Sarah had enjoyed many fine meals there. "I'm Joe. Can you come? Right away?"

"Of course. I'll just need a few minutes to get ready. Please, have a seat," she offered, inviting him into the front room that served as her office.

He didn't sit down, though. They never did. Instead he stood shifting his weight from one foot to the other, restlessly, as if his constant motion would hurry her along. With practiced ease, Sarah checked her medical bag—the one that had belonged to her late husband, Dr. Tom—to make sure all her necessary supplies were packed. Then she went and changed into her working clothes, the dark skirt and jacket that didn't show the stains. Mr. Ruocco helped her with her cape and offered to carry her bag for her.

When Sarah called out that she was leaving, Aggie came running for a good-bye kiss and to give Sarah another pout, just to let her know how much she'd be missed. Even after she and Mr. Ruocco had made their exit, Aggie ran to the front window and pressed her nose against the glass to give Sarah one last wave.

Sarah waved back, her heart so full of love she thought it might burst. Aggie had brought so much joy into her life since she'd found her several months ago at the Prodigal Son Mission on Mulberry Street. Still, Sarah couldn't help worrying. The child had only spoken twice since the day she'd turned up on the mission doorstep. The first time was to call out a warning to save Sarah's life, and the other was when Sarah had overheard her telling young Brian Malloy that her real name was Catherine. Aggie must have thought that was safe to do, since Brian was deaf. Sarah hadn't yet had the courage to admit she knew Aggie's secret. She'd been hoping Aggie would choose to speak on her own before she had to do so, but she was beginning to think that wouldn't happen.

Mr. Ruocco set a brisk pace, and Sarah had to ask him to slow down a bit to accommodate her.

He apologized profusely. "It's just that Mama said to hurry."

"Is it your wife having the baby?" Sarah asked. "Isn't her name Maria?"

"Yes, Maria, but no, she is not the one. It's Antonio . . . *his* wife."

"Antonio?" she echoed in surprise. She'd thought him just a boy, too young to be married already and now with a baby on the way. "Isn't he the youngest?"

"No, Valentina is the youngest. 'Tonio is the youngest boy, though."

"Oh, yes." She'd forgotten about the girl. Valentina didn't spend much time in the restaurant. The Italians kept a close watch on their daughters.

They'd come to the corner, so they had no more opportunity for conversation as Mr. Ruocco helped her dodge horses and wagons and piles of manure in the death-defying process of crossing the street to arrive safely at the other side. Each intersection provided the same challenge, and with Mr. Ruocco practically running in between each one, Sarah learned nothing new about the family or their situation.

At last they saw the weathered red awning that shaded the front of Mama's Restaurant on Hester Street. Because it was too late for lunch and too early for dinner, no hungry customers stood in line, waiting for a table. Instead, the other two Ruocco brothers sat forlornly on the stoop, smoking cigarettes and looking as useless as men usually did when a woman was giving birth.

"This must be the proud papa," Sarah guessed, smiling at the younger man.

They both jumped to their feet, and Sarah saw she'd been right in remembering Antonio as little more than a boy. He couldn't be twenty yet, and the expression in his eyes was pure terror. "You're the midwife?" he asked almost desperately.

"That's right, and I'm sure everything will be fine," Sarah assured him.

"It's too soon. The baby is coming too soon," he informed her.

She glanced at Joe, wondering why he hadn't mentioned this to her, but he avoided her gaze. "Get out of the way, so she can go inside and get to work," Joe said gruffly, and the two men parted instantly to make way.

Sarah noted as she passed that the other brother also looked worried, even if he wasn't as terrified as Antonio.

"Mama!" Joe called as they entered. "Mrs. Brandt is here!"

The dining room was deserted except for two old men in the corner, drinking grappa and arguing. The checked tablecloths had been swept off and straightened from the lunch service and readied for the evening meals that would be served here. In the afternoon sunlight, the room looked like something from the Old World, with its plaster columns where ivy climbed and draped along the ceiling, and the paintings of the beautiful hills of Italy.

Joe turned to Sarah. "Come, I'll take you upstairs."

Like many business owners, the Ruocco family lived above their restaurant. As Joe led her toward the back of the dining room, a small woman burst through the kitchen door and came bustling toward them.

"*Grazie*, Mrs. Brandt," she said, drying her hands on her apron as she came. "You are good to come so quick." Patrizia Ruocco was a legend in Little Italy. Fifteen years ago she'd come to America with her three small boys, not speaking a word of English, and against all odds, she'd built a successful business. "You, Giuseppe, go with your brothers," she said, waving a hand at Joe as if he were a pesky fly. "Give me bag," she added, taking Sarah's medical bag from him before he turned to go. He seemed almost grateful to escape.

"Upstairs, please," Mrs. Ruocco said, leading the way to a door in the corner of the room. Patrizia Ruocco stood less than five feet tall, but hard work had made her strong. She carried Sarah's medical bag as if it were filled with feathers, and she climbed the stairs without even losing her breath. Once her hair had been jet black and probably her best feature, but now it was streaked with gray. Her body was rounded and womanly—still firm even in middle age—but oddly, she gave no impression of softness. Perhaps it was her dark eyes, which seemed as if they could cut right into a person's soul.

The stairs were narrow and twisted around, designed to take up as little space as possible in the house. Two flights up, Mrs. Ruocco opened another door into a hallway. Sarah could see that several bedrooms with neatly made beds and spotlessly scrubbed floors opened onto it. She could also hear moaning.

Mrs. Ruocco stopped and turned back to face Sarah. "The baby, he come too soon," she told Sarah gravely. "This Irish trash . . ." She caught herself, and her face tightened as she tried to control a fierce anger. "This Irish *girl* Antonio bring to us," she continued deliberately, "she is dropping my grandson too soon."

"How much too soon?" Sarah asked, remembering her rash promise to Antonio that everything would be fine.

"They are married only . . . not six months," Mrs. Ruocco said, the admission a vile taste in her mouth. "The baby was started before they marry, but not long before. A month, maybe two."

Sarah nodded. A month, or even a few weeks, could make such a difference—the difference between life and death for the infant. She'd know when she talked to the mother if they had those weeks or not. "Sometimes babies who are only a couple of weeks early don't live," Sarah warned her. "If this one is two whole months early—"

"I will do anything for the baby to live," Mrs. Ruocco told her fiercely. "I will pay anything you ask. I want my grandson."

If force of will could give the baby life, this one would

live to be a hundred. "I'll do the best I can, but God is the one who decides these things, not me," Sarah reminded her.

"He better decide my grandson lives," Mrs. Ruocco hissed before turning and leading Sarah down the hall.

As they approached the last door on the right, the moaning grew louder and a female voice cried out. "It's coming again! Mary, Mother of God, make it stop!" The last word ended in a shriek of agony.

Mrs. Ruocco set Sarah's bag on a chair just inside the door and hurried over to the bed where a girl even younger than Antonio lay, wailing like a banshee. Before Sarah could guess what she had in mind, Mrs. Ruocco drew back her hand and slapped the girl soundly across the face.

The wail ceased instantly, and the girl gaped at her in shock, holding a hand to her burning cheek.

"Stop screaming," Mrs. Ruocco ordered her. "You disturb your husband."

The girl blinked stupidly, but she didn't utter another sound.

Mrs. Ruocco turned to the other woman in the room, whom Sarah hadn't yet noticed. She recognized her as Maria Ruocco, Joe's wife.

"Mrs. Brandt, she here," Mrs. Ruocco told Maria. "Do what she say. If she need anything, get."

"Yes, Mama," Maria replied calmly. If the sight of her mother-in-law slapping her sister-in-law had alarmed her, she gave no indication.

Mrs. Ruocco turned back to Sarah, who still stood transfixed in the doorway. "If you must choose, save baby."

The girl on the bed gasped but quickly covered her mouth

when Mrs. Ruocco turned that razor-sharp gaze toward her again. Satisfied the girl was adequately intimidated, she nodded and took her leave, ushering Sarah into the room and closing the door behind her.

Sarah took a deep breath and somehow managed a smile she hoped was reassuring. "I'm Sarah Brandt," she told the girl. "What's your name?"

"Nainsi O'Hara," she replied in a whisper, then quickly shook her head. "I mean Ruocco. Nainsi Ruocco."

Irish trash, Mrs. Ruocco had called her. She was certainly Irish, with her reddish hair and smattering of freckles. She was probably pretty under better circumstances, and Sarah doubted she was older than fifteen.

"Well, Nainsi, can you answer a few questions for me? Honestly, because I need to know the truth so I can help you."

The girl glanced at Maria, who nodded permission. "All right," she said reluctantly, still rubbing her cheek.

"When did . . . when did your baby get started?"

Again the girl glanced at Maria, and this time a flush rose up her neck and colored the cheek that wasn't already red from the slap. "I . . . August," she said. She'd be embarrassed by that, of course, since she hadn't been married in August.

Sarah's heart sank, but she didn't allow Nainsi or Maria to see her dismay. She went to the washstand and washed her hands thoroughly in the warm water someone had recently carried up, drying them on a crisply ironed linen towel. Then she opened her medical bag and got out the pocket watch that had belonged to her late husband. She handed it to Maria.

"Would you keep track of how often the pains come? It's probably been about four or five minutes since the last one."

Maria took the watch carefully and nodded. "They are still far apart," she reported. "Maybe ten minutes."

"Thank you," Sarah said, relieved to know she'd have a little time. "Nainsi, I'd like to examine you. It's so long before your baby is due that maybe you aren't really in labor at all. Lots of women have false labor pains."

"Her water broke," Maria reported solemnly.

This time Sarah knew there was no hope. The baby would be born, no matter what. "How long ago?"

"About an hour. That's when we sent Joe for you."

"Another one's coming," Nainsi announced, holding the bulge of her stomach with both hands. "Make it stop! It hurts so much!" she cried, biting her lip against the scream that threatened.

Sarah laid her own hands over Nainsi's stomach to feel the strength of the contraction. It was strong enough to qualify as real labor, but certainly not the forceful contractions that would come later. Like most of the young girls Sarah had delivered, Nainsi didn't tolerate pain very well and lacked the self-discipline to deal with it. They were in for a long evening. The thought had no sooner formed in her mind than Sarah noticed something very interesting about Nainsi's baby.

As the contraction eased, Nainsi fell back on the bed, panting. "Don't let me die," she begged. "Please don't let me die!"

"Don't be stupid," Maria snapped. "You will not die."

"*She* said to let me die!" Nainsi whined, obviously referring to Mrs. Ruocco. "She *wants* me to die!"

"She was just reminding me of the Catholic doctrine to save the child first if a choice must be made," Sarah said to soothe her fears. "That's not going to happen to you, though, so you don't have to be afraid. Try to rest now. You'll need your strength later."

Nainsi looked skeptical, and Sarah couldn't blame her for doubting. She apparently wasn't a cherished member of the family.

Sarah began preparing the room. Someone had already covered the bed with an oilcloth and a clean sheet. Sarah ordered some hot water and more clean towels to keep Maria busy. When Maria was gone to fetch them, Sarah finished fluffing the pillows to make Nainsi more comfortable and said, "I'd like to check your stomach again, to make sure the baby is in the right position."

"How can you tell that?" the girl asked, her eyes wide.

"I can feel his head," Sarah said as she began to knead the mound of Nainsi's stomach, tracing the outline of the baby's body. "You can tell a lot of things by just feeling."

"Is it?" Nainsi asked when Sarah was finished. "Is it in the right position? I knew a lady whose baby wasn't, and they had to cut it out of her. She . . . she died." The girl shivered with dread.

"It's in the right position," Sarah assured her. "And it seems awfully big, too."

Nainsi's hands went protectively to her stomach again. "Does it? Does that mean it's too big to come out?"

"No, it should come out just fine. I mean it seems big for only seven months." In fact, it seemed big even for nine months, Sarah thought, but she didn't say it.

Nainsi was a sturdy girl, and from what Sarah could tell, she was carrying low and all around instead of straight out in front. Depending on how they carried, some women hardly looked pregnant even when they were full term. If Nainsi had lied and the baby wasn't early, perhaps it would have a chance.

"Nainsi, could your baby have gotten started earlier than August?" Sarah asked.

Nainsi looked up at her, and for the first time Sarah saw a hint that she might be more clever than she'd seemed. "It could've, but it didn't," she informed Sarah with a hint of satisfaction.

Before Sarah could ask what that meant, Nainsi's eyes widened as another contraction began, and Maria returned with an armload of towels. After that, the contractions came in earnest. Sarah gave Nainsi a towel to bite on so she wouldn't scream and draw Mrs. Ruocco's wrath again. Maria helped Sarah support the girl when the time came to start pushing, and just as the sun was setting, Sarah delivered her of a strapping baby boy.

He wasn't the biggest baby Sarah had ever delivered, but he was certainly one of the biggest. His body was rounded and padded with the fat that forms during the last month of development. His cheeks were full, his chin double, and his head was covered with coal-black hair. He let out a wail to match the one his mother had given earlier as soon as the cool air of the room touched his wet skin. So much for Sarah's fear that he wouldn't be able to breathe. That was the problem that killed so many infants born before their time. But this baby wasn't early at all.

"It's a boy," Maria said happily, showing the first real emotion Sarah had seen. She had towels ready to dry him off, and Sarah handed the baby to her.

As Maria took the baby and cradled him, Sarah couldn't help thinking she looked almost beautiful as the joy lit her face. Under ordinary circumstances, no one would consider Maria Ruocco beautiful. If anything, she was plain, her face round and nondescript. Her figure was squat and would probably run to fat later in life, just as the dark fuzz above her upper lip would eventually become a mustache. Her hair was thick and dark, but it grew low on her forehead, and she wore it parted in the middle and pulled straight back, a style that only emphasized how plain her face was.

"Is it over?" Nainsi asked weakly. So far she'd shown no interest in the baby, only relief that she was rid of it.

"Almost," Sarah said. A few minutes later, Sarah had her cleaned up and resting comfortably in a clean nightdress. "Would you like to hold your baby now?"

Nainsi frowned slightly. "I guess. I don't know much about babies."

"You'll learn," Sarah assured her.

Maria had washed the baby and wrapped him in a blanket that had obviously been purchased for his arrival. Maria had quieted him down, and he now lay peacefully in her arms, staring up at her face in fascination. As it dried, his hair had begun to curl. Sarah thought of the handsome Ruocco boys and their glistening black curls.

"You should try to nurse the baby right away," Sarah said. "It will help you recover more quickly."

Nainsi frowned again, looking askance at the bundle in Maria's arms. "Do I have to?"

"Of course you have to," Maria said sharply. "You are his mother." Even still, she surrendered the child with obvious reluctance. Perhaps she was thinking how eager she would be to nurse her own child. Sarah knew how anxious Maria had been for a baby when she'd first married Joe. That was five years ago, and she still had yet to conceive. She'd consulted with Sarah several times, and Sarah had given her every scientific and old wives' remedy she knew, but to no avail. Not for the first time, Sarah questioned the ways of the world where women like Maria were barren, and girls like Nainsi had babies they didn't want.

"I'll go tell everyone," Maria said when Nainsi had settled the baby in her arms. "It's dinner, our busiest time, but they'll want to know. I should be helping them, too, now that the baby is here."

"Let Valentina help," Nainsi said nastily. "She never does anything but sit on her skinny bottom and complain."

Maria's lips tightened, but she swallowed whatever reply she might have made. She'd probably gotten good at that with a mother-in-law like Patrizia, Sarah thought. "I will send Mama up to see the baby," she said instead, knowing that would have more effect on Nainsi than anything else she could have said.

The girl's face flamed, but Maria was gone before she could respond.

"Let me show you how to feed the baby," Sarah said to distract her.

Nainsi showed no enthusiasm for the process, but the baby's instincts prevailed and soon he was latched on and sucking vigorously. Nainsi looked down at him doubtfully. "I don't think I have any milk."

"It hasn't come in yet. That takes a few days."

"What if it doesn't, though? What if I don't have any at all?"

"You will," Sarah assured her.

"Some women don't. I've heard the old biddies talking. Can't I feed him with a bottle instead?"

"It's not very good for the baby," Sarah warned her.

"Sometimes they even get sick." And die, Sarah thought, but she didn't say it.

"*She* wouldn't like it if it got sick, would she?" Nainsi asked.

Before Sarah could think of an appropriate reply, they heard the stairway door open and the sound of footsteps hurrying down the hall. Mrs. Ruocco appeared in the doorway, and this time she was breathless.

"Maria say he is alive," she said in wonder.

"Yes, he's just fine," Sarah said.

She said something softly in Italian that might have been a prayer and crossed herself, then went the bed where Nainsi was still nursing the baby.

Someone had come along behind Patrizia, more slowly, and now he reached the doorway, too. Antonio looked no less apprehensive than he had when she'd seen him downstairs.

"You've got a healthy son," Sarah told him.

He gave no indication he'd heard her. He was staring at the girl in the bed.

Mrs. Ruocco leaned over and whipped open the blanket covering the child. He was too engrossed in suckling to even notice, but everyone else saw how Patrizia reared back in shock at the sight of the chubby, pink, obviously full-term infant.

She turned accusingly to Sarah. "He is not too early."

Sarah drew a deep breath, choosing her words carefully. "He's healthy and strong. Your grandson will live," she added, reminding the woman that that had been her wish.

Mrs. Ruocco glared down at Nainsi, who had taken a sudden maternal interest in her son. She tucked the blanket carefully back over his bare legs and actually cooed at him. Then she lifted her gaze to her mother-in-law with an odd defiance, as if to ask what she intended to do now.

Mrs. Ruocco turned to Antonio, who didn't seem to have understood the meaning of any of what had happened. She asked him something angrily in Italian, and he answered her defensively.

"What are you saying about me?" Nainsi demanded. "Talk in English so I can understand!"

If Sarah had thought Mrs. Ruocco's gaze intimidating before, it was positively murderous now. "I ask when was the first time he go under your skirt," she said between gritted teeth.

Nainsi's cheeks burned scarlet, but she looked over at Antonio. "And what did you tell her?"

"August," he said, still not certain what it meant. "You should be glad the baby isn't sick," he told his mother plaintively.

"He not sick because you not make him in August," the woman said fiercely. "And if *you* did not, who did?"

"What are you saying?" Antonio asked. "That this isn't my baby?"

"Yes, that is what I say," Mrs. Ruocco informed him.

"She's crazy!" Nainsi insisted. "You're my husband. This is your baby!"

The baby had lost his grip on Nainsi's breast, and he started to cry in protest. No one paid any attention, least of all his mother.

"Don't listen to her!" Nainsi pleaded. "She hates me because I'm Irish. She'd say anything to turn you against me!"

Sarah thought that might well be true, but in this case, she had to agree with the older woman, who was shouting at

Antonio in Italian again. He started shouting back, and they both began waving their hands to emphasize their points. Sarah couldn't understand a word, but she knew exactly what they were talking about. Mrs. Ruocco was jabbing her finger into his chest, and he was throwing his hands in the air to indicate he was as puzzled about the situation as she was.

Between the shouting and the baby wailing, no one heard Maria coming until she stepped in between the two and pushed them apart. "Stop yelling! You're making the baby cry!"

For the first time they seemed to notice it was crying. Maria gave them both a look of disgust and strode over and snatched the baby from Nainsi's limp grasp. Maria started to bounce him and make soothing sounds, but he continued to scream.

"He's hungry," Sarah said. "He won't stop until he gets something to eat."

"I'll get him something from the kitchen," Antonio offered, earning a scornful look from every woman in the room.

Mrs. Ruocco glared at Nainsi. "Feed the bastard, you whore."

Maria gasped in shock. "Mama, what are you saying?"

Her nerves fraying from the baby's cries, Sarah took him from Maria and gave him back to Nainsi, forcing her to offer him her breast again. The baby's cries ceased instantly, leaving the room in silence except for the happy sounds of suckling.

Maria was still gaping at Mrs. Ruocco. "Mama?"

"I know it," the woman said angrily. "Antonio, he just a boy. He not know what to do. She must show him."

Antonio flushed scarlet, revealing the truth of his mother's theory, and he shot Nainsi a glance that could've curdled her milk.

"She is whore," Mrs. Ruocco continued. "She try get husband and home for her bastard. She trick Antonio. She trick whole family!"

"No, Mama," Maria insisted. "You can't know that. Look at the baby. He looks just like Antonio!"

Newborn babies seldom resembled anything more closely than an elderly man who'd lost his hair and his teeth. This one did, at least, have the black curly hair of the Ruocco family, but beyond that, any resemblance would be entirely in the eye of the beholder.

"Look at baby, Maria," Mrs. Ruocco said, pointing an accusing finger. "Is he sick, like baby born too soon?"

Maria looked at the baby, her face reflecting her refusal to accept the truth. "We are lucky, Mama. God has blessed us by making him strong enough to live. That's what you wanted, isn't it?" she reminded her.

"I want my *grandson* to live," Mrs. Ruocco corrected her. "This baby, he nothing to me."

"You can't be sure," Maria argued desperately. "Mrs. Brandt, tell her! She can't know for sure!"

This was what Sarah had dreaded. If she confirmed the truth she knew, she would condemn Nainsi and her baby to abandonment and perhaps even death. A woman with a newborn would fare poorly on the streets, and few families would welcome a daughter back home after such a scandal, if Nainsi even had a family. But if Sarah lied, she would be doing an injustice to Antonio and his entire family. She thought of King Solomon with the sword, ready to cut the baby in two. If only she had his wisdom, and if only one of her choices were the right one.

"Look at her," Mrs. Ruocco said, gesturing at Sarah. "She know truth, but she cannot say. She want protect baby. Look at baby. He too big and too fat. Count to nine, Maria. Nine month was June. Antonio did not know this whore in June."

Tears stood in Maria's eyes, and she looked at Sarah, silently pleading for her to deny it. Sarah still couldn't bring herself to say the words, but she gave Maria the slightest nod.

Maria's face crumpled, and Nainsi howled in fury. "You can't believe her!" she cried to Antonio. "Mama is paying her. She'll say anything to get her money! You know this is your baby. Come and look at him, and you'll see!"

But Antonio was already shaking his head. He'd obeyed his mother all of his life, and he wasn't going to defy her now. He turned and fled the room.

"Come back here!" Nainsi shrieked hysterically. Then she turned to Mrs. Ruocco. "This is your grandson. You have to believe me! He promised!"

This time it was Maria who slapped her into silence. The baby, who had drifted off to sleep, startled and then settled down again into sweet oblivion.

"That husband of yours almost knocked me down the stairs," a new voice said a few moments later, and Sarah looked up to see a buxom Irishwoman in the doorway. Her faded orangey hair and the curve of her face made her an older version of Nainsi. "What's the fuss about, anyway?" she asked of no one in particular, seemingly unaware of the tension in the room. Then she saw the infant cradled in

Nainsi's arms. "Ah, and that would be my grandson, would it?" she asked, a smile breaking across her worn face. "What a handsome lad, and look at all that hair."

Nainsi gaped at her for a long moment and said, "Mommy." Then she burst into tears.

2

Sarah would always remember the next few minutes as a blur of angry hands gesturing and lots of incoherent shouting. Nainsi blurted out the accusations the
Ruoccos had made against her, and Mrs. O'Hara rose to her
daughter's defense, or at least her voice did. The two older
women started screaming invectives at each other in a
variety of languages while Nainsi sobbed and Maria wept
silently.

Sarah took the sleeping baby from his mother, marveling
for the thousandth time how infants could sleep through
anything. She laid him gently in the cradle that had been
lovingly prepared for him, probably by Mrs. Ruocco herself,
and wondered what would become of him. At least Nainsi
had a mother. Judging by Mrs. O'Hara's clean but well-
mended clothes and her work-roughened hands, she might

have a difficult time taking not only her daughter but the baby back into her care—but at least there was a chance they wouldn't end up on the street.

When the din had died down to a manageable level, Sarah said, "Excuse me," startling everyone into silence. When she had their full attention, she continued. "This is an unfortunate situation, I know, but Nainsi and the baby need some peace and quiet and some rest."

Mrs. Ruocco looked at the girl in disgust. "We will not bother her anymore. I want her out of my house, her and her bastard!"

"You dago cow!" Mrs. O'Hara cried. "You'd put her out five minutes after she birthed your grandchild?"

"That bastard is no my grandchild!" Mrs. Ruocco replied indignantly.

"Mrs. Ruocco," Sarah said as calmly and reasonably as she could. "Nainsi and the baby shouldn't be moved tonight. I know you're angry right now, but if anything happened to either of them, especially that innocent baby who has done nothing to deserve it, you'd regret it for the rest of your life."

Sarah wasn't sure if this were true or not, but she hoped Mrs. Ruocco would be willing to assume the finer feelings Sarah had assigned to her.

For a moment, she feared she'd misjudged her, but then Maria said, "Please, Mama. What will people think if we put her out tonight? I'll look after them until . . . until they're strong enough to go." Her voice broke on a sob, and she looked longingly down at the baby, sleeping angelically in his cradle.

Mrs. Ruocco muttered something in Italian and threw up her hands in disgust. "Do what you want, Maria, but

I do not want to see this one's face again. When Mrs. Brandt say, they must go. Both of them."

Maria's shoulders sagged with relief. "*Grazie,* Mama."

"Yeah, thanks for being so generous," Mrs. O'Hara echoed acidly. "You'll regret this, you'll see. My girl ain't no liar, and your boy don't get out of his responsibility so easy. They was married in the church, for life."

Mrs. Ruocco ignored her. "Mrs. Brandt, I am sorry you see this. It is not right. Come downstairs. You will eat before you go. I will fix you special meal."

"Oh, that really isn't necessary," Sarah said politely, longing for the peace and quiet of her own home with her own tiny family. But then her stomach growled audibly.

"You will eat," Mrs. Ruocco decreed, and left the room.

No one spoke until they heard the stairway door close behind her. Then Mrs. O'Hara turned back to Nainsi.

"You stupid cow!" she snapped. "I told you them dagos is nothing but trouble! I guess you think you can come back home with me and I'll take care of you *and* your baby."

Now that her mother-in-law was gone, Nainsi's confidence returned. She drew herself up and smoothed the covers across her lap. "Don't worry about that. I won't be needing any help from you."

"You got some other plans I don't know about?" Mrs. O'Hara scoffed.

"No, I'm staying right here," Nainsi said.

"How you figure that?" her mother asked in amazement.

"She won't throw me out. You'll see," Nainsi replied smugly.

"Stupid, stupid cow," Mrs. O'Hara lamented. "Didn't you hear a word she said?"

"I heard every word, but she didn't hear any from me.

She will, though, and then you'll see. Now I'm tired. You can go along home, Mommy, so I can get some rest."

"Who's gonna look out for you if I leave?" Mrs. O'Hara asked in disgust. "Nobody here's got any love for you."

"Maria will look after me, won't you, Maria." Nainsi seemed to take great delight in the prospect of having her sister-in-law waiting on her, although Sarah couldn't imagine Maria would treat her very kindly.

"Yes," Maria confirmed mildly. "I will take good care of her and the baby. Tomorrow, you come back when she is feeling better and the baby is awake."

"And be sure and tell Brigit I had my baby and that he's a boy," Nainsi said. "Go to her flat and leave her a note so she'll see it as soon as she gets home. I want her to tell all my friends. Don't forget!"

Mrs. O'Hara nodded absently. She didn't look happy, but she didn't argue about leaving. Sarah was sure she found the prospect of spending any more time in the Ruocco house thoroughly distasteful. She walked over to get a last look at the baby. "Sure looks like a little dago, don't he?" she remarked.

No one replied.

Mrs. O'Hara sighed. "I'll be back to see you tomorrow, girl. If you know what's good for you, you'll keep your mouth shut, and not make things any worse. I wouldn't put it past this bunch to slit your throat for you."

Nainsi just smiled serenely as she watched her mother walk away.

SARAH SLEPT POORLY THAT NIGHT. SHE KEPT THINKING about the innocent little baby and wondering what would become of him. Obviously, Nainsi couldn't hope for help from the baby's real father, or she would never have seduced Antonio into marrying her in the first place. She wasn't the first girl to have done such a thing, and she might even have gotten away with it if her baby had been small or sickly. Or even if she'd married a man with no mother to catch her out and expose her lie. But she hadn't, and now she was going to have to suffer for failing to plan more carefully.

Finally giving up on sleep, she got out of bed before dawn and made herself some breakfast. Maeve and Aggie were still sleeping soundly. Sarah decided she'd make her usual follow-up visit to the new mother first thing and then be back in time to enjoy the whole morning with the girls.

Hunched against the morning chill, Sarah made her way over to Little Italy. In earlier times, she would have taken a Hansom cab, but now she had to economize to provide for her new family. Even at this early hour, the streets and sidewalks were alive with traffic as people went to work or to shop. Housewives bartered with pushcart vendors over the price of their wares while draymen shouted at their horses as they fought their way through the crowded streets to deliver their loads.

Mama's Restaurant wasn't open yet, but the family would already be up and about, shopping for fresh vegetables at the market and making the noodles and sauce they would serve later. Sarah hoped Nainsi and the baby had rested better than she had, and she wondered how long she could delay Nainsi's departure from the Ruoccos' home.

The front door of the restaurant was locked, so Sarah knocked. She could hear movement inside, and soon Lorenzo, the middle brother, opened the door. He held a broom in one hand, and for a moment he didn't recognize her.

"I'm here to see Nainsi and the baby," Sarah said, knowing he wouldn't be happy at the reminder of the family crisis.

"Oh, yes, please come in," he said, stepping aside. He wasn't quite as appealing as his brothers, she noticed. Joe had the winning smile and charming manner. Antonio was boyish and sweet. This brother was too mature to be boyish and too serious to be charming. Or maybe he simply wasn't very happy that she was here.

He'd just closed the door behind her when they heard a scream. It was the first in a series that continued, scream after scream after scream, as he raced to the stairway door, Sarah at his heels. Someone else was behind her, but she didn't stop to see who. Fighting her skirts on the narrow staircase, she nearly fell more than once. Gratefully, she flung herself through the open door on the third floor through which Lorenzo had disappeared.

Just as she'd feared, the screams were coming from Nainsi's room. Lorenzo reached the doorway first, but he stopped dead. Sarah tried to see what was going on, and when he wouldn't move, she shoved him aside and pushed her way in.

The screams were coming from a slender young girl who stood just inside the door, paralyzed by what she saw on the bed. She just kept screaming and screaming with each new breath until Sarah took her by the shoulders and turned her around, shoving her into Lorenzo Ruocco's arms.

"Valentina!" he cried, wrapping his arms around her. "What is it?"

She made a strangled sound and began to sob.

Meanwhile, Sarah had seen the reason for her terror. Nainsi lay still on the bed, her eyes open wide and unseeing, her face a ghastly gray. Sarah knew before she even touched her that she was cold and a long time dead. Still, she checked her pulse just to make sure. The body was already beginning to stiffen.

"Is she . . . dead?" Maria asked, peering wide-eyed around her brother-in-law's shoulder.

"I'm afraid so," Sarah said.

Valentina smothered another anguished cry against her brother's chest, and Maria stared in horror, crossing herself. Then she also pushed her way past them into the room.

"She died from having the baby?" she asked Sarah, staring mesmerized at Nainsi's body, which looked like a doll that had been tossed carelessly aside. Her arms lay outstretched, as if she'd just flung herself down on the bed. Her legs were under the bedclothes, but the covers were slightly rumpled, as if she'd been tossing in her sleep.

Before Sarah could answer, Maria suddenly realized her responsibilities. "Lorenzo, get Valentina out of here, and go find Mama. She already left for the market, but she'll be back soon."

"Come along, Valentina," Lorenzo said gently.

"The baby was crying," the girl whimpered. "He was crying so long, I went to see what was the matter."

Both Sarah and Maria looked down at the cradle at the same time. The baby lay still, sobbing almost soundlessly, his little face scarlet and his dark hair damp and bedraggled. As Valentina had said, he'd been crying for a very long time, and now he lay exhausted, barely able to make a sound. Maria scooped him up into her arms.

"He's soaking wet," Maria said in dismay. "Poor *bambino*."

"It's all right," Lorenzo was assuring Valentina. "Let's go downstairs."

"But why did she die?" Valentina asked plaintively as she let her brother lead her away.

"The baby is hungry," Maria said with an edge of desperation in her voice as she tried to soothe him. "What can we do?"

"We'll have to get some bottles and milk," Sarah said. "Can we send someone for them?"

"Yes, Lorenzo will go, if you tell him what we need."

"I'll make the baby a sugar teat in the meantime, and we'll give him a little water. He's probably dehydrated."

Maria's eyes widened again. "Does that mean he will die?"

"Oh, no, it just means he needs some liquid." She grabbed up a handful of diapers and a clean blanket from the dressing table and started to usher Maria out of the room. Then she stopped, remembering the girl lying dead. Quickly, she went back and pulled the covers over Nainsi's ashen face. Maria stood in the doorway, cradling the baby and watching with glistening eyes. Sarah gently guided her out into the hallway, closing the door behind them. No one would disturb Nainsi's body, Sarah was sure. No one in this house had wanted to be near her even when she was alive.

Downstairs they found Valentina sitting at the kitchen table, her eyes red and her face white. Lorenzo was trying to get her to sip some brandy. The large room where meals for a hundred could easily be prepared was redolent of garlic and onions and a dozen magnificent spices that made Sarah's mouth water even though she'd eaten only an hour earlier.

Maria told Lorenzo to go out and get the things Sarah wrote down that they would need for the baby. Then she changed the boy while Sarah made a sugar teat by wrapping a spoonful of sugar in a clean cloth and tying it off with string to make a ghost-shaped object. Then she wet the ghost's head and gave it to the baby to suck. It wasn't what he wanted, but it was wet and tasted good, so he kept after it. The apprehension in Maria's eyes began to fade.

"He will be all right?" she asked.

Sarah didn't want to make any rash promises. "He won't die from this, if that's what you mean, and he seems to be very healthy and strong. Feeding a baby with bottles is dangerous, though. Sometimes they do fine, and other times . . . Other times, they don't."

He wouldn't be Maria's problem anyway, Sarah couldn't help thinking, but she didn't bother to say it. She was too grateful that someone here cared about him.

"He'd be better off dead," Valentina said with an air of authority.

Maria and Sarah gaped at her.

"Well, he would," she insisted righteously, the color returning to her cheeks. "His mother's dead, and he doesn't have anybody to take care of him."

"You are a wicked girl," Maria told her angrily.

"I don't care what you think," Valentina said with a haughty toss of her long, dark braids. "I don't care what anybody thinks. I never wanted that nasty little baby around here anyway, or his mother either. Nainsi O'Hara thought she was better than us, just because we're Italian, but she was only dirty Shanty Irish. She never had a new dress in her life, and she had to work in a factory before she married Antonio. She should've been grateful when he brought her here, but she wasn't. She was mean to him and to all of us."

"Valentina, have a little respect for the dead," Maria said wearily.

"Why? She never had any respect for me."

"You don't deserve any," Maria snapped. "Go away and leave us alone."

With a sniff, Valentina rose and left the room.

Maria sighed. "I'm sorry. She is just a child, and she is very spoiled. Because she's the baby and the only girl."

"Of course," Sarah said politely and started some water to boil in preparation for the supplies Lorenzo would bring.

When Lorenzo returned, Sarah warmed some of the milk and prepared a bottle. Maria offered it, and the baby took to it right away. He gulped down almost all of the milk before falling into an exhausted sleep in Maria's arms.

"He is so beautiful," Maria marveled, gazing down at him lovingly, like an adoring Madonna.

Sarah took the bottle so Maria would have both hands free to cradle him, and once again she considered how unfair life was. If only Maria had given birth to this boy, he would have been welcomed and adored.

"I should put him to bed so he can rest," Maria said after a few moments.

"We'll need his cradle," Sarah said and watched Maria's face fall as they both remembered where his cradle was and what had happened in that room.

Maria looked over to the corner where Lorenzo had withdrawn after returning from the store with the baby bottles. He sat, forearms resting on his knees, watching Maria and the baby intently.

A silent communication passed between him and Maria, an understanding that surpassed words. "I will go," he said, as if responding to a spoken request. Still, he rose reluctantly, unable to conceal his aversion to returning to the room where Nainsi's body lay.

Sarah didn't want to return either, but she needed to see

the body again. She was anxious to discover the cause of Nainsi's death. It was too soon for childbed fever to have developed, and the girl hadn't been ill at all last night when Sarah left. A hemorrhage was a possibility, but she hadn't had a chance to check for that. Sarah was mystified, and she needed to know she hadn't missed anything that could have caused Nainsi's death. If Sarah had been responsible . . .

"I'll go with you," Sarah said.

Surprise registered on Lorenzo's face, but she also saw relief. "There's no need," he said perfunctorily.

"No, not at all," Maria confirmed, her own distaste evident.

"Yes, there is," Sarah replied, and started out of the room before either of them could protest again.

Lorenzo followed her up the stairs this time, and both of them walked more slowly than they had earlier. No one was screaming, and they felt no urgency. Sarah didn't wait for Lorenzo. She opened the door and went on in, steeling herself against the horror of such a tragic death. Not letting herself look at Nainsi's body, she quickly gathered the rest of the baby things she saw stacked neatly on the dresser and placed them in the cradle.

She heard Lorenzo's footsteps stop just outside the doorway. When Sarah looked up, he was watching her, also carefully avoiding looking at the bed.

"Go ahead and take it downstairs," Sarah said, indicating the cradle.

Still without so much as a glance at the dead girl, he quickly came in, picked up the cradle, and made his way out again. Sarah had expected him to bolt, but he hesitated when he realized Sarah wasn't going with him.

"Are you coming?" he asked.

"In a minute. I just have to . . . I have to check something," she said, managing a reassuring smile. She was getting very good at that.

"I'll stay then," he said, even though she could see he hated the thought.

"No, Maria needs the cradle. Go ahead. I'll be fine. I'm a nurse," she reminded him with another smile. "I'm used to death."

It was a lie, of course. She'd never get used to it, but he believed her. Or at least he pretended to and left.

Sarah began her examination, gingerly drawing back the covers to reveal the entire body. She found no pool of blood to indicate the girl had hemorrhaged. An infection wouldn't have had time to work yet, and she'd seen no signs to indicate any kind of distress at all yesterday. Sometimes people just died, Sarah knew, but this death was simply too convenient. No one in this house had liked Nainsi even before they'd discovered how she'd tricked Antonio. Mrs. O'Hara had reminded them last night that Catholic marriages could not be easily dissolved. Antonio could have thrown Nainsi and the baby out, but divorce wasn't an option, even if the baby wasn't his, so he'd never be able to remarry without being banned from the church.

Sarah started to examine the body more closely, looking for any signs of violence. She noticed that one of Nainsi's fingernails was torn, the jagged end not completely ripped off.

Gooseflesh rose on Sarah's arms. Fingernails didn't easily tear like that. She looked at Nainsi's vacant eyes, still staring at nothing, and this time she saw something she had missed before. Red dots, like pinpricks in the whites of her eyes and on her face, too. Sarah wasn't sure what that meant, but she'd never seen dots like that on a woman who'd died in childbirth. Carefully, Sarah closed the girl's eyes.

She was so engrossed in her work, she hadn't noticed the sounds of someone coming down the hall until she heard a howl of anguish that made her jump. Mrs. O'Hara stood in the doorway, paralyzed with horror as Lorenzo had been this morning.

"No, no, no," she kept saying, over and over, as she stared at the body. "Not my Nainsi, it can't be my Nainsi," she insisted as the tears pooled in her eyes. "She's all I've got, the only one left. Not my Nainsi!"

Sarah hurried to comfort her, helping her to one of the chairs Sarah and Maria had brought in for themselves yesterday while they'd been waiting for the baby to arrive. "I'm so sorry, Mrs. O'Hara," she murmured, hating the meaningless phrase but having nothing else to offer.

Still in shock, Mrs. O'Hara continued to stare. "That bitch told me she was dead, but I thought she was lying. They're devils, those dagos. They'll say anything." She drew a ragged breath. "I told Nainsi not to get mixed up with them, but she wouldn't listen. She never listens." Her voice broke on a sob, but she fought the tears, clinging to her anger. "What happened to her?" she demanded of Sarah. "She was fine last night!"

"I don't know," Sarah admitted.

"Was it the baby? My sister died in childbirth," Mrs. O'Hara remembered. "She wouldn't stop bleeding."

"That wasn't it. She didn't bleed any more than normal. She didn't seem to be sick, either."

"So it wasn't childbed fever?"

Sarah hesitated. She knew nothing for certain except that

she couldn't explain Nainsi's death and she'd seen several things to make her suspicious. "Mrs. O'Hara, I don't see anything that would have caused her death."

The older woman's face darkened with fury. "I knew it. They killed her, didn't they? How did they do it? And which one was it?"

"I told you, I don't know how she died," Sarah repeated.

They both looked up at the sound of footsteps in the hallway. Mrs. O'Hara rose to her feet as Patrizia Ruocco appeared in the doorway. Maria was right behind her. Like everyone else, Mrs. Ruocco stopped in the doorway to stare at the body.

"She is dead," she said without a trace of emotion.

"And you killed her," Mrs. O'Hara said.

Mrs. Ruocco looked at her as if she were a maniac. "I did not even know she was dead."

"You and your brood! She was fine last night, and now she's dead. Somebody here killed her."

"*Siete pazzeschi!* She die from the baby. Women die from babies every day."

"*She* says Nainsi didn't die from the baby!" Mrs. O'Hara insisted, gesturing toward Sarah.

Mrs. Ruocco fixed her razor-sharp gaze on Sarah, silently daring her to repeat such a vile accusation to her face.

"I just said I don't know why she died," Sarah hastily explained. "It could have been from childbirth, but I've never had a patient die like this before."

"This is crazy. You are all crazy!" Maria insisted, pushing her way past her mother-in-law into the room. "And why is she lying here like this? No respect!" She grabbed the edge of the covers Sarah had drawn back and jerked them over the dead girl, covering her face.

The violent action knocked several pillows to the floor, and Sarah mechanically bent to pick them up. As she did, she saw something that stopped her breath—a reddish smear on one of the pillowcases. Blood? It could have come from the birth, but Sarah was certain she'd changed all the linen on the bed last night.

As casually as she could, she turned the pillow over before placing it back on the bed, so the smear didn't show. She didn't know what it meant, but if it was connected with Nainsi's death and someone here had killed her, it might disappear.

"Mrs. Brandt," Mrs. Ruocco said angrily, "this girl die from baby. What else could she die from?"

"It could be murder!" Mrs. O'Hara cried. "She was murdered, and one of you dagos killed her!"

"You are just upset," Maria said in an attempt to soothe her. "Did you look at her? She has no marks on her, no bruises or blood. How could she have been murdered?"

This stopped Mrs. O'Hara for a moment, and she looked at Sarah helplessly. But Sarah had no answers, not yet anyway. She also didn't want to incur Patrizia Ruocco's wrath, because if she felt her family was in danger, she'd stop at nothing to protect them. Nainsi's body might just disappear along with any chance of learning the truth.

"I'm sorry. I know this is upsetting to everyone, but if she died from something to do with the birth, something I've never seen before or a mistake I made, I need to know. A doctor could tell for sure how she died," she said. "Just to ease Mrs. O'Hara's mind and my conscience."

"A *doctor*?" Mrs. Ruocco scoffed. "And who will pay for a doctor? Will you pay for him, you Irish pig?" she asked Mrs. O'Hara.

"Yes, I will, you dago cow!" she replied. "And I'll see all of you hanged for what you did to my girl!"

Mrs. Ruocco muttered something in Italian. "Get a doctor then. Just get this . . ." She gestured wildly toward the bed. ". . . this thing out of my house!"

Mrs. O'Hara made an outraged sound and started screaming profanity at Mrs. Ruocco, who haughtily turned her back and walked away. Mrs. O'Hara followed her, threatening to bring down every punishment under heaven upon her daughter's killer.

When their voices died away as they descended the stairs, Sarah turned back to Maria, who looked absolutely terrified. "What will happen?" she asked in a whisper.

Sarah went to her, taking her icy hands. "Nothing, if Nainsi died in childbirth," Sarah said, not wanting to upset Maria any more than necessary.

"I mean the baby," Maria said, apparently not believing for a moment that Nainsi might have been murdered. "What will happen to the baby?"

Sarah had no answer for her.

"You must help me keep the baby," Maria said desperately.

Sarah would have liked nothing more than to give Maria the child she'd longed for, but . . . "I'm not sure there's anything I can do to help."

"What will happen to him if I don't keep him?" Maria asked. "I cannot give him to that woman!"

She had a legitimate concern. Mrs. O'Hara probably didn't have the means to care for a child herself. Bottle-feeding required time and patience and diligence in addition to rigid cleanliness. "Maria, I'm not the one you need to convince. Have you even talked to your husband about this?"

Something flickered deep in her eyes, and her expression hardened. "He will do what I ask."

"And what about Mrs. Ruocco?" Sarah asked, knowing full well she would have the final word.

Before Maria could reply, they both heard a commotion out in the street. They hurried over to the window and saw that in the street below, a small crowd was gathering around a screaming woman. The woman was Mrs. O'Hara. Maria jerked up the sash so they could hear what she was saying.

"Murder! Police!" she was screaming. "They murdered my daughter! Police! Get the police!"

Maria gave an outraged cry, turned, and ran from the room. Sarah took the time to close the window and give Nainsi's covered body one last glance. On impulse, she took the bloodstained pillow and slipped it under the bed. Then she followed Maria, carefully closing the bedroom door behind her.

Down in the dining room, she found all the Ruoccos assembled. Antonio and Joe had finally made their appearance, and from the looks of them, they'd awakened to excruciating hangovers. Only a drunken stupor would have allowed them to sleep through the morning's excitement. Lorenzo stood silently, his face expressionless as he observed the chaotic scene. Valentina was crying loudly, and Maria was pleading with her mother-in-law in rapid Italian, but Mrs. Ruocco ignored all of them. She was staring at the police officer banging on the front door, demanding admission.

For a long moment, no one moved, and then Lorenzo walked over to the door, unlocked and opened it. The policeman entered, followed by Mrs. O'Hara. Lorenzo managed to get the door closed before anyone else could force their way

in, but the crowd outside pressed against the glass door and
the front windows, peering inside.

"There they are," Mrs. O'Hara said, pointing wildly.
"That's all of them. They killed my girl."

"This lady says a girl was murdered in here, Mrs. Ruocco,"
the officer said respectfully, because Patrizia Ruocco was a
prominent figure in the community. Sarah recognized him,
although she couldn't remember his name. But he hadn't seen
her yet.

Mrs. Ruocco stepped forward, fairly radiating indigna-
tion. "This woman is crazy. Her daughter marry my son, but
she die in childbirth."

"No, she didn't," Mrs. O'Hara exclaimed. "Ask the midwife. She's right there!" She pointed directly this time, and
Sarah winced.

"Mrs. Brandt?" the officer asked, peering at her in the
shadows. "Is that you?" Practically all the policemen at Headquarters knew her from her association with Detective
Sergeant Frank Malloy.

"Yes," she said, reluctantly stepping forward and trying
to look more confident than she felt.

"Do you know what's going on?"

"I delivered a baby here yesterday, to Mrs. O'Hara's
daughter," she added, gesturing to the older woman. "She
was married to Mrs. Ruocco's son, Antonio. This morning,
she was dead. I'm not sure why she died—"

"They killed her, that's why!" Mrs. O'Hara screeched,
and all the Ruoccos began yelling in protest.

The officer had to shout and push the Ruoccos back when
they tried to attack Mrs. O'Hara. "Quiet, the lot of you!" he
hollered several times before order was restored. "I got to
find out what happened here. If I don't . . ." He glanced

meaningfully over his shoulder at the curious crowd gathered outside.

Virtually all the faces were Italian, so Sarah didn't think they'd riot over the death of an Irish girl, but who knew what could happen? Riots had started over much less.

Sarah turned to Mrs. Ruocco. "I have a friend who is a police detective. He'll be fair, and he'll find out what really happened to Nainsi."

Mrs. Ruocco frowned suspiciously. "He is Italian?"

"Well, no," Sarah had to admit. Police Commissioner Theodore Roosevelt had opened the ranks of the New York City Police Department to people of all ethnic groups, but she didn't think they had any Italian detectives yet. "He . . . he's Irish, but I promise you he'll be fair," she hastily added.

Mrs. Ruocco made a rude noise. "Do what you want," she told the policeman. "Lorenzo, go find . . ." She hesitated, her face twisting with distaste before she finished. "Go find Uncle Ugo. Tell him come right away."

Sarah winced, and the policeman visibly paled. Ugo Ruocco was a prominent member of the community, too. But not in a good way. Rumor said he was the leader of the notorious gang of thugs known as the Black Hand.

Sarah turned to the policeman. "You'd better get Detective Sergeant Malloy, now."

3

FRANK MALLOY HOPED HE COULD REFRAIN FROM STRAN-
gling Sarah Brandt when he saw her. How many times had
he told her not to get involved in crimes? She seemed to attract trouble like a magnet, though. Too bad Little Italy was
only a few blocks from Police Headquarters. A longer walk
might've helped him calm down a little. Pushing his way
through the crowd that had gathered in the street didn't im-
prove his mood either. He strode into Mama's Restaurant in
full fury.

What he found knocked the fury right out of him and
made him want to turn tail and run flat out to the nearest
gang of criminals armed with brickbats and rocks. At least
he knew how to handle them. He absolutely hated hysterical females, and this room was full of them.

"Malloy," a familiar voice said over the din. "Thank heaven you're here."

His anger flickered to life again as he turned to see Sarah Brandt coming toward him. "Don't blame heaven," he told her grimly. "It's *your* fault I'm here."

She didn't look the least bit repentant. "You're the only one I could trust to handle this."

He winced at the caterwauling of the other women. "I'll have to introduce you to some other detectives real soon, then."

She ignored his sarcasm. "Malloy, a young woman died here mysteriously last night. Well, she was just a girl, actually. I delivered her baby yesterday, and this morning when I got here, she was dead."

Frank felt the old familiar wave of pain threatening to wash over him. His wife Kathleen had died in childbirth. No wonder these women were grief-stricken. But what had Sarah said about how the girl died?

"What do you mean, she died *mysteriously*?" he asked.

"I'm not really sure, but . . ." She lowered her voice and leaned in closer so no one would overhear. "She didn't die from the normal complications women die of in childbirth, and I saw some things that made me suspicious."

"What things?" he asked, taking her by the arm and leading her farther away from the family.

"I'll have to show you, but . . . I'm afraid that she may have been murdered," she whispered.

"Here, in this house?" Malloy asked. He knew the Ruocco family. Everyone in the neighborhood did, and he'd eaten here a hundred times.

She nodded.

"That's impossible. Why would anybody kill a woman

who just gave birth?" For Italians, a new baby was the happiest event in their lives.

"They were very angry with her. When it was born, they realized the baby didn't belong to her husband."

Frank had seen newborn babies. They all looked the same, like tiny, squalling old men, and you couldn't tell anything about them, certainly not who their fathers were. "How would they know that?"

"It's a long story, but the mother was an Irish girl who'd married Antonio Ruocco because she was in a family way and—"

"Irish, you say?" Frank could hear the warning bells ringing in his head.

"Yes, she was Irish, and they knew the baby wasn't Antonio's because—"

"Wait," Frank said, stopping her with a raised hand.

He looked around the room again and realized they were all staring at his Irish face with naked hostility, even the Irish woman sitting alone in the far corner of the room. And the women had stopped crying. The silence was eerie. An Irish girl in an Italian household who'd made someone angry enough to kill her.

He went back to the front door, opened it, and gave an order to the cop who was standing guard to make sure nobody in the crowd got too rowdy. The fellow took off at a run.

When he closed the door and turned back, Sarah Brandt was one step in front of him.

"Where's he going?" she demanded.

"For help," he replied.

"*Help?*" she echoed in amazement, but he didn't bother to enlighten her. He needed as much information as he could get as quickly as possible.

"Now tell me exactly what happened," he said.

"They killed my girl is what happened," the Irish woman cried.

That set off the Ruoccos again, and they all started yelling at once in two languages, with the Irish woman yelling right back. Luckily, Frank had lots of experience dealing with unruly crowds, and this one wasn't even armed. It took a few minutes, but he finally got them settled down again and cowed enough to stay that way, for a little while anyway. He knew he couldn't question Sarah in front of them, though.

"Is there someplace where we can talk in private?" he asked her.

"The kitchen," she said, pointing.

He followed her, and as he passed Mrs. Ruocco, he said, "I sent for another policeman. Let me know when he gets here."

She gave him a withering glare, letting him know exactly what she thought of him and the rest of the Irish policemen.

Frank sighed with relief as the kitchen door swung shut behind him. "Now tell me what happened, from the beginning."

"I came here yesterday to deliver a baby. I didn't even know that Antonio had gotten married—"

"The girl married Antonio?" he asked. "He's just a kid!"

"So was she," Sarah said grimly. "They'd only been married a few months, a little over five, I think. That's why they were frightened when they called me. They thought the baby was coming too early."

"You said they got married because she was in a family way?"

"That's right, but she was supposed to only be about seven months along. That's how long she'd known Antonio."

Frank raised his eyebrows. If he'd been talking to a man, he would've observed that young Antonio hadn't wasted any time playing dip the wick with the girl, but he refrained. "Let me guess, the baby wasn't early."

"No." She walked toward the stove and for a second he couldn't figure out where she was going, but then he saw the cradle sitting beside it. "See for yourself."

She gently drew back the blanket, and he could see a baby sleeping peacefully. He didn't know much about infants, but this one was big and fat. Nothing sickly about him. Even Frank could see he'd been born on time, maybe even a little past time.

"I guess young Antonio was a little surprised," he said.

"He probably wouldn't have known the difference, but of course his mother did. She'd known the baby was conceived before they were married, but no one guessed the girl was much further along than she claimed. Not until the baby was born, that is."

"I can imagine Mrs. Ruocco was pretty mad."

"Everyone was. Nainsi's mother—the lady outside who is claiming they'd killed her daughter—tried to defend her, but Nainsi didn't even try to deny the truth. I guess she was depending on the Catholic Church to prevent Antonio from divorcing her or something. She didn't even seem concerned."

"When did she turn up dead?"

"I got here early this morning to check on her and the baby, and when I arrived, someone started screaming upstairs. Valentina—she's the youngest in the family—had gone in to see why the baby kept crying, and she found Nainsi dead. Her body was cold and starting to stiffen, so she'd been dead a couple hours by then, at least."

"And what makes you think somebody killed her?"

"I said I wasn't sure, but she has a broken fingernail, like she'd been struggling with someone, and then I found a pillowcase with a smear of blood on it."

"There's a lot of blood when a baby is born," Frank remembered all too vividly.

"I'd changed the bedclothes."

"But you might've missed some."

"Malloy, I don't *want* her to have been murdered," she said in exasperation. "If I could think of another explanation, I'd have given it to Nainsi's mother and the Ruoccos and gone home. She didn't die from any of the usual things that women die of in childbirth. I know the signs of all of them."

"And you're an expert in murder, too, I guess."

She glared at him, but it was a pale imitation of Mrs. Ruocco's withering stare. She couldn't begin to compete. The baby made a whimpering sound and distracted her. "He's waking up. I'd better get Maria. She's looking after the baby," she explained. "Then you can go upstairs and look at the girl's body yourself, since you *are* an expert in murder," she added tartly.

He sighed again as he followed her out of the kitchen, this time in exasperation.

As soon as he reentered the dining room, Joe Ruocco approached him. He looked like he'd been on a three-day bender. His eyes were red-rimmed and bloodshot, his complexion a trifle green. He hadn't shaved or bathed yet this morning. Frank could still smell the liquor and the sweat on him.

"Mr. Malloy, this is all a mistake," he said. "Nobody killed nobody here. The girl, she had a baby. Women die from that. This is what happened to her. There is no need for the police."

From the corner of his eye, Frank saw Sarah speak to one of the women, who then hurried off to the kitchen. "If that's what happened, you've got nothing to worry about, Joe," Frank assured him. "What do you know about this girl? From before she met Antonio, I mean."

Joe glanced uneasily at his mother, who was watching the exchange through narrowed eyes. "She's a wild girl. She tricked Antonio. She already had a baby in her, and she tells him it was his. He's a stupid boy, so he marries her." Joe tried to give his brother a meaningful glance, but the boy was slumped over one of the tables, head on his arms, probably passed out. "They go to her priest, an Irish priest, in secret, so Mama doesn't know until it's done. We are surprised, and Mama is angry, but we took the girl in. What else could we do?"

"Antonio must've been pretty mad when he found out he'd been tricked," Frank observed, watching to see if the boy stirred. He didn't move.

Joe knew immediately what he was implying. "Oh, no, he was only sad. He feels like a fool, to be tricked by a stupid girl. I took him out last night, and we got drunk so he wouldn't have to think about what he will do with her and the baby."

Frank couldn't help noting that Joe had conveniently given his baby brother an alibi for the night, just in case his wife really had been murdered.

The front door opened, and to Frank's relief he saw Gino Donatelli come through it. Everyone in the room looked up in surprise, but Donatelli looked straight at Frank. "Detective Sergeant," he said respectfully, removing his hat and nervously smoothing the jacket of his crisply pressed police uniform.

Frank hadn't been too happy when Teddy Roosevelt opened the ranks of the New York City Police Department to Italians, and even Jews, but today he was ready to see the wisdom of it. "Officer Donatelli," he replied, going to him and shaking his hand.

Donatelli was naturally surprised, but Frank had done it to elevate Donatelli in the Ruocco's estimation. Italians would never trust an Irishman. They'd only trust another Italian, and then not completely unless he was a blood relation. Frank's only hope for this case was to use Donatelli to convince the Ruoccos they were being treated fairly.

He turned to Mrs. Ruocco. "Officer Donatelli is going to help me investigate your daughter-in-law's death."

"Murder, you mean!" Mrs. O'Hara insisted.

Donatelli looked at her in alarm, but Patrizia Ruocco distracted him. "You are Italian," she said. It wasn't a question. Donatelli had coal-black hair and an olive complexion, along with a classic Roman nose. He stood taller than any of the Ruocco men, and he was even more handsome.

"Yes, Mrs. Ruocco. My father is Angelo Donatelli, who owns the shoe repair shop on Spring Street."

"He has five sons, yes?"

"Six. I'm the third one."

He'd adequately established his pedigree. Mrs. Ruocco nodded in silent approval.

"We're going up to see the body now," Frank said.

"That's not decent," Mrs. O'Hara cried. "The poor girl just lying there like that with two strange men looking at her!"

"I'll go with them, Mrs. O'Hara," Sarah Brandt offered.

Frank couldn't help the prickle of annoyance he felt, even

though he'd intended to take her with them anyway. She was the one who thought it was a murder, after all.

Joe stood up from the table where he'd been sitting with his brothers. "Should one of us go, too?"

Frank didn't think Joe would even make it up the stairs in his current condition, and he certainly didn't want any of the Ruoccos to hear what Sarah thought. "No, just stay here until we've had a chance to look things over."

Frank gestured for Sarah to precede them, and they trooped up the narrow stairs in silence. As soon as they reached the upstairs hallway, Frank closed the stairway door behind them.

Donatelli cleared his throat. "Detective Sergeant, what's going on here?" Plainly, he meant more than just the facts of the crime. He must have been wondering why Frank had sent for him in the first place.

"Antonio Ruocco married himself an Irish girl who already had a bun in the oven by another man," he said, figuring he didn't need to spare Sarah's sensibilities. He was pretty sure she didn't have any where babies and their creation were concerned. "He didn't know that, of course, and yesterday, the baby was born. That's when everybody figured it out that the baby couldn't be Antonio's. This morning the girl was found dead." He glanced at Sarah. "Mrs. Brandt here was the midwife. She thinks the girl might've been killed."

Donatelli nodded politely. "Pleased to meet you, Mrs. Brandt."

"I'm happy to meet you, too, Officer Donatelli," she replied, but Frank could see the same question in her eyes.

"I sent for Donatelli because if it turns out the girl really was murdered, Mrs. Ruocco would never trust an Irish cop." He turned back to Donatelli. "You know who Patrizia Ruocco's brother-in-law is?"

"Ugo Ruocco," he replied grimly. "Everybody knows that."

"I'm guessing he's already on his way."

"Oh, yes," Sarah confirmed pleasantly. "Mrs. Ruocco sent for him as soon as I sent for you."

"Then we better get this settled before he gets here," Frank said. "Mrs. Brandt, show us what makes you think the girl was killed."

She led them to a closed door in the hallway and opened it. They followed her inside. The figure on the bed had been covered by the blankets.

"Is this how you found her?"

"No, she was lying there with the covers up to her waist, like she'd been sleeping, except her eyes were open and her arms were outstretched like this." She demonstrated.

Without waiting to be asked, Sarah drew the blanket away from the body. The girl had been a healthy little piece, all breasts and hips, and her hair was a pretty shade of red. Frank could see why Antonio had been attracted. She wore a simple nightdress, and her naked feet and ankles were ghostly white.

Donatelli hung back in the doorway, his young face expressing embarrassment at this breach of decorum.

"Come closer, Donatelli," Frank said, "so you can see."

Reluctantly, he did, shifting his hat from under one arm to the other, and hesitantly looking down at the girl on the bed.

Sarah tried to lift the girl's hand, but the body was too stiff. "This hand," she said. "See how the nail is broken? Something violent happened to break it like that, and it must've happened as she was dying. You'd never leave a broken nail hanging like that."

She was right, and Frank felt an odd mixture of pride in her for having figured that out and resentment that she was in a position where she needed to. "Anything else?"

"Those red dots on her face," she said. "There are some in her eyes, too. I never saw anything like that before."

Frank leaned over the corpse to take a closer look at her face. Then he reached down and pulled one of the eyelids up. Donatelli sucked in his breath, but Frank and Sarah pretended not to notice. "See these red dots, Donatelli?" he asked. "That happens when somebody suffocates."

This time Sarah caught her breath.

"Which pillow has the blood on it?" he asked, looking at the collection piled beside the body.

She bent down and pulled one out from under the bed. "I put it there so no one else would see the stain and figure out what it was," she explained. Once again Frank felt a twinge of pride, but he ignored it.

He took it from her and examined the smear. It looked like blood, all right. Then he positioned the pillow above the girl's face, as if he were going to push it down and smother her. The stain lined up with where her mouth could have been if the pillow had covered her face.

"Where did the blood come from?" Donatelli asked.

Frank peered into the girl's mouth. "There's dried blood on her front teeth. Her upper lip is cut on the inside, like somebody pushed something against it really hard."

"So somebody did kill her then," Sarah said sadly.

"Why would they do something like that to her?" Donatelli asked in disgust. "She's just a girl."

"Maybe because the Catholic Church doesn't allow divorce," Frank observed. "Or maybe they just didn't appreciate a Mick dropping her little bastard in their house."

Donatelli flushed and cleared his throat, reminding Frank that a lady was present.

"Excuse me, Mrs. Brandt," Frank said perfunctorily.

"I most certainly will not," she said, making Donatelli's jaw drop and forcing Frank to bite back a grin. "What are you going to do now?"

"We'll need an autopsy to prove she was smothered," Frank said.

"If Ugo Ruocco thinks you're going to blame somebody in this house for killing her, he'll never let you take the body," Donatelli warned him.

"Then we better remove the body before he shows up," Franks said, even though he knew he should wait for the coroner.

"Mrs. Ruocco said she wanted Nainsi out of here as soon as possible," Sarah offered helpfully.

"Then we'll try to oblige her. Donatelli, find out if they've got a phone here, and if they don't, go to a call box and get an ambulance right away to take the body to the morgue."

"Yes, sir," the young man said, and hurried out.

Frank turned back to Sarah. She looked tired and discouraged. Even her eyes had lost their sparkle. "You should go home," he said.

"I hoped I was wrong, you know," she said, ignoring his suggestion as usual. "It doesn't give me any pleasure to find out she was murdered."

He ran a hand over his face. "I know," he admitted. "How do you get yourself into these situations?"

She seemed to consider for a moment. Finally, she said, "I've been wondering that myself, and I want to remind you that I'd never known anyone who was murdered until I met you, Malloy."

"Are you blaming me?" he asked in surprise.

"The evidence speaks for itself," she answered wryly. "Now help me wrap up the body. We'll have to put the pillow in with it. I doubt Mrs. Ruocco will let us walk off with any of her belongings, especially if she realizes it will help prove Nainsi was murdered."

Frank concentrated on the corpse so he wouldn't think about how intimate it was working alone in a bedroom with Sarah Brandt. In a mercifully short time, they had the body tied up in a sheet with the bloody pillow tucked inside, ready for transport.

When they got back down to the dining room, they found everyone still pretty much where they had been before. Donatelli was speaking quietly and very respectfully with Mrs. Ruocco in Italian.

"What's he saying to her?" Mrs. O'Hara demanded of Frank. "They're cooking up some lie, ain't they? Trying to say my girl wasn't murdered."

"I was saying I sent for an ambulance to take her away," Donatelli said loudly, so everyone in the room could hear.

"Where're you taking her?" Mrs. O'Hara cried, jumping to her feet. "Not to some dago undertaker who'll make her disappear!"

"She's not going to disappear," Frank assured her, hoping this was true. If Ugo Ruocco arrived before the ambulance, he couldn't be sure. "She's going to the morgue."

"What will happen at this morgue?" Mrs. Ruocco asked.

"They'll find out how she died," Donatelli explained.

"Mother of God," Mrs. O'Hara murmured, crossing herself. "They'll cut her up, won't they?"

"And if they find out she died of natural causes," Frank hurriedly added, "nobody has to worry."

"How do we know they tell the truth at this morgue?" Mrs. Ruocco challenged. "They could lie to ruin us!"

Donatelli glanced at Frank, asking a silent question. Frank had no right to grant permission, but he nodded anyway.

"I'll go with her and watch everything they do," Donatelli offered. "I'll make sure they do it right."

Patrizia Ruocco looked him up and down, taking in his uniform. He might be Italian, but he was also from the police. "Giuseppe," she said to her eldest son. "You go with him. You watch them cut her up and make sure they do not lie."

Joe gaped at her in horror for a long moment, the color draining from his face. Then he slapped a hand over his mouth, lunged to his feet, and ran from the room. They could hear him retching in the kitchen and a woman's voice chiding him shrilly. Maria, Joe's wife. In another moment she emerged, holding the baby, her expression outraged. "What is going on?"

No one answered her.

"I'll go, Mama," Lorenzo said. He rose to his feet with the enthusiasm of one going to meet his doom.

Mrs. Ruocco nodded her approval.

"Go where?" Maria asked. "Where are you going?"

Outside the crowd was dispersing to make way for the black ambulance wagon. Whatever Donatelli had told them at Headquarters had worked. The attendants jumped down and fairly ran inside, carrying a stretcher.

"You got a body here?" one of them asked.

"Upstairs," Frank said. "I'll show you."

"Go with them, Lorenzo," Mrs. Ruocco said. "And watch. Make sure they do not take anything."

The attendants glared at her, but she just glared right back at them, and Frank had to admit she was probably justified to take precautions. He led them upstairs, and they immediately started grumbling about having to take the body down the twisting steps.

Behind them, Lorenzo said, "There's an outside stairway that's straight. You can use that."

It was the work of a moment to load Nainsi's body onto the stretcher. Lorenzo showed them the door to the outside stairway at the opposite end of the hall, and they started down.

"I'll tell the ambulance to go around to the alley and meet you," Frank said, thinking it was probably better than carrying the girl's body out the front door and into the street for the crowd to gape at.

With any luck at all, they'd be out and away before Ugo Ruocco showed up.

"You," Patrizia Ruocco said to Sarah. "You bring all this trouble."

"I'm so sorry," Sarah said honestly. "I don't want to hurt anyone, but I've got to be very careful in my profession. If one of my patients dies, I have to find out why, or else I could be in trouble, too."

"So you make trouble for us instead," she said bitterly, sitting down at one of the tables. She propped her head in both of her hands.

"You make trouble for yourself," Mrs. O'Hara said, her

voice raw with her pain. "You make up lies about my girl, and then you kill her!"

"Mrs. O'Hara," Sarah said, going to her. "I know you're grieving, but we should wait until we know the truth about Nainsi's death before making accusations."

Someone groaned, and everyone looked over to where Antonio sat. He'd straightened up and was rubbing his face, muttering in Italian. Then he realized everyone was staring at him. "What?" he asked defensively.

"This is all your fault," his mother told him in disgust. "You bring that whore into my house."

"My Nainsi wasn't no whore!" Mrs. O'Hara objected furiously. The Ruoccos ignored her.

"I didn't know, Mama," Antonio whined. "How could I know? You wanted the baby when you thought it was mine!"

As if he knew he was being discussed, the baby made a fussy sound. Instinctively, Maria bounced him gently, trying to soothe him, but Mrs. Ruocco glared at the bundle in her arms.

"I do not want him *now*," she declared. "Let *her* take him!" she added, gesturing at Mrs. O'Hara.

"*No!*" Maria fairly shouted, startling everyone. "No," she repeated more reasonably but with equal finality. "I will keep him."

"You will *not*!" Mrs. O'Hara declared, rising to her feet. "I'll not have my grandson raised by a bunch of ignorant foreigners!"

"Who are you calling ignorant?" Joe wanted to know.

"Stop shouting," Antonio begged them, holding his head with both hands.

"I do not want that whore's bastard in my house," Mrs. Ruocco insisted.

"He's just a baby," Maria argued. "He cannot help who his mother was. Or his father either," she added with emphasis. "I will keep him."

"Like hell you will!" Mrs. O'Hara screeched, making Antonio moan and hold his head again. "Give me that baby! He's mine!"

Before anyone realized what she intended, she hurtled herself across the room. She would have snatched the baby from Maria's arms except Frank Malloy intercepted her as he emerged from the stairway.

"Whoa," he said, forcibly restraining the nearly hysterical woman. "What's this now?" He looked to Sarah for an explanation, but she didn't get a chance to give it.

"They're going to steal my grandson from me!" Mrs. O'Hara wailed. "They killed my girl, and now they want her baby, too."

"She cannot take care of a baby," Maria argued. Frank really looked at her for the first time. She was a plain woman, no one he'd even glance at twice in the street, but fury had brought color to her cheeks and a sparkle to her eyes. She looked like a wild creature defending her young. "If she takes him, he will die!"

"I'd rather have him dead than with the likes of you!" Mrs. O'Hara unwisely cried.

Even Mrs. Ruocco looked shocked.

"You see?" Maria said triumphantly. "You cannot just let him die." She turned to her mother-in-law, her will like a flame that would scorch any who denied her. "Your son cannot give me a child, but you can. I want this baby, and you will give him to me."

Sarah could see Mrs. Ruocco's silent struggle. As much as she hated Nainsi, she also loved her family. Everyone knew how desperately Maria wanted a child of her own. Sarah had seen that desperation before, a longing that bordered on madness, and Maria looked as if she were very close to that edge.

Mrs. Ruocco laid a hand on her heart, as if it pained her. She could not bear to refuse Maria any more than she could bear to consent. Finally, after what seemed an eternity, she said, "Giuseppe, he . . . he must agree." She looked at her oldest son. Everyone looked at him. Mrs. Ruocco must have been certain he would refuse.

"Yes," Maria confirmed in an oddly mocking tone. "Giuseppe must agree."

His face was white, and this time Sarah didn't think it was from his hangover. She almost expected him to bolt again rather than face such a momentous decision, but he swallowed down hard and said, "Whatever Maria wants."

Sarah gasped in surprise, and so did several others, but she didn't have time to notice who. Mrs. O'Hara started screaming and fighting Frank, who still held her back from attacking Maria.

"You can't let them take the boy!" she was telling him. "He don't belong to none of them! He's mine!"

"The law says the baby belongs to the woman's husband," Frank informed her as he wrestled her flailing arms.

"But they said he don't!" she argued. "They said Antonio ain't its father. That's why they killed my girl!"

"It doesn't matter," Sarah explained, going to Frank's aid. "Please, Mrs. O'Hara, listen to me. The law assumes a woman's husband is the father of her children, even if everyone knows he isn't. If she dies or if he divorces her, he still has custody of them. They're his property."

"But *he* ain't the one that wants the boy," Mrs. O'Hara argued, pointing at her son-in-law. "Don't Antonio have no say at all?"

Everyone looked at Antonio again. He still held his head as if it would fly apart if he didn't, and now his face was almost green. Paralyzed with indecision, he looked from his mother to his brother to Maria and back to his mother again. Mrs. Ruocco seemed to be daring him to stand up and be a man. Maria defied him to deny her, and Joe just stared back, helplessly.

Maria whispered, "Joe," and that broke the spell.

As if she'd struck him with a whip, he jerked up to his full height. "You will keep the baby," he informed his brother. "Tell her." He pointed at Mrs. O'Hara.

"I will . . ." Antonio had to swallow. "I will keep the baby," he said obediently, and this time he bolted, heading for the kitchen to be sick.

Mrs. O'Hara gave a primal howl of anguish.

Sarah saw Malloy's desperate plea for help, silent though it was. "Mrs. O'Hara, there's nothing you can do right now. Let me take you home," she said gently, moving to take the woman by the arm.

Defeated, she sagged in Malloy's grasp, and he released her to Sarah. The older woman let Sarah lead her toward the front door.

"It ain't right," she was muttering as she wept loudly and sloppily. "It just ain't right for them to have my girl's baby."

Malloy hurried to precede them and opened the door, holding it for them as he shouted something to the ambulance driver. Sarah murmured comforting phrases as she led Mrs. O'Hara out into the street.

"Where do you live?" she asked.

"Howard Street," Mrs. O'Hara murmured brokenly. "Just past Broadway."

Sarah turned her in that direction, and they started walking. She was starting to believe she would get the older woman away without further incident when Mrs. O'Hara stopped dead in her tracks and breathed a curse.

Sarah looked up and saw only an average-looking, middle-aged Italian man walking toward them, followed by a group of younger men who seemed to be ready for anything. Before Sarah could even comprehend what she was seeing, Mrs. O'Hara said, *"Ugo,"* and turned and ran in the other direction, leaving Sarah standing alone on the sidewalk directly in the path of Ugo Ruocco and his minions.

4

THE AMBULANCE DRIVER MOVED JUST AS QUICKLY AS Frank would have wanted, whipping his horse into motion to pull the vehicle around to the alley to pick up Nainsi Ruocco's body. Frank waited just an instant, to make perfectly sure the wagon was well on its way, before turning back to make sure Sarah and Mrs. O'Hara were well on their way, too. He saw Mrs. O'Hara scurrying past him in the opposite direction and without Sarah.

Instantly, he sensed the change in the crowd. Something had happened, and instinctively, he sought out Sarah to assure her safety. He found her at once, standing with her back to him in the middle of the sidewalk, all alone because the crowd had drawn away, stepping into the street to make way for . . .

Frank almost groaned aloud. Ugo Ruocco and about half

a dozen of his young toughs were heading straight for Sarah. He opened his mouth to call out to her, but someone else beat him to it.

"Mrs. Brandt! Mrs. Brandt!"

Sarah turned toward the young Ruocco girl who had come charging out of the restaurant to summon her.

"Mrs. Brandt, come quick! The baby is sick!"

"Sarah, don't," he tried, but she only gave him a puzzled glance before hurrying by him and back into the restaurant with the girl. He checked to make sure Ugo and the boys were still coming, then he followed her inside. The last person he wanted to see this morning was Ugo Ruocco, but he wasn't going to leave Sarah to Ugo's mercy, unprotected.

He winced when he stepped through the door. The baby was screaming, and even Frank could tell he was in pain.

"He just started crying," Maria said in terror.

"Make him stop!" Antonio begged, hands over his ears. He'd returned from the kitchen, but he looked like he might need to go back.

Sarah took the baby from Maria's arms. He kept screaming, but she didn't seem the least bit concerned. "He's probably just hungry," she said, heading for the kitchen door.

"But I already fed him this morning," Maria protested, following after her.

"He's hungry again," Sarah explained as the door closed behind them, muting the sound of his wailing a bit.

Frank glanced around at who was left. Officer Donatelli waited patiently for his orders. Joe and Antonio were perking up a bit, but they were still a little green. The girl— what was her name again?—stood in the middle of the floor, wringing her hands in distress. Mrs. Ruocco sat at a table, head in hands, looking as if she wanted to be as far away from the rest of this bunch as possible.

Frank went straight to Donatelli and told him in a hurried whisper that Ugo Ruocco was coming and to go out through the kitchen to meet the ambulance in the alley to make sure they got the body away safely.

No sooner had Donatelli disappeared into the kitchen than the restaurant door opened again, and Ugo Ruocco came in. The younger men with him made a little show of jostling each other to be the first to follow, but eventually they were all inside, too.

Ugo wasn't a large man, but his presence seemed to fill the room. He wore a custom-made suit with a snow white shirt, the kind the men on Wall Street wore. No one would mistake him for a financier, though. His broad, olive-skinned face betrayed his heritage. Pock-marked and coarse featured, he obviously came from peasant stock. Only ambition, relentless effort, and a cruel disregard for the welfare of others had elevated him to his current position.

"*Zio!*" the girl cried and ran to him. He caught her in an embrace.

"What is it, *ragazza piccola?*" he asked tenderly, stroking her hair. "What has made you so unhappy?"

"Nainsi is dead, and the police are here!" she informed him indignantly, looking up at her uncle with a theatrical pout.

"What is this about the police?" he asked, looking at Frank with a trace of amusement. He had no fear of the police.

"Uncle, thank you for coming," Joe said, hurrying toward him for a quick embrace. Antonio followed.

When he'd finished with the children, Ugo looked over

to where Mrs. Ruocco stood. She'd risen from her chair but made no move to greet him.

"Patrizia," he said in a tone of mock amazement. "You sent for me."

"Ugo," she said by way of greeting, although she said it with a grimace through gritted teeth. If her children were happy to see their uncle, she wasn't.

"Sit down, Uncle," Joe urged, pulling out a chair for him.

"Is that your baby crying so loud, Antonio?" Ugo asked mildly as he took the offered seat.

Antonio's lip curled in disgust. "You know it is not my baby, Uncle."

Ruocco nodded, and Frank noted that he had already been told about the baby's birth and questionable lineage. When had that happened?

"But it is your wife's baby," Ruocco said. It wasn't a question. "Did Valentina say she died?" he added with appropriate, if false, regret. "That is too bad for you, Antonio, to be a widower so young." He gave the boy a sympathetic glance while he smoothed his lush mustache with one finger. Antonio looked away in embarrassment. "But why does this sad event bring the police to us?"

Everyone in the room looked at Frank. Ruocco's boys had stationed themselves around the room, ready to block any attempt at escape and ready to take any action Ruocco might command of them. Frank hated being in such a vulnerable position, but he knew better than to show fear. Ruocco would smell it like the wolf he was.

"It looks like somebody helped Nainsi Ruocco along into the next world by holding a pillow over her face," Frank said. He pretended not to notice the small gasps of surprise and the wave of animosity that roiled from the rest of the people in the room.

Ruocco didn't bat an eye. "I am sure this is all a terrible mistake. In fact, I will be happy to pay you a reward for your efforts if you will straighten out this misunderstanding."

The offer was a reasonable one, and Ruocco would have every reason to expect Frank to accept it. Everyone knew the police did what they were paid to do, and they certainly weren't paid very much to uphold the law of the land. Who would care if one more poor Irish girl died, after all? And what good would come of bringing her killer to justice? A respectable family would suffer a lot of misery, and the girl would still be dead.

Frank had once believed he had no choice but to follow this logic and live by these unwritten rules. He knew better now, and he wanted to tell Ruocco what he could do with his offer of a bribe. He couldn't though, at least not yet. Sarah was still in the building, and Frank would be no good to her or to anyone else if Ruocco told his henchmen to slit his throat for showing disrespect.

"They already took the girl's body to the morgue," Frank said. "It's out of my hands now."

Irritation flickered across Ruocco's broad face. He turned back to Mrs. Ruocco and demanded something in Italian.

She straightened defiantly and replied, mentioning Lorenzo.

"*Lorenzo?*" he scoffed, dismissing his nephew with a wave of his hand.

"We didn't have any choice, Uncle," Joe hastily explained. "Nainsi's mother ran out into the street screaming for the police when she found out the girl was dead."

Before Ruocco could react, the kitchen door swung open, and Sarah came into the dining room, apparently unaware of what was going on. She glanced at the newcomers and then dismissed them as unimportant, going straight to Mrs. Ruocco.

"Maria is going to need some help learning how to prepare the baby's bottles and take care of him," she said, as if nothing else was more important. "I'd be happy to help her, but if you'd prefer, I can suggest someone else to—"

"Who is this?" Ruocco demanded.

Sarah looked at him in surprise, and Frank noticed she managed to let Ruocco know his behavior was rude.

"She is the midwife, Uncle," Joe hastily explained.

"And she was just leaving," Frank said. "Mrs. Brandt, get your things."

"Brandt," Ruocco echoed thoughtfully, looking her up and down. "You are not German," he added, referring to her name.

"No, I'm not," she replied, offering nothing else. And making no move to leave, either, Frank noted impatiently.

Ruocco stared hard at her, annoyed that he could not classify her. An ordinary midwife he could deal with, but he could see Sarah Brandt wasn't ordinary. Even though she moved among the working classes, she would always carry with her the evidence that she had been born to wealth and privilege, the daughter of one of the oldest families in the city. Ugo didn't know all that, but a man as perceptive as he was, who depended on his ability to judge others in order to retain his power, would sense it.

"Who are you?" Ruocco asked, meaning much more than her name.

"I am the midwife," Sarah said stubbornly. To her, that was the only correct or necessary answer.

Sensing she was somehow getting the upper hand, he changed tactics. "Do you think my nephew's wife was murdered?"

Frank caught his breath, silently begging her not to answer that question.

"I don't know why she died," she said without even looking at Frank for guidance. "I never saw anything like it before."

Ruocco's eyes widened innocently. "Why do you want to ruin this family, Mrs. Brandt?" he asked, his voice suddenly silky with charm as he rose to his feet. "The girl lied to my nephew to give her bastard a name. She deserved to die."

"I think God should make those decisions," Sarah informed him. "I just want to know for certain how she died so I'll know if it was my fault or if I could have done something to prevent it."

"What if it was your fault? What if you killed her yourself?" he challenged, obviously enjoying the verbal duel.

"Then I will take the blame for it and try to learn from my mistake," Sarah replied. "I always want to do my job better. Lives depend on it. I'm sure you can appreciate that, Mr. Ruocco."

Frank wanted to shake her. Didn't she know who she was talking to? This was no upper-class gentleman who would treat her with respect. Ugo Ruocco killed people who displeased him.

But Ruocco seemed more amused than angered by her defiance. "Lives depend on it," he echoed with a small smile.

"Patrizia, I do not know why you send for me," he told his sister-in-law.

"To make the police go away and leave us alone," Mrs. Ruocco snapped, glaring at Frank.

This also seemed to amuse Ruocco. "Will you go away?" he politely asked Frank, stroking his mustache again.

"I'm finished here," Frank said, not wanting anyone to think he was leaving because Ruocco wanted him to. "I was waiting to escort Mrs. Brandt."

"Are you finished, too, Mrs. Brandt?" Ruocco asked with exaggerated civility.

"Yes, she is," Frank informed her. "Get your things, Mrs. Brandt, and I'll see that you get home."

He saw the flicker of rebellion on her face, but she must have realized he was only concerned for her safety. She turned to Mrs. Ruocco again. "Please send for me if Maria has any problems with the baby. I'll be happy to help in any way I can. I'm very sorry about Nainsi . . . about everything."

Mrs. Ruocco betrayed only anger, although it didn't seem to be directed at Sarah in particular. She nodded her head once in acknowledgment of Sarah's words of condolence. "Giuseppe, get Mrs. Brandt's coat."

Joe looked around helplessly as Sarah went and fetched it herself from the chair where she had laid it. He went to help her with it before Frank could move.

As Sarah buttoned her cape, Ruocco asked of no one in particular, "Why does Maria take care of the baby?"

"Maria is going to keep the baby," Joe hastily explained.

Ugo's dark eyes narrowed, and he fixed his gaze on Joe. "You are going to keep the whore's baby?"

Joe blanched. "Maria is barren. She . . . she wants a baby," he stammered.

"The mother was a lying *whore,*" Ugo repeated.

"Will *you* tell Maria she cannot have a baby?" Mrs. Ruocco challenged Ugo with a glare of her own.

"The baby can't help who his parents are," Sarah added, making Frank want to shake her again.

This time Ugo didn't look amused. "You will go home now, Mrs. Brandt."

Frank saw the flicker of rebellion again, but he hurried over and took her by the arm before she could offend Ruocco any more.

"Come on," he said, picking up her medical bag.

For once she did as she was told. No one spoke as they left the restaurant. The crowd outside had retreated a respectful distance, in deference to Ugo Ruocco, but they still lingered in small groups. If something interesting happened, no one wanted to miss it. Still holding Sarah's arm, Frank hustled her along the sidewalk until she finally shook loose of his grip and forced him to stop.

"Slow down. We don't have to *run* away," she snapped.

"It wouldn't be a bad idea, though," he replied. "Do you know who Ugo Ruocco is?"

"I know he has something to do with the Black Hand."

Frank glanced back to see if any of Ruocco's boys had followed. "Keep walking," he told her, steering her toward Mulberry Street.

This time she came along without protest.

"Ruocco runs the Black Hand," Frank said just loud enough for her to hear. "He collects protection money from all the Italians, and if somebody refuses to pay, they get beat up or killed or their store gets bombed, or maybe even all three."

"I know all that," she reminded him.

"Then you should also know he wouldn't hesitate to kill a lowly midwife who annoyed him."

He was glad to see she looked a little bit chastened, but only a little. "What if we're right, and Nainsi was murdered? What will happen?"

"Probably nothing."

"What do you mean, *nothing*?"

He should've known she'd be outraged. "I mean if Ruocco pays off the right people, no one will care if she was murdered or not."

That silenced her, but not for long.

"I don't suppose he'd want his family accused of murder," she said.

"To Italians, family is everything," he explained. "They don't trust anybody who isn't a blood relative, and they stick by family to the death."

"Patrizia Ruocco doesn't seem to like Ugo much," she observed.

"Maybe she doesn't, but she still sent for him when she thought her family was in trouble."

She thought this over for a minute or two. "Poor Nainsi," she mused. "And her mother . . . I can't imagine how awful it would be to lose a child like that, and then to lose your grandchild, too."

"I couldn't believe Mama Ruocco let her daughter-in-law keep the boy," Frank said in wonder.

"I couldn't either. Everybody knows how much Maria wanted a child of her own, though, and the Ruoccos can probably give him a better home than Mrs. O'Hara."

"Mrs. O'Hara won't see it that way," he reminded her.

"I know." She sighed. "But the law is against her. Even if she had the means to fight them, she'd still lose."

They'd reached the Prodigal Son Mission, where Sarah volunteered, and she stopped. "Malloy, I'm going into the mission while I'm here to see if they need anything. Will you let me know what the coroner finds out about how Nainsi died?"

He nodded reluctantly. "For all the good it will do. And don't start thinking about justice for this girl," he warned. "She shouldn't have gotten mixed up with the Italians in the first place, and nobody but her mother is going to care what happened to her."

She frowned, hating what he said but knowing he was right. "Thank you for coming anyway."

He just shook his head. "Be careful. And stay away from the Ruoccos."

She smiled a little, and Frank felt a familiar catch in his chest. "I'll try," she said and started up the front steps to the mission.

When she was safely inside, he headed for police head-quarters in the next block to make his report.

SARAH HADN'T INTENDED TO STAY SO LONG AT THE MIS-sion, but they were having a problem with one of the girls and needed her help. Now she'd have to hurry if she wanted to get home before the streets became completely jammed with people returning from the day's work. She'd missed an-other afternoon with Aggie, too. Thank heaven she had Maeve and didn't have to worry about whether Aggie was safe.

She was skirting the south edge of Washington Square when she heard the first newsboy calling out the headlines.

"Irish girl murdered in Little Italy!" he cried, waving

a penny newspaper to attract the attention of the pedestrians.

Sarah started at the coincidence. She knew he couldn't be talking about Nainsi's death. The penny papers only cared about sensational stories, and Nainsi's wouldn't qualify. As Malloy had said, only her mother would care if she'd been murdered or not.

She reached the corner and turned up the west side of the Square. On the next corner stood another newsboy selling a different paper.

"Dagos slit Irish girl's throat and steal her baby!" he was crying, waving the papers. People were passing him coins and snatching the papers from him as quickly as they could press within reach.

This was too much of a coincidence. Sarah waded into the crowd and emerged with a slightly wrinkled copy of the scandal sheet. Stepping into the square where she could read without blocking anyone's way, she quickly scanned the story. They'd given Nainsi's name the American spelling of Nancy, and they said her throat had been cut, but otherwise, it was her story, all right. According to the paper, Nainsi had been practically kidnapped by the Ruoccos and kept a prisoner until she gave birth. Then she'd been murdered so they could have her baby. The paper had included a drawing of a voluptuous young girl sprawled on a bed in a skimpy nightdress. With one arm she clutched an infant and with the other she tried to ward off a large, dark man wielding a knife.

When Sarah looked up, she realized many others had stopped to read the story, just as she had, and they were murmuring in outrage. Sarah and Mrs. O'Hara were no longer the only ones in the city who cared if Nainsi had been murdered.

FRANK HAD SPENT MOST OF THE DAY INVESTIGATING A suspicious warehouse fire. He stank of smoke and only wanted to get home and have a hot bath, but when he stopped by headquarters to make his report, he found Gino Donatelli waiting for him.

"*Pew,*" the young officer said as Frank approached.

"Warehouse fire," Frank explained. "Was she smothered?"

Donatelli nodded.

"Come with me." Frank led him back to the detectives' area and sat down at a battered desk. Donatelli pulled up a rickety chair beside it.

"Did you stay for the whole autopsy?" Frank inquired knowingly.

Donatelli smiled a little sheepishly. "Didn't have to. Doc Haynes didn't have time for it today anyway. Lorenzo wasn't going to leave without an answer, though, so he started looking the body over to see what he could find."

"He noticed the red dots on her face?"

"Yeah, and he explained to Lorenzo what they meant. He looked at the pillow and the girl's cut lip and the blood on her teeth, and showed Lorenzo how she was smothered, just like you did back in her room."

"Did that convince him?"

Donatelli shook his head. "He was still arguing, so Doc pried the girl's mouth open and started looking down her throat."

"Down her throat?" Frank repeated. "For what?"

"He gets these long pincher things and sticks them in her mouth and pulls out this feather."

"How'd she get a feather in her throat?"

"It was a feather pillow," Donatelli said grimly. "Doc says she must've sucked it right through the pillowcase when she was fighting real hard to breathe."

In the normal course of things Frank knew, feathers frequently worked free of the loose pillowcase ticking. His mother collected them carefully, probably intending to have enough someday to make a new pillow or at least to stuff back into the old one. He'd never inhaled one, though. Now he felt a tickle in his throat and had an unreasonable urge to cough. His discomfort must have shown on his face.

"Yeah, that's how Lorenzo acted, too," Donatelli said with a grin. "He even started gagging. Doc said he could watch while he cut open her chest, just to make sure, and that's when Lorenzo bolted."

"So he'll report back to Mama and Uncle Ugo that she was smothered."

"Doc isn't really going to do the autopsy until tomorrow, but he was pretty sure what he'd find," Donatelli said.

"I'll check with him later and get his report. Thanks, Donatelli," he said generously. "You did a good job."

The young man looked pleased, but he didn't smile. "There's one more thing."

Frank didn't want to hear one more thing about this case. "What is it?"

Donatelli reached into his uniform pocket and pulled out a piece of paper. When he unfolded it, Frank saw it was one of the penny newspapers. Then he saw the drawing.

"What the hell . . . ?" he muttered, snatching the paper from Donatelli. "Her throat wasn't cut," he protested as he read. "Where'd they get this?" he demanded of no one in particular.

"Mama's is only a few blocks away from here," Donatelli reminded him. "Somebody could just go over to the press shacks and tell them whatever they wanted to hear."

The rooms in the two houses directly across the street from Police Headquarters were rented by hordes of reporters who spent their days watching the Black Marias arrive and disgorge their prisoners, hoping one of them would provide a good story. Donatelli was right, somebody with knowledge of a story like Nainsi's would only have to stand outside on the sidewalk and wave to get all the attention he wanted. Or *she* wanted.

"Nainsi's mother," Frank guessed.

"Who else would care?" Donatelli asked. "I don't think the Ruoccos wanted this story in the newspapers."

"She'll be sorry," Frank predicted. "Ugo will make sure of it."

Frank heard somebody calling his name. He swore.

"Maybe it's about something else," Donatelli offered.

"Malloy!" It was one of the Goo-Goos, a brand-new officer, breathless from running through the building in search of him. He sighed in relief when he saw Malloy sitting at his desk. "Commissioner Roosevelt wants to see you right away."

"Yeah," Frank said to Donatelli, rising reluctantly. "He probably wants my advice on running the department or something."

Donatelli rose also and followed Frank down the hall toward the stairs to the second floor where Roosevelt kept his office. "If you need somebody who speaks Italian, you know where to find me," he said in parting.

Frank just grunted and started up the stairs.

Miss Kelly, the girl secretary Roosevelt had hired in a break with decades of tradition of an exclusively male staff, greeted him and told him to go on in. The commissioner was waiting for him.

Frank wished he'd had a chance to clean up first, but Roosevelt would have to take him as he was.

"Been cleaning chimneys, Detective Sergeant?" Roosevelt asked with his toothy grin.

"Warehouse fire, sir," he replied. "I just got back."

"You were down at that Italian restaurant this morning, though." It wasn't a question.

"Yes, sir. I suspected the girl had been murdered, so I sent her body to the morgue for an autopsy."

"Throat cut, eh?"

"Oh, no, she was smothered."

"Then the scandal sheets are wrong."

"They're wrong about a lot of things, Commissioner," Frank explained wearily. "She wasn't kidnapped. She was married to one of the Ruocco boys. He thought he'd gotten her in a family way. When the baby came way too early, he knew it wasn't his. The whole family was pretty mad. The next morning she was dead."

"What about the baby?"

"It's fine, and the Ruocco family wants to keep it. Seems one of the other boys' wives can't have any of her own."

"The girl was murdered, though. No doubt about that?"

"No, sir, no doubt at all, according to the coroner."

"Who did it?"

"We don't have any idea. And it's Ugo Ruocco's family."

Roosevelt grimaced in distaste. "The girl married his son?"

"His nephew. He'll try to protect them though. He'll bribe and threaten whoever he has to."

"A girl was murdered. We can't let a criminal stop us from investigating," Roosevelt insisted.

"He can make sure we don't find the killer, though," Frank said. "If it was somebody in the family—and it probably was—they'll never turn on each other. All they have to do is keep quiet."

Even though he understood, Roosevelt didn't like it. Frank wished he wasn't the one delivering the bad news, but it couldn't be helped.

They could both hear the sound of a paddy wagon pulling up in the street below with its load of boisterous drunks. It was early for that, Frank noted. They didn't start picking up that kind of crowd until long after sundown. Even then, they usually didn't make this much noise.

Roosevelt must have had the same thought. He went to the window overlooking the street, and Frank followed. The men spilling from the wagon didn't look drunk. They were much too feisty and coordinated as they dodged the officers' locust clubs and managed to get in a few licks of their own. One even successfully broke free and raced away down the street to freedom. The officers were too busy to even notice his escape.

"What's this?" Roosevelt muttered. "It looks like a riot!"

Frank thought so, too.

Someone knocked loudly on the office door, and before Roosevelt could answer, it opened.

Minnie Kelly stuck her head in, her eyes wide. "An Officer Donatelli says he has to see you, Commissioner."

"He was with me at the restaurant this morning," Frank said to Roosevelt.

"Send him in," Roosevelt said.

Donatelli didn't wait for Miss Kelly. He was right behind her, and he stepped around her into the room.

"Mr. Roosevelt, sir, there was a riot down at the Ruoccos'
restaurant. I knew Mr. Malloy was with you, and you'd both
want to know right away."

"What kind of a riot?" Roosevelt demanded. "Who was
involved?"

"A group of Irish boys, it seems, sir," Donatelli said.
"That's how it started. They got to reading the penny press
about the girl who got killed, and they were drinking some,
I guess. They worked themselves up into a fever and marched
down to Mama's, started yelling and then throwing rocks. A
window got broke, and then all hell—I'm sorry, sir, then
things started getting really rough. Some of the neighborhood toughs came out with sticks, and a lot of noses got
bloodied. Our boys gathered up as many as they could from
both sides and sent the others packing."

"So that's who they're bringing in now," Roosevelt said.

"Yes, sir, at least the ones that didn't run away."

Roosevelt removed his wire-rimmed glasses and rubbed
his eyes. "I'd better telephone the mayor before he hears this
from someone else. Malloy," he added as he put his glasses
back on, "you're in charge of this investigation. I want the
killer found."

Frank wanted to remind him how he'd just explained
that the task was impossible, but he resisted the self-
destructive urge. "An Irish cop won't get far with those people," he said instead. "They only trust their own."

"I don't have any Italian detectives to send," Roosevelt
reminded him.

"I'll help in any way I can," Donatelli offered. "I grew up in that neighborhood."

"Dee-lightful," Roosevelt said, his good humor restored. "Take this young man, Malloy. Donatelli, is it? Good work, Officer Donatelli. And just tell Conlin if you need anyone else," he added, mentioning the chief of detectives. "I want this matter settled before this little altercation turns into a full-scale war between the Irish and Italians."

"Yes, sir," Frank said, although he had no hope at all that he'd be able to obey this order. One thing might help, though, if he could convince Roosevelt to do it. "Maybe we could start by getting the newspapers to publish the facts instead of all this business about the girl being kidnapped and her throat being cut."

"Yes, yes, good idea, Malloy. Good idea," Roosevelt said, rubbing his hands in anticipation of getting to work. "I'll call a press conference. I'll need a full report with all the details so I can answer questions. I'll get Haynes there to talk about the autopsy, too."

"He, uh, he hasn't actually done the autopsy yet," Frank admitted.

"Then he'll do it tonight. I want the news in the morning papers. I'll need that report right away, Detective Sergeant Malloy."

Frank took the hint and made his escape, Donatelli on his heels.

"I never saw him up close before," Donatelli whispered as they made their way downstairs. "He's something, isn't he?"

Frank didn't answer. He was too busy trying to figure out how he was going to do the impossible and solve Nainsi Ruocco's murder.

5

SARAH TOOK AGGIE FOR A WALK THE NEXT MORNING TO pick up several of the more reputable newspapers. Aggie almost had to run to keep up with her as she hurried back home to see what they had to say about Nainsi's death. When she arrived, she found Mrs. Ellsworth and Maeve in the kitchen with all the ingredients for an English pudding.

"Good morning, Mrs. Brandt," she said cheerfully. "Going to catch up with the news?"

"I want to see what they have to say about a . . . a friend of mine. Maeve, will you take Aggie upstairs for a little while?"

"Mrs. Ellsworth was going to show me how to make a pudding," Maeve said, not wanting to hurt the older woman's feelings. She probably also wanted to *eat* the pudding.

"There's plenty of time for that," Mrs. Ellsworth said

cheerfully. "Give me and Mrs. Brandt a few minutes to talk, and I'll call you down when we're finished so we can start the pudding."

"Yes, ma'am," she said obediently, taking Aggie by the hand.

As soon as they were out of earshot, Mrs. Ellsworth's polite smile faded. "What's wrong?"

"One of my patients was murdered night before last," Sarah said, laying the papers on the kitchen table to sort through them.

"Good heavens," Mrs. Ellsworth said, taking a seat at the table. "I was afraid something like that would happen. I saw a crow on your back fence on Monday morning. It's an omen of death. I didn't say anything, because I know how you feel about my superstitions. I was just hoping you wouldn't have a delivery that day." She shrugged apologetically. "How did it happen?"

Sarah didn't comment on her feelings about Mrs. Ellsworth's superstitions, but she briefly told her what had happened to Nainsi. "Last night when I was coming home, the newsboys were shouting about how she'd been kidnapped by the Ruoccos and had her throat cut because they wanted her baby."

Mrs. Ellsworth made a rude noise. She'd had personal experience with the way the newspapers distorted the facts to make a story more sensational. "Let's see what new lies they're telling today. Hand me one of those papers."

The two women spent the next few minutes scanning the stories.

"Says here Roosevelt himself had a press conference about it," Mrs. Ellsworth reported.

"This paper says that, too," Sarah noted. "I can't understand why he'd take such a personal interest in the death of one poor Irish girl."

"Maybe you should ask him," Mrs. Ellsworth suggested with a sly grin. The Roosevelts had been friends with Sarah's family for generations.

"Maybe I will." They both read on for a minute or two. "Oh, my, does yours talk about the riot down at Mrs. Ruocco's restaurant?"

"Yes. Says they arrested more than twenty men, too. Must have been a real . . . what is it the Irish call a big fight?"

"Donnybrook," Sarah supplied. "The Irish and the Italians hate each other under the best of circumstances. They hardly need an excuse to start fighting."

"Looks like they found one, though. I wonder if Mr. Malloy was down there making the arrests." Mrs. Ellsworth was especially fond of Frank Malloy.

"I don't think he does that kind of thing," Sarah said, wondering what Malloy had thought when he heard about the riot. They'd both been so sure no one would care about Nainsi's death. Then she noticed something particularly disturbing at the end of the news story. "Theodore promises that the killer will be caught," she said in amazement.

"A good thing, too," Mrs. Ellsworth said.

"More like a miracle, and even less likely to happen. They're Ugo Ruocco's family."

"Who's Ugo Ruocco?"

"He's the leader of the Black Hand."

"Heavens! You mean those horrible people who blow things up?"

"They're more likely to beat people up," Sarah said. "They only use bombs if they can't persuade you some other way."

"Persuade you to do what?"

"To pay them money to protect your place of business. The irony is that you're paying them to protect your business from *them*. If you pay, you're safe. If you don't pay, they destroy you."

"How awful!" Mrs. Ellsworth exclaimed in outrage. "Why don't the police do something about it?"

Sarah gave her a sad smile and a moment to figure it out for herself.

"Oh," the older woman said. "I suppose the Black Hand pays for protection from the police."

"Or else the police are afraid of them, too." Sarah sighed. There was so much evil in the world.

Before she could sink into complete despair, she heard small feet running through the house.

"I think Aggie got tired of waiting for her cooking lesson," Sarah said, turning to catch the child in a hug. Maeve was close behind her. The four of them spent the next hour preparing the pudding and putting it on the stove to steam. Sarah was trying to clean Aggie's hands when they heard the doorbell ring.

As usual, Aggie pouted, and Sarah went resignedly to answer it. She recognized the silhouette through the frosted glass, and she was smiling when she opened the door.

"Malloy," she said.

He didn't smile back, which told her he wasn't happy to be here. Which meant he was here on business.

Aggie came running and flung herself at him before he could even remove his hat. Maeve and Mrs. Ellsworth followed at a more dignified pace, but they greeted him just as happily.

"Something smells good," he observed when he'd set Aggie back on her feet.

"Mrs. Ellsworth showed us how to make a pudding," Maeve reported.

"We'd invite you to stay and try some, but it won't be done for another three hours," Mrs. Ellsworth said. "I don't suppose you planned to stay that long."

"I'm afraid not. I'm working on a case. I just need to ask Mrs. Brandt a few questions, and then I have to go."

"Yes," Mrs. Ellsworth said, nodding wisely. "The Ruocco case, I suppose. We were reading about it in the newspapers this morning."

"Did Roosevelt put you in charge of it?" Sarah asked.

"Yes," was all he said, but his look told her that he held her personally responsible for getting him into this mess.

She tried to look apologetic, but he seemed unmoved.

"I'll take the girls upstairs while you two talk," Mrs. Ellsworth said generously. Sarah knew she'd cut off her arm to be allowed to sit in on the conversation, but she'd have to be content to hear about it second hand. "So nice to see you, Mr. Malloy. Maybe you'll bring Brian back this evening for some pudding," she added, referring to his son.

"We'll see," he said politely.

Sarah and Malloy waited until the three of them had disappeared up the stairs.

"Would you like some coffee?" Sarah asked as Malloy removed his coat and hat and hung them up in the hallway.

"I could use some," he said, and followed her into the kitchen.

"I'm sorry, Malloy," Sarah said as she took cups down from the cabinet. "I never imagined anything like this would happen."

He took a seat at the table. "Did you hear about the riot?" he asked, not bothering to hide his annoyance.

"It was in the papers this morning. Was anyone seriously hurt?"

"No, but that doesn't mean it won't happen again. I imagine Ugo Ruocco's got some of his thugs posted down there now, and they'll do some real damage if anybody starts another fight."

Sarah filled the cups and set them on the table. "At least Theodore managed to get the real story into the news today."

"Yeah, but the penny press is still talking about kidnapping and stolen babies," he said. "They don't care about the truth. They just want to sell newspapers."

"And now Theodore has promised everyone you'll solve the case," she said sympathetically, taking a seat opposite him at the table. "What can I do to help?"

"You can't *do* anything, so don't even think about getting involved in this investigation," he warned.

"Of course not," she said innocently. "Why would I?"

She didn't fool him. "I mean it, Sarah. Ugo Ruocco would kill his own mother if she got in his way, and he sure wouldn't hesitate to kill you."

"I'm not in his way," she pointed out. "And I'm not likely to be. Now tell me why you're here. You said you had some questions for me."

He sighed with resignation. "I want you to tell me everything that happened from the time you got to the Ruocco house until you left the night Nainsi was killed."

She'd already told him everything yesterday, but that had been under far different circumstances. She went through the entire sequence of events again, trying to remember every detail.

"You're sure Antonio wasn't the baby's father?" he asked.

"It doesn't seem possible. He didn't even know Nainsi when the baby would have been conceived."

"Wasn't she scared of what they'd do to her when they found out?"

"That was so odd. I thought she would be. I was afraid *for* her, especially when her mother said she couldn't take her and the baby in if the Ruoccos threw her out, but Nainsi wasn't even worried. She told her mother they'd let her stay. She seemed almost . . ." She searched for the right word. "Smug. That's it. She was very confident that Mrs. Ruocco wouldn't throw her out."

"She was stupid then," Malloy observed.

Sarah had to agree. "Someone in the family must have killed her," she pointed out. "But I just can't see why any of them would."

"Why not?" he asked, genuinely curious. She felt a small sense of pride that he valued her opinion.

"Well, because killing someone is so dangerous. What if you get caught? And they didn't need to kill Nainsi to get rid of her. Mrs. Ruocco had already said she'd throw her out as soon as I said it was safe for her to leave."

"But she was married to Antonio in the church," Malloy argued. "He'd never be able to divorce her."

"Antonio is a big baby. I can't imagine he was that interested in getting married in the first place. He might even be glad for an excuse to avoid that responsibility for the rest of his life."

"So you don't think he was outraged enough to have killed her for tricking him?" Malloy asked.

"He wasn't even very angry. He just seemed embarrassed. Besides, he and Joe went out and got drunk that night. They weren't even in the house when she was killed."

"We don't know that for sure yet. We don't really know when they got home or exactly when she died. What about the rest of the family?"

Sarah pictured them in her mind. "Let's see, Mrs. Ruocco had already decided what she was going to do. Why would she change her mind and murder the girl instead?"

"You're right. It doesn't seem likely. What about the others?"

"Joe, Lorenzo, Maria, and Valentina. Why would Joe or Lorenzo or Valentina care that much? And Maria was the only one in the house who was kind to Nainsi. They might have been angry at what Nainsi had done, but why take the chance of killing her? I can't imagine any of them being outraged enough on Antonio's behalf to hold a pillow over Nainsi's face while she fought them with all her strength for however long it took her to die."

"I can't picture it either," he admitted.

"But it had to be someone in the family, didn't it?"

"Not necessarily."

"What do you mean? It was the middle of the night. Who else could've been in the house?"

"Anybody. There's a back staircase that goes right up to the floor where she was killed. That's how they took her body out yesterday."

"Wasn't the door locked?" Sarah asked.

"Wouldn't matter if it was. Even Aggie could've jimmied it."

"But why would someone outside the family want to kill her? Surely, her death had something to do with the baby and the fact that it wasn't Antonio's. Who else would care anything about her?"

"Ugo Ruocco might care."

"Did he even know?" Sarah asked in surprise.

"From what he said yesterday, Joe and Antonio must've gone straight to him that night. He knew the baby wasn't Antonio's, and he didn't seem too upset that the girl was dead, did he?"

"He wouldn't have killed her himself, would he?"

"Not a chance, but he has plenty of men who'd do it for him."

"That would be more understandable if it was someone outside the family," Sarah said.

"But even harder to prove. Nobody in Ruocco's crew is going to say a word, and the family wouldn't tell, even if they knew about it, which they probably didn't. Ruocco wouldn't trust them with a secret like that."

They sipped their coffee in silence for a few moments, each considering various possibilities.

"If one of Ruocco's men could have gone up those stairs, anyone could have," Sarah mused.

"Yeah, but who else even knew she'd had the baby, much less that they'd figured out Antonio wasn't the father?"

"Nainsi's mother, but she wouldn't have killed her." A memory stirred. "Wait a minute, one of Nainsi's friends knew, too," Sarah recalled. "Or at least she told her mother to deliver a message to her. What was her name? Brigit, I think."

"Brigit who?"

"She didn't say, but Mrs. O'Hara would know. Nainsi wanted all of her friends to hear the news, too, and I guess this Brigit would tell them."

Malloy considered. "I wonder if one of her 'friends' was the baby's father."

"Do you really think . . . ?"

"Right now, I only hope," Malloy admitted. "Maybe the father is married. Maybe Mrs. O'Hara told this Brigit what the Ruoccos suspected. Maybe he didn't want Nainsi to tell anybody who he was."

"That's a good story, but do you think it's likely?"

"No," Malloy admitted, "but it would be a lot more convenient if the killer isn't related to Ugo Ruocco."

WHEN MALLOY LEFT, SARAH JOINED MRS. ELLSWORTH and the girls upstairs while they waited for the pudding to steam. They were starting to think about lunch when the doorbell rang again. This time she found Lorenzo Ruocco on her doorstep.

He looked as if he'd rather be standing in front of a speeding train, but he whipped off his cap politely. "Mrs. Brandt, I'm sorry to bother, but Maria, she asks that you come."

Although Sarah was surprised, she couldn't help feeling a little stir of excitement at the prospect of going back to the Ruoccos' house. "What's wrong?"

"The baby, he cried all night. Mama says she will give him to that Irish woman if he doesn't stop, and Maria . . . Mrs. Brandt, you must come. Maria will go crazy if she loses the baby!" He looked positively desperate.

"Of course I'll come," Sarah said. Malloy had warned her about getting involved with the case, but she wouldn't really be investigating. They wanted her there in her professional capacity. If she happened to find out something useful that led to Nainsi's killer, even Malloy couldn't complain.

As quickly as she could, she gathered her things and bid

the girls good-bye. When she came back into the front room, she found Mrs. Ellsworth comforting Lorenzo.

"They say that a baby who cries long will live long," she was saying. He nodded politely and solemnly, although he didn't look comforted.

"Aggie, you be good for Maeve and Mrs. Ellsworth," Sarah told the child. "I'll be back as soon as I can."

Aggie pretended to pout again, but Sarah tickled her and made her smile and gave her a parting kiss.

"Don't worry about a thing," Mrs. Ellsworth said. "We'll even save you some of the pudding."

Still, Sarah felt the same regret she always felt over leaving Aggie.

Lorenzo was more considerate than his brother had been and slowed his pace to match hers. Sarah had no trouble keeping up with him, even though he was just as anxious to get back as Joe had been to get her there the other day to deliver Nainsi's baby.

"I can understand why your mother would be so upset. A baby's cry is the most disturbing sound in the world," Sarah said conversationally. She wasn't sure what she could find out from Lorenzo, but she'd try to get him talking anyway. "That's so people won't be able to ignore it and will do whatever they can to make the baby stop."

Lorenzo almost smiled. "We couldn't ignore him last night."

"I'm sure he kept everyone awake."

"Maria took him downstairs so they could sleep," he said.

"But you didn't sleep," she guessed. The shadows under his eyes betrayed him.

He shrugged, embarrassed. "She . . . she needed help."

"Not many men would sit up with a screaming baby," Sarah observed, meaning it as a compliment.

He did smile this time, sheepishly, and made a small, helpless gesture.

Sarah smiled back. Lorenzo wasn't the first grown man to be captivated by an infant. He hardly seemed the type, but as Malloy had said, Italians were very fond of children.

"Could he be sick? The baby, I mean," he asked, growing solemn again.

"Maybe it's the milk. I warned Maria that some babies don't do well when they're fed from a bottle."

"He cannot die," Lorenzo said gravely. "Maria would. . . . Just tell me what you need, and I will do it, but he cannot die."

Sarah had no answer for that. She could make no promises, and she didn't think Lorenzo's efforts would make much difference. A wet nurse would be the best solution, of course, but even if they could find one and could afford her services, would Mrs. Ruocco allow it? Surely not for a baby she despised.

When they reached the restaurant, they found it doing bustling business with people coming in for their noon meals. Lorenzo took her around to the alley and up the rear staircase to avoid the crowd. This was the staircase Malloy had told her about, the one they had used to carry Nainsi's body out. The wooden steps had been enclosed so they were protected from the weather. An intruder could have climbed them without worrying about being seen, either going or coming. Malloy was right, anyone could have gotten into the house.

Halfway up the stairs, she could hear the baby crying. Poor little thing.

Maria must have heard them coming. She was waiting for them in the hallway when Lorenzo opened the door.

"Mrs. Brandt, you must help," she cried over the baby's screams. She held him in both arms and was swinging him back and forth in a futile attempt to calm him.

Sarah could see Maria was on the verge of hysteria. Her eyes were bloodshot and so shadowed they looked bruised. Sarah started crooning meaningless phrases of reassurance to her while she quickly set down her medical bag, shed her cape and thrust it at Lorenzo. Then she took the baby from Maria's arms.

The sudden shift startled him into silence for a moment, and he looked up at her in surprise. "There, now," she said softly. "You must be tired of crying."

He whimpered but didn't start screaming again. Sarah knew that sometimes just being held by someone calm could quiet a hysterical infant.

"Have you tried feeding him?" Sarah asked.

"He ate no more than an hour ago. Then he started screaming. I tried offering him more, but he wouldn't take it."

She'd been right, it was probably the milk. "Lorenzo, would you go out and try to find some goat's milk?"

"Goat's milk?" he echoed stupidly.

"Yes, some babies don't do well on cow's milk, and goat's milk seems to be easier on their stomachs. You said you'd do anything to help," she reminded him gently.

"Oh, yes, of course. I will. I will get it," he said, handing Sarah's cloak to Maria and heading back down the stairs. Maria pushed the door shut behind him. Sarah noticed she didn't lock it.

"Will that help?" Maria asked, her voice taut with exhaustion and fear.

"It might," was all Sarah could promise. "And if it doesn't, we'll try something else." The baby was starting to fuss again, screwing up his face for a full-fledged scream. "In the meantime, could you fix a hot water bottle? A small one to hold on his tummy?"

While Sarah walked the baby and let him suck on her finger, Maria went and found a small glass bottle, filled it with warm water, and wrapped it in a diaper.

The hot water bottle seemed to relieve some of the baby's discomfort, and Sarah continued to walk with him. She made Maria sit down, but the poor woman couldn't relax. She perched on the edge of the chair, ready to jump up the instant the baby might need something. After a while, the child finally fell into a fitful sleep, and Sarah laid him in his cradle, which Maria had put in the bedroom across from the room where Nainsi had died.

Maria gave a shuddering sigh and fought back tears. "He must stop crying. Mama doesn't want him here, and if he cries all the time . . ." She bit back a sob.

"Don't worry," Sarah said, patting her shoulder. "And I want you to get some rest, too. Lorenzo said you were awake all night, and you look it."

Maria automatically touched a hand to her hair as if to check the validity of Sarah's assessment. "Lorenzo was with me," she said, as if that had somehow made a sleepless night less of a sacrifice.

"He's a good man," Sarah said. "Not many men would tolerate a screaming infant all night."

"No," she agreed, a far away look in her eye. Fatigue was claiming her. "Not many would."

"You need to take a nap now, while he's sleeping," Sarah said.

"I could not," Maria protested. "Sleeping in the daytime? Mama would never allow it."

"She doesn't have to know. Besides, the baby could be up all night again, and how will you stay awake if you don't get any sleep at all?"

"What if he wakes up while I'm sleeping?" Maria asked, the edge of desperation back in her voice.

"I'll sit with him and wait for Lorenzo to get back. Is there another room where you can lie down?"

She frowned, not wanting to cooperate. "Valentina's room, I suppose," she said reluctantly.

"Good, then go there. I'll call you when he wakes up," she lied. He might wake up in just a few minutes, but she'd let Maria sleep as long as possible.

After a bit more coaxing, Maria finally went down the hall and retreated into one of the other rooms, closing the door behind her. Sarah checked on the baby and found him sleeping, although he didn't look content. If his stomach was bothering him as much as she guessed, he'd have succumbed to sheer exhaustion for the moment, but it wouldn't last long. His little body jerked, as if he'd dreamed he was falling, but the movement set the cradle rocking lazily, and the motion soothed him again. A wonderful invention, cradles, Sarah mused.

Satisfied she could do nothing more for the baby, she took the opportunity to look around the room. The double bed and large dresser were fairly new and of good quality. The shaving stand gave silent proof that one of the room's usual occupants was a man, while the brushes and hairpins on the dresser belonged to a woman. This must be the room where Maria and Joe slept. Maria had naturally put the cradle in here.

The door to Nainsi's room was closed, and Sarah had no desire to open it. The girl would have shared that room with Antonio for the few months they were married. What would that marriage have been like? Had Nainsi really thought no one would discover her secret, and that she could pass off her baby as Antonio's? Sarah remembered how confident the girl had been the afternoon before she died. Why had she been so sure Mrs. Ruocco would let her and her baby stay here? Could she really have been that naïve?

Sarah glanced down the hall. Four doors opened onto it. She knew one was Valentina's bedroom, where Maria had gone. The fourth door stood open. If Malloy were here, he'd investigate to see who else slept on the same floor where Nainsi had died, so Sarah walked down to take a look. This room was furnished as a parlor. The furniture here was older and looked comfortable and well used. A pile of mending lay in a basket near one of the overstuffed chairs and a stack of ladies' magazines sat on a table. Over the fireplace hung a picture of a beautiful sunlit landscape. Sarah imagined it was a picture of Italy. If so, she could understand why the Italians spoke so lovingly of their homeland. On the opposite wall, where the sunlight wouldn't hit it directly, hung an elaborately framed photograph of a man. His unsmiling face looked familiar, and when Sarah looked more closely, she realized he bore a family resemblance to Ugo Ruocco. He was much younger, of course, but the photograph was obviously old. This must be Patrizia's husband, Ugo's brother.

Everyone knew the story of how Patrizia and her children had come to America and she had started the restaurant. What had become of her husband? Had he died in Italy and

Ugo brought the family over here to take care of them? Or had he died during the crossing? Many immigrants did, she knew.

Sarah picked up one of the magazines and sat down in the chair closest to the window to wait for the baby to wake up. She'd read most of a second magazine when she heard someone coming up the inside stairs. Thinking it might be Lorenzo, she went out to meet him so he wouldn't accidentally wake Maria or the baby. Instead she encountered Patrizia Ruocco. She looked almost as weary as Maria had.

The older woman started in surprise. "Mrs. Brandt," she said, not pleased to see her. "Why are you here?"

"Lorenzo came for me. Maria thought the baby was sick."

Patrizia's expression hardened, and she glanced around. "Where are they?"

"I sent Lorenzo for some goat's milk. I think it might agree with the baby more than cow's milk."

Her lips flattened into a thin line. "Maria?"

"I . . . I made her lie down for a while. She was exhausted," Sarah added quickly, remembering Maria's fear that Mrs. Ruocco wouldn't approve.

"She want to be a mother. This is what happen," she said sourly. "The baby?"

"He's asleep."

The woman reached up and rubbed her forehead as if it ached.

"You should probably get some rest, too, Mrs. Ruocco," Sarah ventured. "I know what happened here last night, the Irish boys and the fighting in the street. You've been having a difficult time."

"Rest will not help," she said bitterly. "That girl, I know

she is trouble. I tell Antonio he is fool, but he is married already. What can I do?"

Sarah wasn't sure how welcome her sympathy would be, but good manners demanded she respond. "You did the right thing, Mrs. Ruocco."

"The right thing," she scoffed, but her venom was gone. She rubbed her forehead again and this time she swayed slightly.

Sarah instinctively caught her. "Come in here and sit down," she commanded, taking the older woman firmly by the arm and leading her into the parlor.

"I cannot leave boys alone in kitchen. I only come up for a minute," she protested, but she didn't resist when Sarah put her in a chair and brought a footstool for her feet.

"I'm sure the boys will be fine, and you won't be any help at all if you faint and fall down the stairs."

"I not faint," she insisted, but without much spirit.

"When did you eat last?" Sarah asked, checking her for fever.

She waved the question away as if it were a pesky fly.

"I guess that means you don't remember," Sarah said. She took her pulse. No fever and her pulse was only a little fast.

"My stomach . . . I am not hungry," she said dismissively.

"Your stomach may not be hungry, but the rest of you needs some food. Stay here, and I'll get you something from the kitchen."

"I go myself," she tried, starting to get up, but Sarah shook her head.

"You almost fainted just now. I'm not going to let you back down there until you've eaten something."

With that she left, hoping Mrs. Ruocco would have the sense to stay put and rest, at least for a few minutes.

The crowd in the dining room had thinned, and almost everyone seemed to have been served, which was probably why Mrs. Ruocco had felt she could safely come upstairs to check on Maria. The scene in the kitchen was still chaotic, but everyone seemed to know just what they were doing. Valentina was dishing up food, and Antonio and Joe were serving. All three of them looked up in surprise when Sarah came in.

"Where's Mama?" Joe asked.

"She's resting. I came to get her something to eat."

They stared at her as if she were insane.

"It's lunchtime," Valentina said, gesturing toward the busy dining room. "We need her help!"

"Mama never rests," Antonio added.

"She's been under a lot of strain," Sarah reminded them. "Could you give me some soup and maybe some tea or coffee to take up for her?"

Everything else stopped while the three of them began to argue over what Mama might like. After a minute or two of this, Sarah started lifting pot lids herself, and that spurred them to action. Almost instantly, they arranged a tray of food for their mother, including bread and soup and a plate of spaghetti and a pot of brewing tea. As Sarah hoisted the tray, Joe poured a glass of wine and added it to the tray.

"For her blood," he said. Then he held the doors for her and waited until she'd disappeared beyond the first turn in the staircase.

Sarah moved slowly and carefully so she wouldn't spill anything. Relieved that she arrived at the third floor with

most of her load intact, she made her way quietly down the
hall to the parlor. When she stepped into the room and
looked around, she almost dropped the tray.

Mrs. Ruocco had moved. She now sat in a rocking chair
on the far side of the room, and in her arms she held the
baby.

6

WHEN FRANK MALLOY LEFT SARAH'S, HE WENT TO SEE Nainsi Ruocco's grieving mother. He would put off visiting the Ruoccos as long as he could.

He was furious at Mrs. O'Hara for going to the newspapers with her story, but he had to admit, from her point of view, it was a wise move. As he'd told Sarah yesterday, no one would be interested in finding out who'd killed Nainsi if Mrs. O'Hara hadn't made the girl's death a public scandal. Seeing her side of it didn't help Frank's temper, though. He was still stuck with the thankless and probably impossible task of finding Nainsi's killer.

Mrs. O'Hara lived in a rear tenement a few blocks from Mama's Restaurant. The rear tenements got little sunlight and less air, so they were cheap. Those few blocks were also a world away. The Irish and the Italians didn't mix much. Frank found Mrs. O'Hara in her fourth-floor flat.

"I suppose you're here to tell me you ain't found out who killed my Nainsi," she grumbled when she opened the door, and she immediately went back inside, letting Frank find his own way in. She'd been sewing men's ties by the feeble light from a window that faced a narrow alley. A bundle of fabric lay at one end of her kitchen table and a pile of finished ties lay at the other. He closed the door behind him.

She picked up her needle and began to sew again, letting him know she wasn't happy to be interrupted. He knew she'd earn only about fifty-cents a dozen for sewing the ties, and a dozen was a good day's work. She wouldn't want to waste any time in social pleasantries with him.

"I'm working on figuring out who killed your daughter, Mrs. O'Hara, but I need to know more about her first." He pulled up the only other chair and sat down across the table from her. She spared him a skeptical glance.

"All you need to figure out is which of them dagos killed her," she said, stitching the fabric with practiced ease. "It had to be one of them."

He glanced around the flat. Through the doorway he could see a large stack of bedding in the other room. "You have lodgers, Mrs. O'Hara?"

"Of course I got lodgers," she said. "You think I can keep myself by making ties?"

Many people in the tenements rented floor space for a few cents a night to those even less fortunate than themselves. Frank pictured the flat as it would be when they were here, the floor filled with men and Nainsi sleeping only a short distance away. "Must've been hard, keeping the lodgers away from your daughter," he remarked, remembering they hadn't yet solved the mystery of who had fathered her baby. He still entertained a small hope that the father might be involved in her death.

"Wasn't hard at all," Mrs. O'Hara snapped. "My Nainsi, she didn't want nothing to do with them bums. She was smart, that one. Knew better than to waste herself on a man couldn't give her nothing. Wanted to better herself, she did."

"How did she plan to do that?" Frank asked mildly.

Mrs. O'Hara glared at him, her faded eyes narrow with hatred. "Not what you're thinking!"

"I'm not thinking anything," Frank insisted. "I'm trying to figure out how she ended up in Little Italy with Antonio Ruocco."

"I don't know. To this day, I don't know. It started when she got herself a job at a sweatshop, sewing men's shirts. They didn't pay her hardly anything, but it was more than she ever made helping me do this." She gestured at the stack of ties.

Frank knew what happened when a girl like Nainsi suddenly got a taste of freedom and a little money in her pocket. "She made new friends at the shop, I guess."

Mrs. O'Hara snorted. "Silly little biddies, every one of them."

"Did she have a special friend? Somebody she'd want to know about the baby?" Frank asked. He already knew the answer, but he wanted to see what Mrs. O'Hara would say.

"Funny you should ask," Mrs. O'Hara said in surprise. "She did want me to tell Brigit Murphy right away."

"This Brigit is somebody she worked with?"

"Yeah."

"Did you tell her about the baby, like Nainsi wanted?"

"Well, I wasn't gonna go out of my way, but I saw her

right when I was coming home—she lives downstairs—so I did. She was coming home from work, and I told her."

Frank wanted to know more about Brigit, but he'd get that information from the girl herself. "I guess Brigit and Nainsi went out in the evenings."

"Nainsi was a good girl," Mrs. O'Hara insisted angrily. "She never walked the streets or anything like that!"

"I didn't think she did. I'll bet she liked to go out and have a good time, though. Maybe she went to dance houses with her friends."

She sewed a few stitches, paying more attention than necessary to the tie she was working on.

"Lots of girls do that, Mrs. O'Hara. You can't blame them for wanting to have fun. Maybe that's where she met Antonio."

She shrugged one shoulder, still not looking up. "Maybe. Like I said, she didn't tell me. All I know, she comes home one day to get her stuff and tells me she's married. Says she'll never be poor again. This boy's family, they got a business, she says. A restaurant. At least I know she'll eat regular. But then I see Antonio, and I know them dagos don't take to outsiders. I know she's in for misery."

She reached up quickly to dash a tear from her eye, but she never missed a stitch.

"Antonio wasn't the only man she knew," Frank reminded her. "He wasn't the father of her baby."

"That's what them dagos say, but my Nainsi was a good girl," she repeated.

Frank didn't bother to point out that good girls didn't get pregnant before they got married. "Did she ever mention any other man to you? Someone she liked before she met Antonio?"

"She never said nothing to me. Why're you wasting your time here? I didn't kill Nainsi, and I don't know who did. You should be talking to them Ruoccos."

"All right, which one of them do you think did it?" he asked.

"How should I know? I wasn't there."

"How did she get along with them? Was there one she fought with a lot?"

"The girl, Valentina. She and Nainsi fought like cats and dogs. The girl was jealous of everything Nainsi got. I guess she's spoiled, being the youngest and the only girl, but she's just plain mean. No call to be like that."

"What about the others?"

"She didn't like any of them, you ask me. Never had a kind word to say about them anyhow. Maria, she was nice enough, I guess. Always acted polite when I was there, and she treated Nainsi all right. But the mother . . . she's a bitch, that one."

"How did Nainsi get along with Antonio? Did he ever hit her?"

Now he had her full attention. "You think he did it? Makes sense, don't it? He thought she lied to him, and a man don't like to be tricked that way."

"Did he ever hit her?" he asked again.

She considered the question. "I don't think so. She never said if he did, and I guess she would've. She complained about everything else he did and didn't do. She didn't have much patience with him."

"What do you mean?"

"I mean them Italian boys, they're handsome all right, but their mamas spoil 'em something awful. Big babies, the lot of them."

Frank remembered Sarah had said the same thing about Antonio. "Joe and Lorenzo, too?"

Mrs. O'Hara made a disgusted face. "They wouldn't piss without asking Mama's leave. You want to know who killed my Nainsi, you ask the old woman. If she didn't do it, she ordered it done."

Sᴀʀᴀʜ ᴄᴏᴜʟᴅɴ'ᴛ ʜᴇʟᴘ sᴛᴀʀɪɴɢ ᴀᴛ Mʀs. Rᴜᴏᴄᴄᴏ ʜᴏʟᴅ-ing the baby.

"He woke up," she said. She seemed a little defensive, as if she were afraid Sarah might think she'd changed her mind about the child.

Sarah tried not to let her amazement show. "I didn't think he'd sleep very long. His tummy hurts, poor little fellow." She set the tray down on the table with the magazines.

Mrs. Ruocco looked at the baby. "The water in the bottle is cold," she said, pointing to where she'd set the hot water bottle on the floor beside the rocker.

"I'll take care of it," Sarah said, going over to get it.

The baby had been crying, but Mrs. Ruocco had managed to soothe him. She would have had lots of experience, and a woman never forgot how to hold a baby.

"He's pretty, isn't he?" Sarah said as she picked up the bottle. "Look at those curls."

Mrs. Ruocco looked down at the baby as if to verify Sarah's opinion. "My boys, they had curls," she remembered. She didn't look happy at the memory. Or maybe she didn't like making a comparison between her sons and this baby.

Sarah started to walk away, but Mrs. Ruocco caught her by the sleeve. When Sarah looked down at her, she saw fear in her dark eyes.

"Will he live?" she asked.

Sarah didn't want to raise false hopes, and she wasn't even sure what answer Mrs. Ruocco wanted to hear. "He's strong and healthy," she hedged. "If we can find some milk that agrees with him, he could do just fine."

"But if you cannot?" she challenged.

Might as well say it. "If he doesn't eat, he'll die. The only other choice would be to try finding a wet nurse. Maybe one of the women in the neighborhood would feed him along with her own baby, to earn some extra money."

She'd expected Mrs. Ruocco to protest such an expense, but she just stared back, her dark eyes unfathomable. After a long moment, she said, "Maria is good girl."

"Yes, she is," Sarah agreed, not knowing what she meant.

"She is like daughter to me. She is better daughter than my own. She is good wife to Giuseppe."

"I'm sure she is," Sarah said uncertainly.

"She need baby, Mrs. Brandt. Some women, they can accept. Maria cannot. She need baby."

Sarah nodded, thinking she understood. "She'll be very grateful if you let her keep this one."

Mrs. Ruocco waved her words away again. "I do not do this for *grateful*. I do this for Maria. So she has happiness. She has no other happiness."

"She'll be a good mother," Sarah tried.

"But the baby must live," Mrs. Ruocco said fiercely. "You will help her?"

"Yes," Sarah promised with all her heart. "Yes, I will."

They heard someone coming up the outside stairs, and Sarah went to see who it was. Lorenzo came in carrying a paper sack. Sarah held a finger to her lips, warning him to be quiet so he wouldn't wake Maria, and led him into the parlor. He glanced over to where his mother sat holding the baby and almost dropped his package.

"You get milk?" she asked sharply. "Goat milk, like Mrs. Brandt say?"

"Yes, Mama," Lorenzo said uncertainly. He looked at Sarah, as if for an explanation for this amazing thing.

She simply smiled benignly and said, "Be sure to put the milk in the icebox when you go downstairs."

He glanced around. "Where is Maria?"

"She sleep," Mrs. Ruocco said. "You, go help your brothers in the kitchen. It is busy time."

He turned to Sarah with a worried frown. "Is Maria all right?"

"She's fine, just a little tired. I made her lie down."

He seemed relieved, but still unhappy. He looked at his mother again, as if to verify that she was indeed holding the baby.

"Go!" Mrs. Ruocco said impatiently.

Lorenzo went.

Sarah went to where Mrs. Ruocco sat. "I'll rock him while you eat something," she offered.

Mrs. Ruocco was staring at the baby's face. "In one minute."

FRANK FOUND THE SWEATSHOP WHERE NAINSI HAD worked. As he'd hoped, the girls were just taking their lunch break. Most of them would skip lunch, he knew, trying to stretch their meager wages so they'd have a nickel or a dime extra for admission to a dance in the evening. Frank found the boss, a man in his forties with thick dark hair plastered down with pomade and a perpetual scowl. For all of that, he was good looking, in a fancy-Dan kind of way. He probably got a lot of attention from the girls who worked for him. Frank had no doubt he took advantage of his position, too.

He introduced himself and learned the fellow's name was Richard Keith. Keith wasn't happy to see a cop. "You won't find nothing illegal here," he claimed, a little too defensively.

Frank was sure he could, if he tried, but he wasn't interested in that. "I'm here about one of your girls."

"Which one? We don't keep girls that get in trouble with the law."

"This one's dead," Frank said.

"Then it's not one of my girls. They're all here today," he said confidently.

"This one doesn't work here anymore. She quit a while back to get married. Maybe you remember her—Nainsi O'Hara."

Frank saw the surprise register on his smooth features, surprise and something else. Guilt? "Nainsi, you say? But she . . . I mean, that's terrible."

"You remember her then," Frank said. It wasn't a question.

"Well, yeah," he said, a little flustered. "She was . . . a good worker." A red flush crawled up his neck.

"Maybe she was good at other things, too," Frank said mildly. "The girls here, they must be anxious to keep you happy so they can keep their jobs. Was Nainsi one of the girls who kept you happy?"

"I don't run that kind of shop," he said, his face scarlet now. His expression was definitely guilty.

"You know why Nainsi got married?" Frank asked.

He blinked stupidly. "I . . . I guess she found a fellow wanted to marry her."

"And she was going to have a baby," Frank said.

Keith gave a little shrug, feigning indifference. "Most of them are when they get married. That's how they get the fellow to come around."

"Except the fellow she married wasn't the father," Frank said.

Beads of sweat were forming on Keith's forehead. "Why are you telling me this? And why are you here at all?"

"Did you know she had her baby?" Frank asked mildly. "And that she died?"

"I . . . I didn't," he claimed. "Well, maybe I heard something . . ."

"Who told you she had her baby?"

"I . . . I don't remember," he claimed. "One of the girls told everybody in the shop. I overheard. Nobody said she died, though."

"She didn't just die," Frank said. "She was murdered."

Keith's eyes widened and the blood drained from his face. "Who killed her?"

"I was thinking it might be the man who fathered her baby."

Keith wasn't a stupid man. "It wasn't me!" he cried. "I never . . . My girls don't get pregnant, because I don't . . . None of them do. If she said it was me, she was lying!"

How very interesting, Frank thought. "She didn't say anything, Mr. Keith. I'm only trying to figure out who it might've been. I guess I'll add you to my list."

The color flooded back to his face. "*It wasn't me.* I got a wife and family. I don't need a lot of little bastards wanting money from me, too. I might have some fun with the girls, but none of them got a baby from it. I'd swear to it."

Frank could find out easily enough what his reputation was. That wouldn't prove he wasn't the father of Nainsi's baby, but at least it would give him an idea of the likelihood of it. "Thanks for clearing that up for me," Frank said with just the slightest trace of sarcasm. "Now I'd like to talk to Brigit Murphy."

"Why?" he challenged, assuming some of his bravado again.

"To find out more about Nainsi O'Hara," Frank said. "If you'd like to point her out, I'd be grateful. If you don't, I'll have to start trying to find something illegal in your shop," he added with a grin.

Keith looked like he wanted to punch Frank, but he pointed to a group of girls gathered in the back of the room. "She's the tall one with the curls."

Frank didn't thank him. He strolled down the length of the room to where the girls stood talking. One of them noticed his approach and motioned for the others to be quiet. By the time he reached them, they were all staring at him in wide-eyed terror. They'd recognized him as a cop. People always did, even though he wore a suit just like any businessman in the city. Maybe it was the way cops carried themselves. He'd never been able to figure it out, but people always knew.

"Hello, ladies," he said as kindly as he could. "I'm Detective Sergeant Frank Malloy. I'm investigating Nainsi Ruocco's murder."

One of them made a little squeak, but the rest of them just stared.

"Miss Murphy," he said, addressing the tall girl. Her hair was light brown and not so much curly as wild and frizzy.

She'd made an effort to pin it up neatly, but it was defiantly springing loose every which way. She'd be a handsome girl if she didn't look like somebody was holding a knife to her throat at the moment. "Nainsi's mother said you were good friends with her."

Brigit nodded uncertainly.

"Did the rest of you know her, too?"

The other girls nodded reluctantly.

"You don't have to be afraid. I'm trying to learn more about her so I can figure out who killed her."

"Wasn't it one of the Ruoccos?" the shortest girl asked.

Frank dearly hoped not, but he said, "I don't know who it was yet. That's why I'm trying to learn more about her—and her friends."

"Didn't none of us kill her," Brigit cried in alarm. "Why would we?"

"I didn't think you did. I'm more interested in finding out about her . . . *gentlemen* friends."

One of the girls snickered, then slapped a hand over her mouth.

Brigit glared at her, but the girl said, "Wasn't none of them *gentlemen*."

"But she did meet men at the dance houses," Frank said.

"Well, sure, that's why we go there," Brigit said before any of the others could speak. "We all meet men there. That's who we dance with."

Frank knew the men would also treat them to drinks and cigarettes and even buy them gifts, in exchange for favors promised or actually delivered. "Did she have any special men that she met outside the dance house?"

"Antonio Ruocco," the short girl said, making the rest of them giggle.

"This would've been several months before she met Antonio," Frank pressed. "Last spring or summer."

The girls exchanged puzzled looks. "That's when she met Antonio," Brigit said. "I don't know when exactly, but it was early spring. The weather was just getting warm."

"That's right," another girl agreed. "She'd just started wearing that straw hat. We told her it caught his eye."

Brigit nodded. "She told us all about him, and he was her only special fellow all summer long. Some of the places, they don't let the Italian boys in, so she'd go out with us, then slip away and meet him someplace."

According to what Sarah had told him, that didn't make any sense. He'd have to question Antonio and find out the truth. "When she found out about the baby," Frank said, "she must've talked to you about it."

The girls looked a little embarrassed to be discussing such a delicate subject.

"She was real scared, and she cried all the time, even at work," the short girl offered.

"Who wouldn't be scared?" Brigit snapped. "She was scared *at first,* but we all told her not to be a goose. Tell him and make him marry her, we said. When she finally told him about the baby, he did, too, even though his mother didn't like it."

"Her mother didn't like it either," one of the other girls said.

"Who cares?" Brigit asked angrily. "They was in love. That's what matters."

That wasn't the picture Frank had of the union, but he didn't want to distract the girls. "Could I speak with Miss Murphy alone for a minute?" he asked the others.

They couldn't dare deny him, but they moved away with

obvious reluctance and only far enough to give the illusion that they weren't trying to listen in.

"Miss Murphy," Frank said, still trying not to frighten her. It was a wasted effort, though. His mere presence was terrifying. "Mrs. O'Hara said she told you about Nainsi's baby being born that night when you were coming home from work."

"Yeah, that's right," she confirmed, puzzled by the question.

"Who did you tell?"

"Who . . . ? What do you mean?" she hedged.

"I mean, who did you tell that Nainsi's baby was born?" he said impatiently.

"I . . . The girls," she said, gesturing to the group hovering nearby.

"Anybody else?"

Now Brigit looked truly frightened. She glanced toward the front of the room where Keith still stood, watching and glowering.

"Please, mister, I'll lose my job. I gotta get back to work."

The bell hadn't rung yet, but Frank didn't point that out. Plainly, she knew something she didn't want to say in front of Keith.

"Go, then," he said, and she scurried away, back to her seat.

He'd have to find Brigit someplace else and get the answer to his question, although he already knew it. For some reason, she'd told Richard Keith directly about the baby's birth. But if Keith couldn't possibly be the baby's father, as he claimed, why would he have been interested?

* * *

WHEN THE BABY STARTED FUSSING AGAIN, MRS. RUOCCO took him downstairs while Sarah fixed a bottle in the kitchen, so his crying wouldn't disturb Maria. By the time the bottle was ready, he was screaming lustily. Luckily, the luncheon diners were all gone, except for a few elderly men still gossiping over their grappa. The screaming had driven Joe, Antonio, and Valentina away. For some reason, however, Lorenzo stayed, even though the baby's cries obviously distressed him.

Breathing a silent prayer, Sarah accepted the baby from Mrs. Ruocco and sat down to feed him the goat's milk. The baby took the nipple and suckled greedily. Milk leaked out the sides of his mouth, and he choked a little until he got the rhythm. His mouth working mechanically, he finally settled down, his little fists clenched tightly against his cheeks, his eyes squeezed shut in bliss.

"He seems to like it," Lorenzo observed hopefully, but he was wringing his hands.

"He like milk," Mrs. Ruocco said dismissively. "He know nothing."

"We'll have to wait to see if it agrees with him," Sarah concurred.

Lorenzo sighed and kept wringing his hands.

"Mrs. Brandt, you must eat," Mrs. Ruocco said, pulling an apron down from a hook on the wall and tying it on. "I will cook." Sarah knew better than to protest. Besides, she really was hungry.

The baby fell into a contented sleep when the bottle was almost empty, and by then Mrs. Ruocco had prepared a plate of spaghetti for Sarah. Mrs. Ruocco took the baby up to his cradle while Sarah ate the delicious meal. Lorenzo had followed his mother out of the kitchen, leaving Sarah alone, so when she was finished, she went back upstairs.

She wasn't sure how much longer she could stay without wearing out her welcome. If the goat's milk agreed with the baby, they wouldn't need her anymore, so this might be her last chance to learn anything of interest. The third floor was quiet. She found the baby sleeping peacefully in Joe and Maria's bedroom, and no one was in the parlor. Perhaps Mrs. Ruocco had gone down to the second floor where her bedroom must be. The family probably had another sitting room down there as well. Counting up the members of the family, Sarah realized Lorenzo's bedroom must also be on the second floor. Of course, any of them could have slipped into Nainsi's room and smothered her in the night. It was a silent crime. Or anyone could have come up the back stairs from the street below and no one would have heard, either.

Sarah was standing in the hallway, considering all the possibilities when a door opened behind her. She turned to see Maria emerge from Valentina's bedroom. Her hair was mussed and her face puffy from sleep.

"Mrs. Brandt," she said in alarm. "Is something wrong? Is the baby all right?"

"He's fine. He woke up, and we fed him some goat's milk, and now he's sleeping peacefully again."

"Why didn't you call me?" she asked in dismay. "I would have helped you."

"Mrs. Ruocco helped me," Sarah reported with a smile.

"Mama?" Maria didn't believe her.

"She even rocked him for a while," Sarah told her. "I think she may be starting to like him."

Maria stared at her for a long moment, uncomprehending. Then her eyes filled with tears, and she started to cry. Sarah slipped an arm around her shoulders and led her into the parlor. By then she was fairly sobbing, and Sarah seated them both on the sofa, patting her back and murmuring words of comfort. She'd seen many new mothers reduced to tears after a sleepless night or two. Maria may not have given birth to this baby, but she'd experienced everything else—the doubts and the fears and the numbing exhaustion and the despair of not being able to soothe the little one's anguish and pain. She'd also experienced her sister-in-law's murder and a near riot at her doorstep. Maria had earned the right to weep.

"It wasn't supposed to be like this," she sobbed. "I did not dream it would be like this."

"Of course not, but you're doing very well at being a mother, Maria."

"I want a baby of my own," she said, scrubbing the tears from her cheeks. "I always want one, as long as I live, but it does not come. Then Nainsi marries Antonio. She is a foolish girl, but I am happy for her. I am happy to have a baby in the house. I think I will help her take care of her baby and play with it. He will love his *Zia* Maria more than anyone. But I did not want her to die!"

She started sobbing again, and Sarah murmured words of comfort. "Of course you didn't, but it was very generous of you to take him. Not many women would, under the circumstances."

"What else can I do?" she asked between sobs. "I cannot let that woman have him, and . . . and he is my only chance to have a baby of my own."

"Oh, Maria, you shouldn't give up hope yet," Sarah said kindly. "You're still young, and—"

"No, it will not happen for me," she insisted. When she looked up at Sarah, the tears had stopped and her eyes were dark with anger. "Joe, he . . . he does not come to me anymore. I will never have a child . . . except for this one."

Sarah's heart ached for Maria's humiliating secret pain, and for the circumstances that had caused her to reveal it to a stranger.

"If he's going to be your son, you should find a name for him," Sarah said in an effort to distract her from her unpleasant thoughts.

It worked. The anger drained from her face. "A name," she echoed in wonder. "I didn't think of that."

"You can't call him 'baby' forever," Sarah said with a smile. "Is there someone you'd like to name him after?"

She considered for a moment. "Maybe," she said with a touch of irony, "we should name him for his father."

GINO DONATELLI WAS MUCH TOO CHEERFUL FOR FRANK'S taste. Frank couldn't even remember being that young and excited about working on his first big case. Maybe he never had been. Gino, however, was taking great pleasure in having been selected to assist Frank with the mysteries of Little Italy.

They'd met at a coffee shop a safe distance from Little Italy, where they wouldn't encounter any of Ugo Ruocco's crew.

"As soon as Commissioner Roosevelt assigned me to this case, I started asking around about the Ruocco boys," Gino was saying.

"And you found out they're good Catholic boys who

never got into any trouble and who respect their mother," Frank guessed.

"How did you know?" Gino asked in surprised.

Frank sighed. "Did you find out anything useful?"

"Well, everybody knows that Mrs. Ruocco and her brother-in-law don't get along too well. They even say . . ." He glanced around to make sure nobody was listening, then leaned in closer and lowered his voice to a whisper. "They say he makes her pay protection money just like everybody else."

Frank swore in surprise. "I guess that would explain why she doesn't like him."

"He gets along good with the rest of the family, though," Gino added. "Ugo never had any kids of his own, so he dotes on his niece and nephews. He spoils Valentina rotten, and he's always getting the boys out of trouble, starting with ten years ago when Joe and Lorenzo knocked over a pushcart. A bunch of Jews chased them through the streets until they ran into Ugo's saloon. So now whenever they have a problem, they go to *Zio* Ugo, and he takes care of it."

"And we know Joe and Antonio went straight to Ugo the night Nainsi's baby was born." Frank rubbed the bridge of his nose. He'd thought he had trouble when it looked like one of the Ruocco family members had killed the girl. If Ugo had sent one of his henchmen, they'd never solve the case.

"We're going to have to visit the Ruoccos and find out exactly what happened the night the girl was killed."

"Right now?" Donatelli asked hopefully.

"No. We'll wait until they're too busy to object."

7

Maria had washed her face and regained her composure. She'd seemed a bit embarrassed about her earlier outburst, but she quickly recovered and began to ply Sarah with questions about caring for the baby. While they talked, Maria picked up a half-finished baby shirt and absently started stitching on it.

Sarah was beginning to think she ought to at least mention that she should be going home when they heard someone running up the stairs. The light footsteps clattered down the hall as Maria jumped up to caution whoever was coming to be quiet.

"You will wake the baby," she warned Valentina, who stopped dead at the sight of Maria and Sarah in the parlor doorway.

"I don't care if I do wake him," Valentina informed them. "I hate that baby. I wish it had never been born!"

"You are a wicked girl," Maria replied in a tone that told Sarah she'd said those words many times before. "Why are you running in the house? You are too old to act like a child."

"I'm trying to get away from all the yelling downstairs," she said petulantly. "Everybody's screaming at everybody else, and it's making my head hurt."

"Who is screaming?" Maria asked with a frown.

"*Zio* Ugo and Mama and Joe and Lorenzo. *Zio* was so mad at them that he forgot to bring me a present. He *always* brings me a present!" she added in outrage.

"Why are they arguing?"

Valentina's young face twisted into an ugly smile. "About you. And that baby. *Zio* wants to throw it in the river!"

Maria made a strangled sound in her throat and grabbed Valentina by the shoulders. "Liar!" she cried, forgetting her own admonition about waking the baby. "You should burn in hell!"

"That's what he said!" Valentina insisted, and Maria gave her a violent shake.

Valentina tried to twist free, but Maria shook her again, making her teeth snap together.

"Lorenzo won't let him, though," the girl quickly admitted, frightened now. "That's why they're fighting. Lorenzo and Joe, they said you were keeping it."

Maria thrust the girl aside and fairly ran down the hallway to the stairs. Sarah stared after her helplessly. This was none of her business, and she certainly couldn't do anything to help. She turned back to Valentina, who was rubbing her arms where Maria had grabbed her.

"Would your uncle really kill the baby?" she asked.

"How should I know? It's just a little bastard. It doesn't belong to anybody here."

"He belongs to Maria now," Sarah said.

"I don't care if he does or not. He's a lot of trouble, and he makes too much noise, and *Zio* Ugo never forgot to bring me a present before he came along."

She really was a wicked girl, Sarah decided.

They both heard a tiny mewling sound coming from Maria's bedroom.

Valentina made a disgusted sound and stalked off to her own bedroom, slamming the door behind her. Sarah went to see about the baby.

He lay in his cradle, staring intently at the flowers on the wallpaper, and Sarah watched him for a few long moments. Few newborns were even attractive. The birth process usually left them with temporarily misshapen heads, and immaturity made their features indistinct. This baby was among the fortunate ones, however. Perhaps because he was so chubby and had such thick curly hair, he looked like a tiny cherub.

As she watched him lying contentedly, an idea formed in her mind. She went to the pile of baby clothes that Nainsi and Maria had prepared and found a bright yellow gown with satin ribbon ties. Then she picked the baby up and started to change him. A few minutes later, she donned her cloak, picked up her medical bag with one hand while holding the baby tucked in her other arm and started down the stairs.

She could hear the raised voices and knew the argument was still going on. The words were in Italian, but she could tell from the tone of them that Ugo was trying to prevail.

When she reached the bottom of the steps, she drew a forti-fying breath and pushed the door open.

Her sudden appearance had the happy effect of silencing everyone in the dining room. The unhappy consequence was that everyone's attention immediately turned to her. They weren't pleased about being interrupted, and when they saw who the intruder was, they were even less pleased. Sarah had a fleeting memory of Malloy's warning that Ugo Ruocco would kill his own mother. Then she forced her face into an apologetic smile.

"Excuse me for intruding, but I really need to be going," she said. Then she looked at Maria. "The baby woke up, and I didn't want to leave him alone upstairs so I brought him down."

She lifted her arm slightly, displaying him to his best advantage. She'd fluffed his curls with her fingers and the yellow gown was darling. He was still gazing around in wide-eyed wonder at this new and fascinating world. Then, as if he were aware of her plan and had waited until every-one was staring at him, he smiled with all the sweet inno-cence of a newborn.

Mrs. Ruocco made a small sound, and Maria swooped in to claim him, taking him from Sarah with loving hands and cradling him to her chest protectively.

"I saw that little gown, and I couldn't resist trying it on him," Sarah confessed.

"I made it," Maria said with a touch of pride and more than a touch of possessiveness. She looked up defiantly at Ugo. "For my son."

One of the boys said something in Italian and walked over to stand with Maria, but to Sarah's surprise, it was Lorenzo, not Joe. Only after Lorenzo glared at him did Joe join his brother beside Maria, shamefaced but presenting a united front.

Mrs. Ruocco still stood on the far side of the room, her face twisted in anger. She said something to Ugo in challenge, and Sarah didn't need to speak the language to understand that she was daring Ugo to tear his family apart.

Sarah watched his broad face flood with rage, but he threw up his hands in surrender as a curse exploded from his lips. He pointed a finger at Mrs. Ruocco and gave her some sort of warning, then turned to leave, but he paused for a moment when Sarah came into his line of vision. His eyes narrowed with hatred, and Sarah couldn't stop the frisson of fear that tingled up her spine before he completed his turn and stalked out of the restaurant. A phalanx of his minions closed around him as he strode down the street.

Only then did Sarah realize she'd been holding her breath, and she let it out in a whoosh.

"Grazie," Maria said, looking up in gratitude—at Lorenzo.

He didn't reply. He just gave his brother a look that spoke of how disappointed he was that Joe hadn't jumped to his wife's defense. Joe looked down at Maria, but she was fussing with the baby and didn't spare him a glance.

"I really must be going," Sarah repeated. "Maria, if you need anything, send for me."

"Oh, Mrs. Brandt, thank you so much for coming," Maria said earnestly. "I will never forget you!"

"Remember to make sure the bottles are clean and boiled each time you use them. I'll stop in and check on you in a few days, if I don't hear from you before that."

"Wait," Mrs. Ruocco said. "You will take some cannoli with you."

After a few more minutes spent wrapping the cannoli and thanking Sarah again and again, they finally let her go. By then customers had started arriving for supper, and Sarah had to work her way through the crowd gathering at the door to get out into the street.

She couldn't help glancing around to make sure Ugo Ruocco wasn't waiting for her outside, but she saw no sign of him. She did see a few young men loitering on the corner, smoking cigarettes and eyeing everyone who walked by with suspicion. They would be more of Ugo's men, set to guard the restaurant from another invasion of Irish hoodlums.

As she walked down Mulberry Street, she gave a moment's thought to stopping at the mission, but she'd already been away from home all day. She missed Aggie, and the thought of having supper with her tonight was much too inviting. She had just crossed Prince Street, within a block of Police Headquarters, when she saw a familiar face in the crowd approaching her.

"Mrs. Brandt," Frank Malloy said with just a trace of censure. He glanced up at the direction from which she'd come and frowned. "I don't suppose you were delivering a baby in Little Italy today."

Sarah tried to look innocent. "As a matter of fact, Maria Ruocco sent for me. The baby wasn't doing well. He'd been crying all night."

People making their way down the sidewalk were jostling the pair and muttering impatiently since they were blocking progress. Malloy took her arm and led her to a doorway where they'd be less of an obstacle.

"Sarah," he said, the frustration thick in his voice. "I told you not to go down there. You could've told them to call a doctor if the baby was sick."

"He wasn't sick," Sarah said, sympathetic to his concern but knowing she was justified. "Besides, if I'd told them to call a doctor, I wouldn't have found out anything that might help you find Nainsi's killer."

"And did you?" he challenged.

"I'm not sure yet. But if I didn't this time, I can find out next time I visit. You'll just have to tell me what you need to know."

Few people were as ungrateful as Frank Malloy, Sarah observed. Instead of thanking her, he looked like he might cheerfully strangle her. Fortunately, he wasn't likely to do so on a public street. "Where are you going now?" he asked through gritted teeth.

"Home to have supper with Aggie."

"Then you'd better get going before I decide to lock you up for your own safety."

"I'm fine, Malloy," she assured him. "No one is interested in me."

"Unless you start meddling in other people's business, and then they'll be very interested in you. Ugo Ruocco doesn't care who your father is or how many times you've dined with the Astors. If he thinks you're a nuisance, he'll have you killed."

"I'm not a nuisance," she protested. He looked like he was ready to argue the point, so she added, "You should know that he's got some of his men posted down by the restaurant. If any Irish boys try to start trouble again, they'll be ready for them this time."

Malloy sighed. "Go home, Sarah, and stay there."

"Don't you want to know what I found out today?"

He rubbed a hand wearily over his face. "Not right now. Right now, I want you to go home."

Sarah took pity on him and went, giving him a cheerful little wave which he ignored. Perhaps it was just as well he didn't want to meet with her tonight. She needed some time to think about everything she'd seen and heard at the Ruoccos house today. Maybe if she took some time to remember everything, she'd figure out what would be really helpful.

Aᴛᴛᴇʀ sᴇɴᴅɪɴɢ Sᴀʀᴀʜ ᴏɴ ʜᴇʀ ᴡᴀʏ, Fʀᴀɴᴋ ᴍᴇᴛ Gɪɴᴏ Donatelli on the corner nearest Mama's Restaurant, as they had previously arranged.

"Wipe that grin off your face," Frank warned him.

He sobered instantly. "I didn't realize—"

"And stop thinking this is fun. It's not fun," Frank added sourly. "I know it's your first big case, and you're thinking about finding the killer and being a big man, but nothing good ever comes of murder."

"But punishing the killer—" he tried.

"Doesn't bring the victim back to life," Frank reminded him. "You can't fix something like that. Punishing the killer might keep him from killing somebody else. It might even make another person think twice about taking somebody else's life, but the dead person is still dead. There's no justice for that, and sometimes . . ."

"Sometimes what?" Gino prodded when Frank hesitated.

"Sometimes punishing the killer makes innocent people suffer."

Gino frowned. "What do you mean?"

"I mean if you put a man in jail or execute him, he might have a family that's left to starve . . . or worse. Half the children living on the streets have a father in jail and a mother who died after selling herself too many times. Now do you still feel like grinning?"

"No, sir," Gino replied, properly chastened.

"Good. We're going to visit the Ruoccos. Your job is to translate if they say anything in Italian and to help me make sure they answer all my questions."

"Yes, sir," he said.

Gino followed him respectfully for the short distance to Mama's Restaurant. Frank noticed the young men loitering on the street corners. Sarah was right, they'd make sure the Irish didn't get very far if they tried to start another riot. None of them would meet Frank's gaze, and he walked into Mama's unchallenged, with Gino on his heels.

The aroma of garlic and tomatoes washed over them, making Frank's stomach clench with longing. The dining room was starting to fill up, and Frank saw Joe and Lorenzo moving through the room with trays held aloft, delivering plates heaped with mouth-watering food to the diners.

"Looks like we came at a bad time," Gino observed. "They're all busy."

"That's good," Frank pointed out. "The rest of the family won't have time to interfere when we question our suspects."

When Joe's tray was empty, he looked over to see who had come in. The welcoming smile froze on his handsome face. He called something to Lorenzo, who frowned when he saw the cops. Lorenzo hurried back into the kitchen as Joe made his way across the room to meet them.

"What do you want?" he demanded.

"We've got a few questions for some members of your family," Frank said.

"It's suppertime. We are very busy. Come back tomorrow."

"We don't want to come back tomorrow. We want to ask our questions right now," Frank informed him with a glare that drained the antagonism right out of him. "Where's Antonio?"

"In . . . in the kitchen," Joe admitted reluctantly. "He's helping Mama."

"Tell him we need to see him." Frank glanced around the noisy room. "And we'll need someplace private to talk to him, unless you want everybody here to know what we're asking him about."

Joe looked like he wanted to punch somebody, but he said, "I'll tell him to take you upstairs. I'll get him."

The people in the restaurant were starting to notice Frank and Gino, and the noise level in the room lessened considerably as people stopped conversing and started whispering and staring. Frank gave them his best effort at intimidation, and soon most of them were at least pretending to mind their own business.

"Here he comes," Gino said softly, and Frank looked over. Antonio had come out of the kitchen, pulling off a sauce-stained apron. He glanced around the room nervously and found to his horror that everyone was staring at him. Then he spotted Frank and Gino near the front door, and paled noticeably. He motioned for them to join him at the stairway door. By the time they got there, he'd opened the door and started up the stairs. They followed, closing the door decisively behind them.

Antonio stopped at the first landing on the second floor, and led them down a short hallway into a family parlor. "What do you want with me?" Antonio asked before they were even in the room. "I don't know anything."

"I'm sure you know a lot of things, Antonio," Frank said,

taking stock of the room. The furniture was comfortably shabby. A shawl hung over the back of a chair and a pair of slippers had been left in front of the sofa. A pillow rested at one end of the sofa, and a blanket had been folded up and laid on top of it, as if someone had been sleeping there. "Tell me how you met Nainsi, Antonio," Frank said.

Antonio frowned. "Why does that matter now?"

"Everything matters now," Frank snapped. "Answer my question."

"I . . . At a dance. I used to go to the dance houses with my brother, and I met her there."

"When was this?"

He frowned, as if trying to remember exactly. "August. I remember because it was right after Valentina's birthday."

"That's a lie, Antonio," Frank moving toward him. "I don't like people who lie to me."

"It's the truth, I swear," Antonio cried, his voice shrill and his eyes wide with fright. He flinched and tried to cover his face when Frank raised his hand, but he only used it to push the boy down onto a chair.

"Then why did Nainsi tell her friends she met you in the spring?"

"I don't know," he claimed, looking up at Frank in desperation. "She couldn't have told them that. I didn't even know who she was back then."

"It's true," a voice said from the doorway behind them. They all turned to see Maria Ruocco standing there. Frank had thought Patrizia was the matriarch of this family, the formidable one they'd have to outsmart, but seeing Maria right now, he reconsidered. For such a small, plain woman, she radiated an amazing amount of authority.

"Excuse me, Mrs. Ruocco," Frank said politely, in deference to the power he sensed in her. "But how would you know such a thing?"

"Because Antonio never went to the dance houses before that. Mama wouldn't allow it until . . . until Joe said it was time he started acting like a man."

"When was Valentina's birthday?" Frank asked her.

"August fifteenth."

This didn't make sense. Nainsi's friends knew about Antonio months before that. "Maybe he was sneaking out so his mama didn't know," Frank suggested, giving Antonio another glare.

"No, I swear! Maria, tell them. I never went out at night before that."

"He would not have dared disobey Mama," Maria confirmed. "What does it matter now, anyway?"

"Because," Frank said, still respectful to her, "if Antonio wasn't the baby's father, he had a good reason for killing Nainsi."

"I wasn't even here when she died," Antonio reminded him. "Joe took me to see Uncle Ugo and then . . . We were with him all night!"

"Why did you go see Ugo?" Frank asked. "Did you want *him* to get rid of your wife for you?"

"No! I mean . . . I don't know why we went. It was Joe's idea. He said Ugo would know what to do."

"Antonio," Maria snapped.

"Thank you for your help, Mrs. Ruocco," Frank said, moving toward her in a slightly menacing manner that forced her to step back until she was out in the hallway. "We'll send for you if we need you again." He closed the door in her surprised face. Then he motioned for Gino to come over to guard the door and turned his attention back to Antonio.

"What did Joe want Uncle Ugo to do?" he asked when he was standing over the boy again.

"He didn't want him to do anything," he claimed. "Joe just told him that Nainsi had the baby and I wasn't the father."

"What did Ugo say?"

Antonio winced at the memory. "He said I was stupid to trust a whore, and I got what I deserved. He said a lot of things like that. I don't remember all of it. He gave me some whiskey to drink, and we sat there for a long time, drinking. He and Joe were talking, but I was just drinking. I don't remember much after that. Next thing I know, I wake up right there." He pointed at the sofa.

"That's convenient," Frank observed. "You don't remember what you did for the rest of the night?"

"No, I don't!"

"Then for all you know, you came home, went up to your bedroom, and put a pillow over Nainsi's face and smothered her."

"I didn't! Why would I?" he cried.

"A lot of reasons. Because you didn't like being made a fool of by a cheap little mickey bitch. Because you didn't like being stuck raising somebody else's bastard. Because you didn't want a wife who'd lift her skirts for any man who gave her a smile or bought her a drink."

The boy lunged to his feet with a roar of outrage, but Frank grabbed his shoulders and slammed him back down into the chair.

"Isn't that what happened?" Frank challenged. "Did she do it for just a smile, or did she make you buy her a drink first?"

Antonio's eyes glowed with loathing, and his handsome face twisted with rage. "It wasn't like that!"

"Wasn't it?" Frank demanded. "Did she even tell you her name first?"

"I knew her name!"

"Did you know she was carrying somebody else's baby?"

That stopped him cold. Frank watched the rage drain out of him, and he was a boy again. "She said . . . she said it was her first time."

"Of course she did."

"She said she liked me," he remembered sadly.

"Maybe she did," Frank allowed. "She was looking for a husband, so she would have wanted somebody she could live with."

Antonio grimaced. "She didn't like me after we got married though. She didn't even want me in her bed. She said she was sick from the baby, and didn't want me to touch her. She was mean to everybody else, too. Mama hated her. Lorenzo said I never should've married her."

"No one would blame you for killing a woman like that, Antonio," Frank said reasonably. "They'd probably throw you a parade."

The boy's eyes filled with tears. "I wish I had killed her. Nobody would laugh at me then. They wouldn't say I was stupid and weak for getting tricked like that."

His shoulders started to shake and the tears ran down his cheeks. Frank had to look away. At least he could be pretty sure Antonio hadn't killed Nainsi. He was too young and still too innocent to hide such a grievous sin. He might've been too drunk to remember, but if he'd been that drunk, he wouldn't have been able to overpower the girl.

"Go back downstairs and tell your brother Joe to come up to see me," Frank said in disgust.

Antonio looked at him in surprise, scrubbing the tears from his face with his palms. "Joe? Why do you want to see Joe?"

"Because I do. Now go get him before I decide to take the easy way out and lock you up."

Antonio sprang to his feet and rushed out, practically shoving Gino aside as he jerked open the door and ducked through it. Maria Ruocco still stood in the hallway outside. She watched Antonio race away, then turned back and came to the doorway again.

"He didn't kill the girl," she said urgently. "He doesn't have it in him."

"Then he doesn't have anything to worry about," Frank said. "Mrs. Ruocco, would you answer a few questions for me?"

She stiffened in silent resistance, but she lifted her chin and said, "I don't know what I can tell you."

"You and your husband sleep upstairs in the room across from where Nainsi died, don't you?"

"Yes." She folded her hands tightly at her waist, offering nothing more.

"Did you sleep there the night Nainsi died?"

"Of course. I always sleep there."

"When was the last time you saw Nainsi?"

She frowned, her heavy brows knitting as she considered the question. "I'm not sure. I . . . helped her with the baby for a while . . . after Mrs. Brandt left. Mama said Nainsi could stay until she was recovered."

"I guess Nainsi must have been upset about having to leave with her baby," Frank suggested.

She took a moment before answering this question, too. "No, she wasn't. She . . . she thought Mama would let her stay. She was married to Antonio, and she thought we would have to let her stay."

"Even after your mother-in-law told her she'd have to leave?"

Maria shrugged. "She was a foolish girl, and young. She did not know anything."

"About what time did you leave her?"

"I went down to help Mama with dinner. That is our busy time."

"Who else helped?"

"Everyone. We always do."

"You're sure? Everyone was there?"

"Yes, I'm sure."

"Antonio said he and Joe went to see their uncle."

Maria nodded. "They did. After dinner was over and we closed."

"What did everyone else do?"

"We . . . we cleaned up. Mama was angry because Joe and Antonio didn't stay to help. After that, we came up here, like always."

"To this room?"

"Yes."

"Did anybody go to check on Nainsi?"

"Valentina took some supper up to her earlier."

"Do you know when that was?"

"I'm not sure. Probably near seven o'clock. The crowd was thinning out, and that's usually when it happens."

"What about after everyone came up here? Did you or anybody else go up to see how she was?"

Maria looked down at her clasped hands. "I . . . I wanted to, but Mama . . . She said we should do nothing for her."

"But when you went up to bed, you couldn't resist checking on the baby, could you?" Frank guessed.

Maria's head snapped up. For a moment, he thought she would deny it, but then she sighed. "I looked in. I just opened the door a little. I could see the baby was asleep in his cradle. Nainsi was . . . She was asleep, too."

"Did you actually see her?"

Some emotion flickered across her face and then was gone. "The room was dark, and I thought she was . . . asleep. I didn't want to disturb her."

"So she might've been dead by then?"

For a second she looked frightened, and Frank knew she was wondering who she might have implicated. Then she remembered something, and her shoulders sagged in relief. "No, she was alive. I remember now. When Joe came in later, he tripped on something and almost fell. He was . . . drunk," she explained in embarrassment. "He made a loud noise, and Nainsi called out to him to be quiet."

"When was this?"

"I don't know. I was asleep, and the noise woke me, too. I helped him get into bed, and then we both went to sleep."

"Did you hear anything else that night?"

"No, nothing that woke me up. And Joe, he was with me all night. I would know if he got up," she added in anticipation of Frank's impending question.

She turned at the sound of footsteps in the hall. Joe appeared in the doorway. "Maria? Why are you talking to this man?" he demanded.

"I was just asking her some questions about what happened the night Nainsi died," Frank explained.

"She knows nothing about that. None of us do. How many times do we have to tell you?"

"Mr. Ruocco," Frank said with a trace of sarcasm. "A woman was murdered in this house. That woman was married to your brother. *Somebody* in this house knows *something* about it."

The color rose in his face, but he knew better than to argue with the police. If one of them accidentally broke your jaw, none of the authorities would care. Uncle Ugo might exact revenge for it, but your jaw would still be broken. "Maria, go upstairs and take care of the baby," he said.

Maria took the opportunity he offered and left. She didn't look back.

"Antonio said you wanted to talk to me," Joe said belligerently.

"Tell me what you did that night after Nainsi's baby was born."

He looked puzzled, but he made an effort to remember. "I . . . We all served dinner, like we do every night. All the time I was trying to think of some way to . . . to help Antonio."

"So you decided to kill Nainsi?"

"*No!* I could think of nothing, so I went to see my uncle."

"Ugo," Frank supplied. "Did you go alone?"

"No, Antonio went with me."

"What time was this?"

"I don't know. After all the customers left. Maybe eight o'clock. Maybe later. I don't know."

"So you went to see Ugo. Where did you go?"

"He owns a place on Mott Street. That's where you go to find him."

Frank knew it well, a saloon where men could talk and not worry about outsiders hearing them. "What did you tell him?"

Joe sighed. "I told him about the baby, and how Mama wanted to throw them both out into the street."

"And Ugo suggested it would be much neater if you just killed the girl."

"No! Nobody said anything about killing her. Why would they?"

"Because she was married to Antonio. You know how hard it is for a Catholic to get a divorce."

"He . . . he didn't want to divorce her," Joe claimed.

"Why not? Don't tell me he was going to forgive her and raise the baby as his own?" Frank scoffed.

"He . . . We were talking," he said, his hands moving nervously. "Trying to decide . . . what was the right thing to do."

"Your mother already decided. She was going to throw Nainsi and the baby out of the house," Frank reminded him.

"But . . . Nainsi was Antonio's wife," he said, gesturing helplessly.

"A wife who'd tricked him into marrying her so her bastard would have a name," Frank reminded him.

"But . . ." He glanced around as if trying to find the correct reply written someplace in the room. "Maria," he finally decided and nodded in approval at his choice. "Yes, Maria, she didn't want Nainsi to leave. She didn't think it was right. The girl is so young, she said. And the baby . . . Who would take care of them?"

"Maria wanted them to stay?" Frank asked in amazement.

"Yes, that's right. She wanted them to stay, but she couldn't say this to Mama. So I went to my uncle. I thought he would know what to do."

"And did he know what to do?" Frank asked, managing not to betray his skepticism of this unlikely tale.

"No," Joe said, heaving another sigh. "No, he did not."

Frank opened his mouth to ask another question, but a shout and the explosion of shattering glass stopped him. "What the . . . ?" he cried, running to the window.

"What is it?" Gino and Joe both demanded, close behind him. They jostled each other for a better view of the street below over Frank's shoulders. The glow of torches illuminated the mob that was swarming down Hester Street. Frank knew it was too early in the evening for them to be drunk enough for this to be a spontaneous act. Someone had organized them, whipping the Irish lads into a frenzy and probably arming them with sticks and stones and enough liquor to make it seem like a good idea to march down to Little Italy and teach the dagos a lesson.

"Gino, go down the back stairs and get everybody you can find at Headquarters," Frank said.

"What are you going to do?" Gino asked.

"Try to stop this."

8

BY THE TIME FRANK GOT DOWN TO THE DINING ROOM, the fighting had already started. Ugo Ruocco's guards had done their job and gotten reinforcements to meet the mob in the street outside. The remaining dinner customers were screaming in terror as Antonio and Lorenzo frantically tried to herd them into the kitchen so they could escape out the back into the alley. Joe had followed Frank down the stairs, and he hurried off to help.

"Turn out the lights!" Mrs. Ruocco was yelling to no one in particular as she reached up to turn off the nearest gas lamp.

Realizing he'd be wasting his time and endangering his life for no reason if he tried to intervene in the melee outside, Frank started turning off the gas jets in the front of the room.

"The door!" Mrs. Ruocco cried as someone slammed against the front window. "Lock it!"

Frank hurried over and shoved home the bolt. "I'll pull the shades, too," he said. He didn't add that it was a safety precaution. If they smashed in the windows, the shades would keep the glass from flying too far and injuring someone inside.

"What's happening?" a woman cried from the shadow of the stairway. Frank looked over to see Maria Ruocco holding the bundled baby. Her eyes were wide with terror.

"They've come to kill us," Valentina informed her hysterically as she emerged from the kitchen. "All because of that damn baby!"

"Valentina!" Mrs. Ruocco chastened shrilly.

"I don't care! I hate that baby! We should throw it out there and let them have it so they'll leave us alone!"

Something thudded against the front window, and Valentina screamed. Joe came out of the kitchen, his brothers close behind him.

"Turn off the rest of the lights," Mrs. Ruocco shouted as glass shattered on the doorstep.

Valentina screamed again and this time she didn't stop. Mrs. Ruocco strode over to her, lifted a hand, and slapped her soundly across the face, silencing her instantly. Frank winced, but he was too glad to have her quiet to worry much about it.

"Mama," Joe said, throwing an arm around Valentina and pulling her close. "We need to get out of here."

"We cannot leave our home!" Mrs. Ruocco replied, outraged.

"Joe's right, Mrs. Ruocco," Frank said. "They might set the place on fire."

Valentina made a sound like she was going to scream again, but Joe tightened his grip, silencing her.

"Maria and the children should leave," Lorenzo said sensibly. "Maria, you take Valentina and the baby out the back and over to Mrs. Pizzuto's."

"I will not leave," Mrs. Ruocco informed him.

"Did I say you should go?" he countered. "Come on, Maria. Hurry before somebody thinks about going around to the back."

"Mama?" Maria asked uncertainly.

"Go," Mrs. Ruocco said. "You cannot help here."

Valentina was already hurrying toward the kitchen, and Maria followed her with obvious reluctance.

"One of you men, go with them and make sure they get there safely," Frank added. Lorenzo went after them.

"You are police," Mrs. Ruocco reminded him with a scornful glance. "Why you no do something?"

"I sent Officer Donatelli to Police Headquarters. They'll be here soon."

She snorted in disgust.

"Come away from the windows, Mama," Joe said, taking her arm and trying to get her to move.

She shook him off. "I tell you turn off lights!"

Joe and Antonio finished the task, and soon they stood in shadowy darkness, relieved only by the flickering reflections from the torches outside.

"Mama, you should leave, too," Antonio said, the fear thick in his voice. "Come on, I'll take you."

"Go, if you are afraid," she said. "I will stay."

"We should've let that Irish woman take the baby," Antonio said, looking toward the front of the restaurant where the shadows of the men outside danced across the shaded window. "Do you know what they're saying about us in the newspapers?"

"I no care what they say," Mrs. Ruocco cried. "Do you have no pride?"

"I have pride for my family, but that baby is not our family," Antonio argued, his voice quivering with terror. "Why should we die for somebody else's bastard?"

"Shut up, Antonio," Joe said. "We aren't going to die."

"He said they'd set the place on fire!" Antonio cried, gesturing toward Frank.

"Then run away with the other baby," Joe said in disgust.

"This is all your fault!" Antonio was shouting now. "You were the one who said I should marry that bitch!"

"You tell him that?" Mrs. Ruocco demanded in surprise.

"The baby!" Joe threw up his hands in frustration. "What else could he do?"

"He could do *nothing*!" Mrs. Ruocco informed him. "He is boy!"

"I'm not a boy, Mama!" Antonio protested. "I'm a man!"

Something struck the front door, shaking it in its frame and startling Mrs. Ruocco into crying out.

"Mama, Antonio is right. You must get out of here," Joe said, moving toward her.

Frank had already stepped between her and the door. He picked up a chair, ready to swing it as a greeting to intruders. "Take your mother out the back," he shouted at Joe.

They heard a door slam behind them and the sound of running feet. Someone burst through the door from the kitchen. "Maria is safe," Lorenzo reported. "What's happening?"

"Take Mama away," Joe said as the front door shook again under the assault of someone trying very hard to break it down. "Quick!"

"No!" Mrs. Ruocco cried, slapping away Joe's hands when he tried to push her toward his brother. "I stay!"

"Get her under a table then!" Frank shouted as the front door shuddered one last time before bursting open. He didn't see what happened to her because he was too busy swinging the chair at the first body through the door. It landed with a satisfactory thud, driving the fellow backward into the bodies behind him. Since the mob kept surging forward, no one could retreat or even stop, and the bodies pouring through the doorway all started falling over each other like dominoes.

Frank raised the chair and brought it down again on the first man to struggle to his feet. It shattered in his hands, so he shook loose one of the legs and started swinging. He wasn't sure how long he could keep the rioters at bay with a chair leg, but fortunately, he finally heard the blast of a police whistle outside, followed by a chorus of echoing bleats that signaled the arrival of the cops.

"Get out of here before I lock you all up!" Frank shouted to the writhing mass of men lodged in the restaurant doorway. He could hear the satisfying sound of locust clubs striking flesh and bone and the howls of pain from the rioters in the street. Someone else had picked up another piece of the broken chair and was helping him beat back the invaders. For what seemed a long time, none of them were able to move because the crowd outside was blocking their escape. But suddenly, as if a cork had been pulled from a bottle, the mob fell away and those stuck in the doorway scrambled or dove or crawled outside to the relative safety of the street. Frank followed, still swinging his club to encourage them on their way. The street was already clearing except for those lying senseless on the cobblestones or being thrown into the paddy wagons.

Gino came running over to Frank. "Is everybody all right?"

"I think so," Frank said, a little winded from his exertions. "Maria took Valentina and the baby to a neighbor's. The old woman wouldn't leave, and the boys are still inside, but nobody got any farther than the front door."

"We are all fine," Lorenzo reported, coming up beside him, still holding his chair leg. So he'd been the one who rushed to help. Frank had expected Joe.

Behind them they could hear Patrizia Ruocco shouting in rapid Italian. Her tone spoke of outrage over the attack on her property and her family. Joe was trying to calm her without much success.

Gino went back to helping his fellow officers clear the streets by throwing every rioter too injured to run into a wagon for transport back to the station. In a surprisingly short time, the Black Marias rumbled away, leaving only the discarded clubs and broken beer bottles as evidence of what had transpired. The sergeant had come over to get Frank's version of what happened. When he was finished, the last of the police officers drifted away, leaving only Frank and Gino Donatelli.

"Lorenzo," Mrs. Ruocco snapped. "Help Giuseppe fix door." She was carrying a broom and a dust pan and had begun sweeping up the broken glass around her doorstep.

"I should go get Maria and let her know it's safe to come home," Lorenzo said.

"I send Antonio already," his mother said.

Lorenzo headed back into the restaurant.

"Mrs. Ruocco, if you like, I can get some police officers to guard your house tonight," Frank offered.

She made a disparaging sound. "Police no good. We take care ourselves. You, go home. Leave us alone."

Frank was only too happy to oblige.

"Should I stay?" Gino asked in a whisper.

"If you want to, but I doubt anybody will bother them again tonight. Those fellows will be nursing sore heads for a day or two. They might want to come back when they feel better, but not real soon."

"Gino," Mrs. Ruocco called. "Go home to you mama. We no need you help."

"Come on, Gino," Frank said, slapping the young fellow on the back. "It's been a long day."

THE NEXT MORNING SARAH WOKE TO THE SOUND OF someone banging on her back door. Only her neighbors used the back door, so Sarah hurried to answer it, hoping no one was sick. She saw Mrs. Ellsworth's silhouette on the glass and threw the door open.

"Have you seen the newspapers?" Mrs. Ellsworth demanded, holding one up. "Oh, I don't suppose you have," she added, noticing Sarah was in her nightclothes. "I'm so sorry to wake you, but when I saw this article—"

"Come in, come in," Sarah urged, closing the door behind her. "What is it?"

"Another riot at the Ruoccos' restaurant last night," she said, holding up the paper again. "I heard the newsboy shouting about it when I was on my way to the market. I bought it and came right here to show you. It's bad luck to go back, you know, but since I wasn't going to my own house, I don't think that counts, does it?"

Sarah had no idea. She took the newspaper Mrs. Ellsworth handed her and scanned the story.

Supposedly, the Irish lads who had been arrested claimed they were only trying to rescue the baby the Italians had kidnapped. According to the report, none of the Ruoccos were injured, although Sarah knew that newspaper reports were notoriously inaccurate. Did she dare go down to Little Italy to check on the family? She knew what Malloy would say, but she really was worried about Maria and the rest of them, too. Maria was already under a strain with Nainsi's murder and caring for the baby. Now she must be terrified as well, knowing a mob had wanted to take the boy from her.

"I should go down there," Sarah said. "Make sure everyone is all right."

"Oh, dear, I don't think that's wise," Mrs. Ellsworth said with a frown. "Who knows who might be lurking around. Besides, the family might not appreciate visitors right now, after what they went through last night."

"I guess you're right," Sarah said, knowing she was. "I suppose if they need me, they'll send for me."

"Of course they will, dear. And if you simply can't stay away, you might consider a visit to the mission a little later on. Surely, someone there can tell you everything you'd want to know," she added with a wink.

FRANK WASN'T SURPRISED AT THE SUMMONS TO ROOSEvelt's office when he arrived at Headquarters the next morning. Old Teeth and Spectacles was in early this morning, and Frank had a feeling he probably hadn't gotten much sleep last night. When he saw him, he was sure of it.

"Mr. Malloy, we can't have the Irish and the Italians rioting in the street," he said before Frank had even closed the door behind him.

"No, sir, we can't."

"Have you made any progress on the Irish girl's murder yet?"

"No, sir. I was at the Ruoccos' last night, questioning the family, when the riot started."

"Do you still think one of them is the murderer?"

"That's the most logical solution, but it's hard to figure out why they would kill her. The boy she was married to had the best reason, but I'm almost certain he didn't do it. By all accounts, he was passed out drunk that night anyway, and I don't think he'd even realized yet what all this meant for him."

Roosevelt removed his spectacles and rubbed the bridge of his nose. "I had a visit from Tammany Hall last night," he said grimly. "And Commissioner Parker." Tammany Hall was where the Democratic politicians held court. He meant that someone in power there had accompanied Parker. Although Roosevelt liked people to think he was in charge of the department, he was only one of four police commissioners. Parker was another of the four, and as a loyal Tammany soldier, he was the bane of Roosevelt's existence. "They came to my *home*," Roosevelt added with quiet outrage. "They want this matter settled, and they want the girl's mother—what's her name?"

"Mrs. O'Hara."

"Mrs. O'Hara. They want Mrs. O'Hara to have the child."

Frank managed not to wince. "But the law says—"

"I know what the law says. I also know that this O'Hara woman has been raising Cain down at Tammany Hall, and the penny press has got everybody in an uproar. When we questioned the rioters we arrested last night, we found out they'd been organized by the Ward Heelers!" The Heelers were the political hacks assigned to organizing voters and making sure they made it to the polls to vote for the proper—that is, Democratic—candidates, as well as performing whatever other duties might be required of them. Frank hadn't realized that starting riots was one of those duties.

"Are you saying Tammany Hall is behind all the trouble? Why would they care about one baby?"

"I think they want to demonstrate to their constituency that they have the power to control even me," Roosevelt admitted. Frank could see how much this infuriated him. "The trouble is, I can see the justice in this woman's claim. If someone in that house killed the baby's mother, then they've got no right to the child."

Frank had to agree with that, too. "We don't know if one of the Ruoccos killed her, though."

"Do you have other suspects?"

"Not any good ones." Frank thought of the foreman at the sweatshop where Nainsi had worked.

"I don't know how long Tammany will wait before they organize another riot, and the next time the Ruoccos might not be so lucky. Would it be possible to convince them to give the child to Mrs. O'Hara?"

Frank remembered Maria Ruocco holding the baby in her arms. She wouldn't give the boy up willingly, but she wasn't the power in that household. "Maybe," Frank said, "but they wouldn't listen to me."

"What about Officer Donatelli?"

"They don't trust the police, even when the cop is Italian.

They don't trust anybody else with authority, either. According to Donatelli, they only trust their own blood relatives."

"But there must be someone else they'd listen to," Roosevelt argued. "Or at least someone who could reason with them. It could save their lives!"

Frank gritted his teeth. He wouldn't say her name. He wouldn't even think it, not even to save every last one of the Ruoccos. "Maybe Donatelli knows somebody," he offered. "Somebody Italian who could influence them."

"Dee-lightful," Roosevelt declared. "The boy is upstairs in the dormitory. The desk sergeant told me they didn't get finished with the prisoners until early this morning, so he stayed here." He hurried to the door and ordered Miss Kelly to send for him.

While they waited, Frank filled Roosevelt in on everything he'd learned so far in the case. Hearing how little it was discouraged even him. He'd said before that all the Ruoccos had to do was keep quiet, and they'd never find Nainsi's killer. He'd gotten them to talk, at least a little, but he was still no closer to the truth.

Donatelli appeared a few minutes later, looking as if he'd only had a few hours of sleep—which he had. His uniform, Frank noticed, looked a little less crisp than usual, but not too bad under the circumstances. Roosevelt quickly explained why they'd summoned him.

"Oh, yes, sir," Donatelli said, his voice still thick from sleep. "I know who could talk to them—Mrs. Brandt."

Frank almost choked.

Roosevelt pulled off his spectacles again. "Mrs. *Brandt*?" he echoed with an accusing glance at Frank that caught him mid-wince. "Mrs. Sarah Brandt?"

"I don't know her given name, sir," Donatelli said, "but she's the midwife who delivered the baby."

"You didn't mention Mrs. Brandt was involved in this case, Mr. Malloy," Roosevelt said, less than pleased.

"She isn't involved," Frank lied. "She just delivered the baby."

"But she also—" Donatelli began but caught himself when Frank glared at him.

"What did she also do?" Roosevelt asked Frank in a tone that brooked no evasion.

"She helped the Ruocco woman take care of the baby after the mother died," Frank admitted reluctantly.

"They'd trust her, then?"

Frank doubted it. "I don't know," he said instead. "And I'm not even sure Mrs. Brandt would be willing to ask them to give up the baby. The Ruocco woman is pretty fond of it, I understand."

"But Sarah would see the wisdom of it," Roosevelt argued, using her first name to remind Frank he'd known her all his life. "She'd understand that it's to protect the family and for the good of the whole city."

Frank suspected Sarah would choose the good of one baby over the good of a whole city any day of the week, but he refrained from saying so. "Mrs. O'Hara doesn't really have the means to take care of a baby," he argued.

"Tammany is going to give her some kind of a pension, I'm told. They want this badly, Malloy. They aren't going to let the matter rest, and if they don't, I imagine Ugo Ruocco will make sure they have a fight on their hands. We can't have these two factions rioting in the streets every night."

Frank thought Roosevelt was right about Ugo putting up a fight. He wouldn't sit by and see his family attacked, but he certainly had no loyalty to the bastard child of a woman who had lied to his nephew. He'd help put pressure on the family.

"I'm not sure it's really safe for Mrs. Brandt to go down to Little Italy," Frank tried, grasping at his last straw.

"Then you and Officer Donatelli will accompany her. Take as many officers as you think you'll need to protect her, too. We must get this settled, Mr. Malloy. Every night that passes gives Tammany another opportunity to stir up more trouble."

"I'll go see her this morning, sir," Frank said, giving Donatelli a dirty look he didn't understand.

"Dee-lightful. Please give her my regards and my personal thanks for her efforts," Roosevelt said.

SARAH WAS TRYING TO DECIDE IF SHE SHOULD TAKE Aggie and Maeve with her to visit the mission when someone rang her front doorbell. Her heart quickened when she saw Malloy's silhouette through the door, and she smiled as she pulled it open.

"Malloy," she said in greeting, but her smile faded when she saw his expression. "What's wrong?" she asked in alarm.

"Let me in, and I'll tell you," he replied sourly.

Aggie and Maeve had heard the bell and now came running to greet him. He put on a good show for them, teasing and grinning, until Sarah sent them upstairs and took Malloy into the kitchen. She poured coffee without asking and set it in front of him.

"I saw the story about the riot in the newspaper. Did something happen to the Ruoccos? To the baby?"

"No, we managed to keep the rioters out of the restaurant until the police came."

"You were there?" she asked in amazement.

"Donatelli and I were there questioning the family when it started."

"How is Maria? And the baby? She must be terrified!"

"Everybody was fine, or at least nobody got hurt. They sent Maria and the baby and the daughter to a neighbor's house."

"Did you find out anything when you were questioning them? About who might have killed Nainsi?"

"Nobody confessed, if that's what you mean," he said grimly.

She could see the discouragement in his eyes. "I wish I could help. I've been trying to figure out if anything I learned when I was there was important."

"What did you learn?" he asked, surprising her.

"Maria is determined to be a good mother to the baby. She doesn't think she'll ever have any of her own because . . ."

"Because what?" he prodded when she hesitated.

"Because Joe doesn't do his husbandly duty anymore," she told him with just a touch of glee, knowing he'd be embarrassed. He didn't like discussing such things with her.

He reached up and rubbed his eyes, probably to keep from having to look at her. "All right," he said with more than a touch of discomfort. "So Maria is claiming the baby for herself because she can't have one of her own."

"I didn't really expect the rest of the family would be too happy about it, but even Mrs. Ruocco has come around."

"The old woman?" he asked in surprise.

"Yes, she's very fond of Maria and wants her to be happy. She must know that Joe isn't much of a husband and Maria doesn't have any other joy in her life. This is her one chance to have a child."

"I can't believe Joe went along with it."

"I can't either, but maybe he has a guilty conscience. He'll let her have her way so she's too busy to bother him anymore."

"Valentina doesn't seem very pleased to have the baby there," Malloy remarked. "She wanted to give it to the mob last night so they'd go away and leave them alone."

"Oh, my! I know she's a spoiled brat, but I never would have thought her capable of such a thing. Do you think she was serious?"

"Yes, I do," he confirmed gravely. "She hates that baby. I wouldn't leave her alone with it for a second."

Sarah considered this information. "Do you think she could have hated Nainsi that much, too?"

"I thought you said she was the one who discovered the body."

"She was, but . . . She was screaming like a banshee. I thought she was genuinely terrified."

"Maybe she didn't realize she'd killed Nainsi. Maybe she just put the pillow over her face to shut her up or something. Then she went in the next morning and found her dead. She'd be pretty upset."

"It's possible, I guess. I'd hate to think someone so young could do such a thing, though."

"You'd be surprised what kids can do," Malloy said. "Sometimes they're worse than adults because they aren't smart enough yet to even think about the consequences of the things they do."

Sarah shuddered at the thought.

"So we've got Mama Ruocco, Maria and Joe in favor of keeping the baby. Valentina is very much against it."

"I don't know how Antonio feels," Sarah said. "I haven't heard him say anything on the subject."

"He wanted to give the baby to Mrs. O'Hara last night when the mob was trying to break down their front door."

"That seems logical," Sarah mused. "He wouldn't feel any connection to the baby, and he wouldn't be overly concerned about Maria's happiness. Lorenzo was, though," she remembered.

"What do you mean?"

"I mean that when Ugo wanted Maria to give up the baby, he stood up for her."

"When did this happen?" he asked, unable to keep the anger out of his voice.

She sighed in resignation. "Yesterday. Ugo came to the restaurant in the afternoon. I'm sure he thought all he had to do was tell them to give the baby to Mrs. O'Hara and they'd obey. Maria refused him to his face, though."

"And Lorenzo defended her?"

"Yes, he and Joe and Mrs. Ruocco, all of them. Lorenzo took the lead, though. He actually shamed Joe into joining him."

Malloy took a long swig of the cooled coffee and set the cup down with a clunk. "If they didn't listen to Ugo, they probably won't listen to anybody else, either."

"Listen to them about what?"

Malloy gave her a long, level look, as if judging her in some way.

"Malloy, what are you talking about?" she prodded, letting her annoyance show.

"I'm talking about getting them to give the baby to Mrs. O'Hara to make peace."

"Mrs. O'Hara can't take care of an infant," she protested. "She couldn't even support herself and Nainsi."

"Tammany is going to give her a pension so she can," he reported.

"Tammany Hall? What do they have to do with this?"

"It's an Irish baby. They say it was kidnapped by Italians who killed its mother."

"Nobody kidnapped him!"

"Somebody killed his mother, though."

"Maria certainly didn't!"

"Are you sure?"

"Of course I'm sure!"

"Who did, then?"

"How should I know?"

Malloy scowled at her. "Then why are you so sure it wasn't Maria? It could've been her just as easy as anyone else."

Now Sarah rubbed her eyes. "This is crazy, Malloy. First Valentina and now Maria. Next you'll be accusing the baby!"

"He didn't have a motive," Malloy pointed out dryly.

"Neither did anybody else," she snapped back. "Not enough of one to kill her, at any rate. Antonio was the only one who had a reason to be angry enough. She'd made a fool of him and ruined his life."

"He was too drunk," Malloy said.

"How do you know that?"

"Don't you remember how hungover he and Joe were that morning? Besides, I questioned them both."

"Then tell me everything you found out. Let's compare notes and see what we know about the night Nainsi was killed. Maybe we're missing something."

Frank glared at her, but after a few seconds, he gave in. "We both know what happened up until you left that night."

"That's right. Maria was with Nainsi, helping her with the baby."

"According to the ones I questioned, Maria went downstairs with everybody else to help serve dinner to the customers that night. Nainsi was fine then. After the crowd left, Joe and Antonio went to see Ugo, while the rest of the family cleaned up. Then the family went up to the second floor. There's a parlor there, where they usually sit."

"Did someone check on Nainsi after they came upstairs?" Sarah asked.

"Maria said Mrs. Ruocco wouldn't let them. Valentina had taken some supper up to her earlier, but no one saw her again until Maria went up to bed."

"But Maria saw her then?"

"She said she looked in and saw the baby was sleeping in his cradle. The room was dark, and she thought Nainsi was asleep, too, so she didn't say anything to her."

"Then she could have been dead already," Sarah said.

"Not according to Maria. She said that when Joe came in later, after she'd gone to sleep, he made some noise and woke her and Nainsi up. Nainsi called out for him to be quiet."

"That means she was still alive when Joe and Antonio came home. Do we know what time it was?"

"No one paid any attention."

"Of course they didn't," Sarah sighed. "But now we know everyone was at home when she died. What else do we know about Joe and Antonio? You said they went to see Ugo. Do you know why?"

"Joe said he and Antonio went to tell Ugo what had happened and ask him how they could keep the baby for Maria."

"That doesn't sound right!" Sarah exclaimed.

"I know. I think Joe's lying about that. Probably, they went to ask Ugo how to get rid of Nainsi and her baby, but he didn't want to say that to a cop."

"We'll probably never find out for sure what they talked about. Ugo certainly isn't going to tell you that."

"No, he won't. None of them will. They do admit that Antonio drank a lot that night and passed out when he got home. He says he slept on the sofa in the second floor parlor, so he wasn't anywhere near Nainsi. Maria claims Joe got into bed after Nainsi called out for him to be quiet, and neither of them got up again."

"Then that's it. Don't you see? Joe and Antonio went to Ugo to ask him to get rid of her, and he sent someone over to kill her. You said yourself how easy it would be to sneak up the back staircase."

"It's a good theory," Frank agreed. "The problem is proving it. Ugo isn't going to tell us who he sent over, and nobody is going to confess. Meanwhile, the Irish will continue thinking the Ruoccos killed the girl and kidnapped her baby, and they'll keep going down to Little Italy and causing trouble until they get the baby back."

"That's ridiculous! They'll get tired or forget all about it."

"Not if Tammany Hall keeps them stirred up. It's politics, Sarah. Tammany wants to put the Italians in their place. They're going to keep organizing riots—"

"*Organizing?*" Sarah cried in outrage.

"Yes, the Ward Heelers got that group together last night. And they'll keep doing it until Roosevelt helps them get what they want."

"Roosevelt? He'll never go along with this." Sarah had known him all her life, and she knew he could never be coerced.

"He can't stand by and watch people riot in the streets. He doesn't have a choice, Sarah. He has to keep the peace, and the Ruoccos don't have any right to that baby."

"But the law—"

"*Morally,* they have no right to it," he insisted. "Especially if somebody in their family killed Nainsi . . . or ordered it done."

Sarah felt tears stinging her eyes as fury flooded her. "You can't just pass a baby around like it's a . . . a loaf of bread!"

"We're going to give him to his grandmother, his only known relative," he pointed out reasonably.

"You'll never convince Maria to give him up," she warned him furiously.

"I know," he said. "That's why you have to do it."

9

FRANK HADN'T EXPECTED SARAH TO GIVE IN SO EASILY, which made him really suspicious. "You do understand what you need to do, don't you?" he asked her as they rode downtown toward Little Italy in a Hansom cab.

"Of course I do. You made it very clear. I'll have a few sharp words to say to Commissioner Roosevelt when next we meet, though."

Frank was sure she would. "He's got to do what's best for the city," Frank tried. "Innocent people are getting hurt in the riots. It's only a matter of time before somebody gets killed. It could even be one of the Ruoccos. Or maybe they'll burn the restaurant and half the street down."

"You can stop explaining. I understand, Malloy," she said tartly. "That doesn't mean I have to like it, though."

She didn't have to add that she *didn't* like it. That was

obvious. They rode the rest of the way through the city in uneasy silence. Frank hoped she was thinking about what she would say to the Ruoccos, and he hoped it would be convincing.

The cab dropped them off at the corner.

"What if they aren't home?" Sarah asked uneasily.

"They'll be getting ready for the lunch customers," he pointed out.

She looked around, noticing the signs of last night's riot. He could see her shock and was glad for it. Maybe that would soften her up a bit.

"Come on," he urged. "Let's get this over with."

The front door was locked and the shades drawn, so he knocked. He saw Sarah eyeing the patch on the door frame where it had been ripped out last night. The edge of the window shade moved a bit, as if someone was peering out to see who was there, and then the door opened.

"Mrs. Brandt," Lorenzo said in surprise. Then his gaze cut to Frank, and his eyes darkened with suspicion. "What are *you* doing here?" he asked Frank.

"We need to speak with you, Lorenzo," Sarah said before Frank could answer. "We need to speak with your whole family, all together."

"Mama said not to let the police in," he protested.

"Mr. Malloy is escorting me today, to make sure I'm safe because of the trouble last night. I have something to explain to you, something that could end all this trouble and get your lives back to the way they were before. Please, Lorenzo. It's very important."

Lorenzo looked unconvinced, but he said, "Come in. I'll ask Mama."

He locked the door behind them and then went to the

kitchen, leaving Sarah and Frank standing in the empty dining room.

"They did a good job getting the place cleaned up," Frank observed. The patch job on the front door would do for now, and all the debris was gone.

"I can't believe the mob actually broke down the door," she said.

"They only broke it in, not down. Next time they'll probably smash the windows and loot the place."

She gave him a murderous glare, but luckily, Mrs. Ruocco came out of the kitchen like a small whirlwind, with Lorenzo and Joe right behind her.

"What you want?" she demanded of Frank. "I tell you go home, not bother us!"

"Mrs. Brandt is the one who wants to talk to you," Frank defended himself, taking a step backward to show he was no part of it.

"How is the baby doing?" Sarah asked, skillfully diverting her attention.

Mrs. Ruocco forced herself to be polite to Sarah. "The goat milk is good for him. He sleep now."

"That's wonderful," Sarah said with genuine relief. "And Maria? Is she getting enough rest?"

Mrs. Ruocco shrugged one shoulder.

"She's doing better now that the baby is sleeping," Lorenzo reported, earning a disapproving look from his mother.

"Is she here?" Sarah asked with the kind of confidence that had to have been bred into her for generations. "I'd like for her to hear what I have to say, too."

"Is about baby?" Mrs. Ruocco asked suspiciously.

"It's about the trouble you've been having," Sarah said.

"I think we can put an end to it, but Maria should be here before I explain."

Mrs. Ruocco studied her for a long moment, probably trying to judge her sincerity. Apparently satisfied, she gave Joe a nod, and he went hurrying away up the stairs to find his wife.

"We are busy cooking for customer," Mrs. Ruocco warned while they waited. "We must earn living."

"Of course," Sarah agreed. "I won't take up very much of your time, but I know you're anxious to stop these riots."

No one spoke, and in the silence, they could all hear Joe's footsteps as he climbed the stairs and then came back down again. A second set of footsteps followed. Joe emerged from the stairway, and he seemed a bit shocked to see everyone still standing exactly as he'd left them all staring at him. He turned and made sure Maria negotiated the final steps. She carried the baby, who was wide awake, taking in everything around him with the watchful somberness of the newly born.

"Mrs. Brandt, what's wrong?" Maria asked, looking around uncertainly.

"You look much better today, Maria," Sarah said with a small smile.

"He only woke up once last night," Maria reported. "Why are you here? Did something happen?"

"Nothing new," Sarah assured her. "I just . . . I wanted to speak with you about this situation you're in. You may not know it, but the politicians from Tammany Hall are the ones organizing the rioters. They are buying them drinks and getting them stirred up until they're brave enough to come down here and attack the place."

"Why would the politicians do that?" Joe challenged. "Why would they care about us?"

"Mr. Malloy explained to me that Tammany Hall wants to show its power over the Italians."

Joe and Lorenzo made outraged noises.

"*Silenzio,*" Mrs. Ruocco snapped. "Why they come here?"

"Because Nainsi's death put your names in the newspapers, and everybody knows you now. Because they've told lies about you and made the Irish angry. They're saying you murdered Nainsi so you could have her baby."

Maria made an anguished sound and covered her eyes with one hand, holding the baby tightly with her other arm. Mrs. Ruocco said something in Italian that Frank was glad nobody translated, and Joe and Lorenzo muttered ominously.

"How can we stop them?" Joe demanded.

"Commissioner Roosevelt has suggested that in order to satisfy the Irish and take away their reason for attacking you, you give the baby to Nainsi's mother," Sarah said as gently as if she'd been suggesting a walk in the park.

This time Maria was the one who cried out. "*No!*" she shrieked, startling the baby. "She cannot have him! She can't buy the milk for him! She can't keep the bottles clean! She lives like a pig! He will die!"

The baby's tiny face screwed up, and he began to wail. Maria started bouncing him absently as she continued her rant. "Mama, you cannot let that woman have him. You cannot let him die!"

To Frank's surprise, Lorenzo went to her and took the baby out of her arms. "Stop it, Maria," he said gently, as he awkwardly shifted the crying infant into the crook of his own arm. "We will *not* let him die." As if he understood the words, the baby stopped crying and gazed up at Lorenzo in wide-eyed wonder.

"But what can we do?" Joe asked, his voice an annoying

whine. "Even Uncle Ugo's men can't protect us! Last night they broke in here. Who knows what they will do tonight or tomorrow night?"

"Then I will take the baby away someplace," Maria said, her voice quivering with anguish. "He will be safe, and they will forget about all of you when he's gone, and then *you'll* be safe," she added with a touch of contempt to her husband.

"I have a better idea," Sarah said, startling everyone, especially Frank.

He looked at her with apprehension, trying to read the serene expression on her lovely face. She hadn't told him about any other ideas, and he certainly hadn't given her permission to have any.

"Mrs. Brandt, we should go now," he tried, but she ignored him completely.

"The reason the newspapers got everyone so angry in the first place is because Nainsi was murdered in your house," she reminded them. "They're saying you don't have a right to her baby because you kidnapped and killed her to get it."

"That is lie!" Mrs. Ruocco cried.

"Of course it is, but people believe it because they don't know the truth."

"What truth?" Lorenzo asked skeptically.

"They don't know who really killed Nainsi," she said, making Frank wince. "When her killer is caught and punished, everyone will understand you had nothing to do with it."

They all stared at her, dumbfounded. Frank felt pretty dumbfounded himself. Her logic was so reasonable—and so wrong! They still didn't know for sure who had killed Nainsi. If one of the family members had done it, all hell would break loose. Didn't she realize that? No, she didn't, he remembered, because she thought one of Ugo's men had killed Nainsi.

Frank watched their faces as they began to comprehend her argument. Joe and Lorenzo didn't quite know what to think. Maria's face seemed to glow with a desperate hope. But Mrs. Ruocco . . . She understood. She knew someone in her family must have killed the girl, and the truth would destroy them.

"Get out my house!" she said furiously, pointing one gnarled finger at the door. "Get out *now*!"

"But Mama," Maria pleaded. Mrs. Ruocco silenced her with a gesture.

Before she could protest, Frank grabbed Sarah's arm and hauled her to the door. She almost stumbled, but he didn't loosen his grip or slow his pace. He had to throw back the bolt one-handed, but he got them both outside.

"What are you doing?" she demanded, outraged. "We have to convince them to cooperate, or you'll never find Nainsi's killer!"

He just kept walking, dragging her along with him until they'd crossed the street into the next block. Then she finally dug in her heels and forced him to stop.

"What are you doing? Don't you *want* to solve this case?" she asked breathlessly, her cheeks scarlet with fury.

"Of course I do, but that's not the way to do it!"

"You won't find the killer without their help," she insisted.

"And they won't help if the killer is one of them."

"But one of Ugo Ruocco's men killed her," she argued.

"Maybe, but we don't know anything for sure. Did you see Mrs. Ruocco's face? She isn't sure either. She knows as well as I do that it might've been one of her children and she'd cut off her arm before she'd help us find out."

"But if it wasn't one of her children—"

"She's not going to take that chance," Frank said. "She'll protect them the way Maria is protecting that baby. If she knows who did it . . . if any of them know . . . it's a secret they'll take to their graves."

So much for Roosevelt's plan to have Sarah reason with them.

"You SHOULD'VE TAKEN ME WITH YOU," GINO DO-natelli said later, after Frank had escorted a chastened Sarah back home and returned to Headquarters. "I might've been able to convince them."

"First of all, you didn't see Maria Ruocco with that baby. She isn't giving him up, no matter who wants her to," Frank said. "Second, none of them are going to help us find the killer because they're all afraid it's somebody in the family. Third, that's true in any language, so you couldn't have helped."

"But I know how they think," he argued.

"So do I," Frank replied acidly. "They think we want to put one of them in jail, and they're right."

Gino ran a hand over his face in exasperation. "Maybe Mrs. Brandt was the wrong person to deliver the message," he said.

"I think we agree on that," Frank said sarcastically. "Who else would you suggest? Maybe Commissioner Roosevelt would go down and talk to them."

"They'd never listen to him, either," Gino said as if Frank had made a serious suggestion. "They'd listen to Ugo, though."

"Mrs. Brandt said he already told them to give the baby up, but they refused."

"Things weren't so bad then. The stakes are higher now. He doesn't want his men fighting the Irish in the streets any more than we do, and he must know he can't beat Tammany Hall."

"He's not going to turn in one of his own family members, and his men won't follow him anymore if he turns in one of them," Frank pointed out.

"No, but he might force Maria to give up the baby to make peace, and then . . ."

"And then what?"

Gino grinned smugly. "And then she'll hate all of them so much, she'll help us find the killer."

SARAH WALKED FAR ENOUGH TO MAKE MALLOY BELIEVE she was going home, but as soon as she was out of sight, she cut over to Broadway and turned south again. She didn't know exactly where she was going, but she knew that on a pleasant day like this, plenty of people would be out in the street, and someone would be able to give her directions.

Howard Street teemed with life. Teamsters guided their wagons through the narrow passage, shouting and swearing. Homeless urchins darted in and out of the traffic, dodging wheels and horses' hooves. Women argued with street vendors over prices and gossiped on porch steps.

Sarah only had to make three inquiries before she found the right tenement. As she made her way up the dark stairs, stepping carefully to avoid tripping over refuse and heaven knew what else, she could easily imagine how a young girl would grasp at any chance to escape such a dreary place. The Ruoccos weren't really rich, unless you compared them to this.

The door to the flat stood open to catch the breeze, and Sarah saw a woman sitting at the kitchen table with her back to the door. The room held only the rickety table and chairs and a battered stove, which was cold on this spring day. Crates nailed to the walls held a few kitchen utensils and dishes. The walls were an indeterminate color beneath years of grime.

"Mrs. O'Hara?" she called, tapping lightly on the door frame.

Nainsi's mother turned in her chair to see who was calling. "Mrs. Brandt," she said in surprise, pushing herself to her feet. "Is something wrong?"

"Nothing new," Sarah said with a smile. "I just thought I'd stop by and see how you're doing."

"Is the baby all right? Have you seen him?" she asked anxiously. "They won't let me near him, them damned murdering dagos."

Sarah managed to maintain her cheerful smile. "He was a little colicky at first, but we tried feeding him goat's milk, and that helped a lot. The last time I saw him, he seemed to be doing fine."

She murmured something that might have been a prayer and crossed herself. "It ain't right," she said bitterly. "They got no claim to the boy at all. He's nothing to them. Why would they even want him?"

"If it's any comfort, Maria is taking very good care of him," Sarah said.

"It's a little comfort," Mrs. O'Hara admitted. "I wouldn't put it past the rest of them to let him die, just for spite, but that Maria, she wouldn't let it happen, I know. She's a good girl, for being Italian and all."

"How are you doing, Mrs. O'Hara?" Sarah asked. "I know this has been very hard on you."

She waved away Sarah's concerns. "I'm doing all right, all things considered. Take more than this to do me in, I'll tell you that. Well, now, where's my manners? Come in and sit down. Can I get you something?"

"Oh, no. I'm fine, thank you," Sarah said, knowing the woman wouldn't have any food to spare. She took a seat at the table. She saw that Mrs. O'Hara had been working at making men's ties.

"I won't have to do this anymore once I get the baby," she told Sarah, moving her work aside. "I don't even have to take in lodgers anymore. Them politicians, they already give me some money, and they said they'd make sure I got a regular pension so I can take care of the boy proper."

"That's very nice of them," Sarah remarked, wondering why the politicians would have taken such an active interest in a woman like Mrs. O'Hara, much less champion her cause.

"Ain't nothing nice about it," she sniffed. "They seen a chance to get a leg up on the Italians, and they took it. They gotta make folks think they're doing something important, or they won't get reelected."

Sarah had to admit this was a rather astute observation from a female who couldn't vote and probably couldn't even read. "I would never have thought of asking for that kind of help," she admitted.

"Don't know why not," Mrs. O'Hara said in amazement. "That's what everybody does. Got some trouble, you go down to Tammany Hall, and they fix you right up."

"I had no idea!"

"Well, they can't fix everything, mind you. But lots of

things. A word here or there to the right people, and life goes a little better. That's why people vote for 'em. I didn't know what they'd've said about Nainsi's baby, but I guess after I told my story to them reporters and it was in the papers, they didn't have much choice."

Once again, Sarah was impressed by Mrs. O'Hara's political astuteness. "It's a shame about the riots, though," she tried, hoping to make Mrs. O'Hara see the unpleasant results of her efforts. "A lot of the Irish boys ended up in jail."

"Wouldn't be the first time," Mrs. O'Hara said philosophically. "If it wasn't for that, they'd be in for something else. Besides, we need to scare them Ruoccos so they know they gotta give up the baby."

Sarah still had one weapon left in her arsenal. "Yes, well, another reason I came today was to talk to you about taking care of him."

"I know how to take care of a baby," Mrs. O'Hara scoffed. "I raised Nainsi, didn't I? She had a brother, too. He'd be twenty now, but he got the diphtheria and died when he was four. I don't need no lessons in how to take care of a baby."

Sarah smiled sympathetically. "Of course you don't, but taking care of this one will be a little different. I'm sure you nursed your children, but your grandson will have to be fed with a bottle unless you can afford a wet nurse for him. That means you've got to buy milk for him every day."

"Every day?" she asked doubtfully.

"Yes, because it needs to be fresh, and as I said, he needs to have goat's milk or else he'll get sick. You've probably never used baby bottles, so I wanted to be sure you understand that they have to be thoroughly washed and boiled after each use."

"Boiled? Whatever for?"

"If you leave milk in the bottles, even just a little bit, it will go bad and make the baby sick. I know you don't want that to happen."

Mrs. O'Hara glanced around the kitchen, and Sarah knew what she was thinking. No one in the tenements used their stoves in the summertime. The buildings were already unbearably hot. The residents would buy their food from the vendors in the streets, which was actually cheaper than buying fuel and hauling it up to their flats.

"Well, maybe Tammany will help you pay for a wet nurse," Sarah went on. "That would be the best thing anyway."

"I don't know about that," Mrs. O'Hara with a frown. "I don't know about any of this. Nobody said he needed anything special."

"I know, that's why I came. Maria would have explained it all to you, I'm sure, but I didn't want you to be surprised. Or unprepared."

The older woman raised a hand and rubbed her forehead. "I never thought . . ."

"Mrs. O'Hara, I know how worried you must be. You've already lost your daughter, and I don't want you to lose your grandson, too," Sarah said. "That's why I came. I know it's a lot to take in, but I'll be happy to help in any way I can."

"I never dreamed it'd be so hard," she said.

"Taking care of a baby under the best of circumstances is difficult," Sarah reminded her. "The sleepless nights, the diapers, keeping them safe. I'm sure you remember that from your own children."

"I lost two others, too," she admitted sadly. "I don't like to remember them. One was stillborn, and the other . . . the other just died. We never knew why."

Sarah felt the other woman's grief like a lump in her own

chest. "I'm sorry." Then she waited, giving Mrs. O'Hara a chance to make the right decision.

The other woman stared at something only she could see for several minutes, and then her eyes hardened with resolution. "I love that baby, Mrs. Brandt. It would kill me if anything happened to him."

Sarah nodded, holding her breath and silently praying.

"But those people got no right to him. He's my flesh and blood, the only family I got left. I can't leave him in that house, Mrs. Brandt, because somebody in that house killed my Nainsi."

Sarah let out her breath on a sigh. She'd done her best, but she'd lost.

In all the years he'd been a cop, Frank had faced many dangerous situations, but none quite so dangerous as bearding Ugo Ruocco in his own den. He could feel the wave of hostility wash over them when he and Gino entered the saloon where Ugo held court. Every eye in the room turned toward them, all filled with hatred.

One of the men challenged them in Italian, and Gino replied in Italian, his tone polite but firm. Several of the men got up from their tables and walked slowly toward them, their expressions taunting as they formed a loose circle around them. The threat of violence was blatant, but Frank knew better than to show a trace of fear. He glared back at them, silently daring them to risk attacking the police. They might win this battle, but they would start a war that would bring down the wrath of the Irish and the police and the city government, too. Frank sincerely hoped they realized that.

After a long moment, an older man sitting at a table on the other side of the room stood up and gave a curt order. He was short and round with graying hair and a well-worn face. The thugs fell back, opening a corridor between him and them. "You want to see the *Padrone,* Gino Donatelli?" he asked.

"Yes, we do," Gino replied. Frank had to admire the way he refused to be intimidated. Maybe letting dagos on the force wasn't such a bad idea after all.

"I will ask if he will see you," the man said, his tone implying that he sincerely doubted that would happen. He turned and walked through a door at the back of the room, closing it softly behind him.

As they waited, Frank could hear the words "fool's errand" echoing in his head. That's what his mother would've said about him walking into a dago saloon. Frank carefully made eye contact with each of the men in the room, silently letting them know they didn't scare him one bit.

Even if it was a lie.

After what seemed like an hour, the older man returned and motioned for them to follow him. Gino led the way. The thugs closed in a bit as they passed, letting Frank and Gino feel their presence without actually making any threatening moves. Frank figured ordinary citizens would be terrified.

Although the saloon itself looked exactly like every other saloon in the city—its furnishings plain, functional, and worn with hard usage—the back room was clearly the office of an important man. Velvet drapes hung at the windows and a handwoven carpet covered the floor. Gilt-framed pictures of European landscapes hung on the wallpapered walls, and Ugo Ruocco sat at a large round table with a bottle of wine and a half-empty glass before him.

Their escort held the door for them and then closed it behind him, standing with his back to it to observe their meeting and prevent interruption.

"Gino," Ruocco said with apparent good cheer. "What brings you here? And who have you brought with you?"

Gino whipped off his hat and nodded slightly in greeting. "Good afternoon, *Padrone*," he said with more respect that Frank would have shown. "Thank you for seeing us."

"How could I turn you away? I would never know why you came, and I am very interested to know that. Please, sit down," he said, waving magnanimously at the empty chairs at the table. "You, too, Detective," he added less enthusiastically.

Gino exchanged a glance with Frank before taking one of the offered chairs. Frank took the one beside him. Frank sized up Ruocco across the expanse of tablecloth that separated them. He was a man supremely confident in his place in the world and the power he wielded. Someplace else, he might not be so confident, but here he was in total control of everything and everyone. Frank and Gino were suppliants come to beg a favor of the great man. The knowledge burned like gall in Frank's mouth, but he knew better than to betray it.

"*Padrone,* Detective Sergeant Malloy has come because he has something important to discuss with you," Gino said.

"I am sure it is about my family," Ruocco said with a small smile that didn't quite reach his eyes.

"You probably know by now that Tammany is behind the riots," Frank said.

Ruocco nodded once, his eyes hard and suspicious. "I have heard this, yes."

"They want to show everybody that they can keep the Italians in their place."

Ruocco's smile disappeared. "Have you come only to tell me what I already know?"

"No, I came to ask you to put an end to the trouble."

"I have men guarding the restaurant," Ruocco reminded him impatiently. "They could not stop it."

"Tammany Hall wants Nainsi's mother to have the baby. If that happens, the riots will stop."

Ugo considered this for a moment. "One small baby to cause so much trouble," he mused. "But we cannot trust them. They also say my family killed Nainsi to get the baby. They will want the murderer, and they will not stop until they get him."

"The *police* would like the murderer," Gino said, completely violating his agreement with Frank to keep his mouth shut during this discussion.

"If we found the killer," Frank clarified quickly, "then Tammany wouldn't have any reason at all to cause more trouble."

"Tammany will always cause trouble," Ruocco corrected him bitterly.

"But they'd cause it for someone else's family," Frank said.

Ruocco saw the logic in this, but he was unmoved. "Poor Maria, I told her to give the baby to that woman, but she would not. If I take the boy now, her heart will break."

Frank didn't think Ruocco cared a whit for Maria's broken heart. "The only other way to get them to call off their dogs is to punish the killer, then," he said, knowing Ruocco would never agree to that.

"Yes," Ruocco said wisely. "That is what we must do."

Frank didn't bother to hide his surprise, and Gino's jaw actually dropped before he caught himself and snapped it shut again. Frank recovered first. "Are you telling us you know who killed Nainsi?"

Ruocco smiled. It wasn't a pretty sight. "I will tell you what I know. I know my brother's wife hated the girl. She made Antonio a fool. He married a whore and gave his name to her bastard child. The girl hurt one of Patrizia's children, and Patrizia will do anything to protect her children."

"Most women will," Frank noted.

"Will most women kill? Patrizia killed my brother to protect her children," he said, and the loathing in his eyes chilled Frank.

"Are you saying she murdered her husband?" Frank asked in disbelief.

"She sent him back to Italy to die alone so her children could stay here," Ruocco said. "It is the same thing."

Not exactly, at least to Frank's way of thinking. This sounded more likely than outright murder, and it certainly didn't make Patrizia Ruocco a killer. "Did Mrs. Ruocco kill Nainsi?" Frank asked.

"I am telling you what I know," Ruocco reminded him sharply. "Do you think the boys do something without Patrizia knowing? Do you think Maria or Valentina can kill like that? No, only one in that house can kill. Patrizia, she is the one."

10

"Do you really think Mrs. Ruocco killed the girl?" Gino asked as he and Frank made their way back to Headquarters.

"Ugo wants us to think so. What was he talking about when he said she sent her husband back to Italy to die?"

"I don't know. She's been a widow as long as I've known her."

Frank reviewed what Ruocco had told them. Frank had considered Mrs. Ruocco a suspect, of course. She had a good reason to want Nainsi dead, the same reason everyone else in the house had. What Ruocco said about the boys was probably true, too. They'd do only what she told them, unless some irresistible passion drove them. If any of them was capable of an irresistible passion, Frank hadn't seen any evidence of it yet.

"You can't believe Mrs. Ruocco did it," Gino was saying. "She's a woman."

"Women can kill," Frank assured him. "They do it for different reasons than men, but they do it just the same."

"Whores do," Gino argued. "But not respectable women like Mrs. Ruocco."

Frank sighed at his naïveté, but he let it go. "Do you know anybody who'd remember the story about what happened to her husband?"

"My mother might. Do you want me to ask her?"

"Yeah, I do. How soon can you talk to her?"

"Right now, if you want. I'm off duty."

Frank looked at him in surprise, pleased at his dedication to pursue this case on his own time. "Good. Find out everything you can, then come and tell me. I'll be at Headquarters doing some reports."

Gino gave him a mock salute and headed off at a sprint. Frank sighed, wondering if he'd ever been that young and eager. He reached the corner and glanced down the street toward Mama's Restaurant. Everything seemed peaceful enough in the waning evening light. A movement in the shadows caught his eye, and a uniformed patrolman stepped forward.

" 'Evening, Detective Sergeant," he said.

" 'Evening, Officer. Keeping an eye on things?"

"Yes, sir. Commissioner Roosevelt, he ordered that we station a couple of men down here in case there's more trouble. He wants to be sure we get officers down here quicker than we did last time . . ."

"I doubt you'll see another mob so soon," Frank assured him. "Most of the troublemakers from last night are still recovering. But if anything does happen, anything at all, let me know. I'll be at Headquarters."

"You'll be the first to hear about it then," the officer promised with a grin.

IN THE SILENT, DESERTED ROOM WHERE THE DETECTIVES had their desks, Frank was feeling sorry for himself. Grumbling about the paperwork, he was wishing he'd gone home to have supper with his son when Gino found him. He'd changed out of his uniform into casual clothes and a soft cap, and as usual, he looked much too excited.

He set a paper sack down on the desk in front of Frank. "My mother sent you some supper."

Frank's stomach growled in response to the aroma of garlic and fresh-baked bread. He tried not to look as grateful as he felt as he pulled open the sack to peer inside.

"What did you find out?" Frank asked. Inside the sack were two thick slices of bread covered with tomato sauce and melted cheese. Frank pulled one out and took an enormous bite. It tasted even better than it smelled.

"I found out that Patrizia and Ugo hate each other."

Frank swallowed. "We already knew that," he reminded Gino grimly.

"Yeah, but now I know *why* they hate each other."

"The protection money," Frank guessed.

"Oh, no, it's about her husband. A story I never heard before."

Frank sighed. "I'm betting it's a long story."

"Not real long," Gino said with far too much glee, pulling up a chair next to Frank's desk. "You see, Ugo came over from Italy first, about twenty years ago. Back then, a lot of men came over to work for a few years and send money home. When they saved up enough to buy some land there, they'd go back to Italy. Most of them never intended to stay here very long."

Frank couldn't understand why somebody would prefer a foreign country to America, but there was no figuring out Italians. "Let me guess, Ugo decided to stay."

"Yeah, he found out he could be a big man over here. He was nothing in Italy and never would be, but here people listened to him. He made lots of friends and lots of money."

"So he brought over the rest of his family." Frank reached into the bag for the other piece of bread.

"No, not all of them, only his brother. At least that was the plan. He was going to bring Ernesto over to work for a while, too. Then they would send for their families. But it didn't work out that way."

"Why not?" Frank asked between bites.

"Because Patrizia Ruocco refused to stay in Italy. By then Ugo's wife had been left alone for almost five years. Patrizia didn't think Ugo was going to send for his wife at all. Some men did that. They'd get here and forget all about their wives back home. Sometimes they'd even get married to another woman. The wives back in Italy, they called them white widows. Patrizia wasn't going to be a white widow."

"So she came along with her husband?"

"She convinced Ernesto not to come without the whole family, even Ugo's wife. Ugo was plenty mad, but in the end he gave in because he wanted his brother here. Like I told you before, family is very important to Italians, and he needed somebody he could trust to help him in his business."

"And Ugo never forgave Patrizia for making him bring over his fat, ugly wife?" Frank guessed.

"No, he never forgave her because when they got here,

Ernesto couldn't get in. Turns out he had consumption. He was dying, so they sent him back to Italy."

Now Ugo's accusation against Patrizia made sense. "Patrizia sent him back alone?"

"That's right. Ugo thought she should go home with him, to take care of him, but she wouldn't. She wanted her children to live in America, and she wouldn't leave them here with Ugo. Ernesto asked Ugo to take care of them all, so he did. But Ugo never forgave Patrizia because Ernesto died alone back in Italy just a few months later."

Frank considered this information. "So Ugo would have a good reason for trying to get Patrizia in trouble."

"We call it a vendetta," Gino explained. "When you carry a grudge against somebody until you figure out a way to get revenge."

"Fifteen years is a long time to wait," Frank observed.

"Not for an Italian," Gino assured him with a grin. "Ugo might see this as his big chance to punish Patrizia by blaming her for Nainsi's death."

Frank licked the last of the sauce off his fingers thoughtfully. "Or maybe she did kill Nainsi, and he sees this as his big chance to turn her in for it."

Gino scratched his head. "Even if she did, we still have the same problem. How can we prove it? Ugo's word isn't enough. He wasn't even in the house, so he can't know for sure or have any proof. Her children aren't going to tell us anything about her, and all she has to do is keep her mouth shut."

"We won't get anything out of any of them as long as they're holed up in their house together. We need to separate them, get the boys away from Mama. If we can scare them, maybe—"

"Detective Sergeant Malloy," a voice called. Frank looked up to see the officer he'd spoken with earlier on the street near Mama's Restaurant. "Wanted you to know, I saw two men leaving the Ruocco house a little while ago."

"Two men? Customers, you mean?" Frank asked.

"No, sir. There was hardly any customers tonight. Nor at noon either. Guess folks are scared there might be trouble. They'd already closed up for the night, turned out the lights down in the restaurant, and then two men come out."

"Who was it?"

"Couldn't see for sure, but it must've been two of the boys."

Gino muttered a curse. "They'd leave their mother alone and unprotected after what happened last night?" he said in outrage. "What kind of men are they?"

"Stupid and selfish ones," Frank supplied. "Did you see where they went?" he asked the officer.

"Yeah, O'Malley followed them. They went to some dance house on Broadway."

Frank looked over at Gino. "Like Antonio said he used to do with Lorenzo. That's how he met Nainsi. Now's our chance to catch them away from their mama."

THE DANCE HOUSE WAS ABOVE A SALOON. DECENT girls wouldn't dare enter the saloon, but the room above presumably provided respectable entertainment, so they could go up there. A band played dance music for short periods of time, during which the men in attendance would select a partner. Then the music would stop, and the men would have a long interval during which to ply their part- ners with drinks from the bar. This was the only type of establishment in the city where unescorted females could meet men without being labeled prostitutes.

Shop girls and factory girls would pay the nickel or dime admission fee for the chance to have a few hours of fun, some free drinks, and perhaps find a man to marry so they could escape their hopeless lives.

Once the dance houses had sprung up all over the city, however, many men quickly learned that the girls were desperate for more than a good time. Their meager wages barely covered the cost of food and shelter, leaving little for clothing and nothing for the occasional luxury, like a new hat or piece of jewelry. Many of the girls, who were usually younger than sixteen, would willingly trade sexual favors for the gift of an article of clothing or some geegaw. Frank wondered what the man who had impregnated Nainsi had given her for the privilege.

When they arrived at the crowded, overheated, and smoke-filled upstairs room, a musical number was just ending, and all the dancers were making their way to the bar for some refreshment. The man at the door tried to collect an admission fee from Frank and Gino, but Frank flashed his badge.

"We ain't doing nothing illegal here," the man cried, holding up both hands in silent surrender. "You got no call to raid us."

"This isn't a raid," Frank said, already scanning the room for sign of the Ruocco brothers. "We're just looking for somebody."

"I don't want no trouble," the man whined. "It's bad for business!"

"When we find him, we'll take him out real quiet," Frank promised. "Do you see them?" he asked Gino.

Gino shook his head. The mass of bodies at the bar was four or five deep, but Frank would've thought they could see the Ruoccos' heads above the crowd because of their height.

"We'll circle the room," Frank said. "You go that way, and I'll go this way. We'll keep an eye on each other and signal to the other if we see them."

"Right," said Gino, and he started off, eyeing the crowd. He hadn't gone three feet before a girl accosted him, though. Frank couldn't hear what she said, but he understood the look in her eye all too well. Gino was a handsome man, and if he was here, he must've come to meet girls. Frank waited to see if he could extricate himself. He did, but he didn't get far before two more girls latched onto him.

With a weary sigh, Frank started in the opposite direction. If he found the Ruoccos, maybe Gino could at least help take them into custody. He scanned the crowd for tall men with dark hair as he walked slowly around the perimeter of the room, but none of the men who caught his eye were the ones he wanted. He'd just mentally dismissed yet another one when he noticed that the girl he was talking to looked very familiar.

She was Nainsi's friend, Brigit. She looked different tonight, with her cheeks flushed and her eyes bright from alcohol. She was shaking her head, refusing whatever the man was offering. She didn't notice Frank's approach.

"Brigit," he said, startling her.

"Is *this* the fellow you're waiting for?" the man scoffed, looking Frank over with contempt. "Find yourself another girl, old man. I'm taking this one."

"Are you?" he asked mildly, but gave the man a look that sent the blood rushing from his face.

"I . . . I'll see you later," the man said and scurried away.

"What're you doing here?" Brigit asked in alarm, glancing around as if searching for someone to help her.

"I was looking for Antonio Ruocco. Have you seen him?"

"*Antonio?*" she echoed in surprise. "No, not tonight. Not for a long time, either. At least since he married Nainsi."

"Was this where they met up?"

"Mostly, I guess," she said, twisting her hands in front of her nervously and glancing around again.

He remembered something else he'd wanted to check. "When did you first meet Antonio?"

"Me? I don't know," she said plaintively. "I can't remember." She didn't want to talk to him, but she was afraid to run away.

"You said she started seeing him last spring. Was that when you met him?"

She shook her head. "Nainsi said she didn't want us stealing him away. She wouldn't ever bring him around us."

"But she told you she was seeing him?"

"Sure she did, like I told you before. She was bragging about how she was going to marry a rich Italian. Can I go now? My fellow's gonna be back in a minute."

"Antonio says he never even met Nainsi until last August," Frank said, watching her reaction.

She didn't have one. "He's lying then, and he'll burn in hell for it, because it got Nainsi killed, didn't it?" she said impatiently. She was still looking around. "Please, let me go. My fellow won't like me talking to you."

"When did Nainsi first trust you to meet Antonio?" Frank continued relentlessly.

"I already said, I don't remember!"

"Was it when she told you they were getting married?" Frank guessed.

She gave the question a moment's thought. "I guess it was," she recalled in exasperation. "She said it was safe then, because they was already promised. She wanted us to see how handsome he was and be jealous. Then they got married a few days later."

She looked up again, over Frank's shoulder, and her eyes grew wide with apprehension. She tried to warn away whoever was coming, but Frank turned and spotted him before he could comprehend the warning.

Richard Keith's jaw dropped when he saw Frank. He was carrying two glasses of beer, one of which was half empty, both of which he forgot about as he turned to flee. He ran right into another man, and the beer went flying in every direction, splashing on several of the other customers who were none too happy about it. They started shouting and shoving and before Frank could rescue Keith, someone had socked him right in the jaw and sent him sprawling at Frank's feet.

"Police! Police! Get out of the way!" someone was yelling over the commotion, and Gino burst through the crowd like an avenging angel.

"Step back, all of you," Frank commanded, and the shocked crowd obeyed, giving Frank and Gino room to pull Keith to his feet.

"Let's get him out of here," Frank said, and Gino helped him half drag, half carry Keith through the crowd, outside, and down the stairs to the street.

"Why did you hit me?" Keith asked, glaring blearily at Frank.

"I didn't hit you . . . yet," Frank said, standing him up on his feet and glaring at him, while Gino stood by to catch him if he fell. "Tell me, Mr. Keith, what is a happily married family man doing in a dance house with one of the girls who works for him?"

Keith's eyes widened as he realized his predicament. "I . . . I like to dance," he claimed. "I just happened to see Brigit there and . . . and . . ."

"And you thought you'd buy her a drink and diddle her a little, is that it?"

"No! I never . . . I don't . . ."

"Yeah, I know, the girls don't get any bastards from you," Frank said in disgust. "Doesn't stop you from getting plenty from them, though, does it?"

"I . . . They don't mind, though," Keith insisted.

"I'll bet they have a different opinion," Frank said.

"They don't, really! I never make them actually do it," he claimed virtuously.

"How did Nainsi get pregnant then?" Frank demanded.

That sobered him instantly. "I didn't . . ." he tried, but the words caught in his throat. "I couldn't help it! It wasn't my baby, though," he added hastily. "I don't care what she said. It couldn't have been!"

"And why is that?" Frank asked with genuine interest.

"Because she . . . It didn't happen until July. That was too late. Brigit told me." Frank noticed he was sweating even though the evening was pleasantly cool.

"What did Brigit tell you?"

"When the baby was born, she told me it was full-grown. I've got kids of my own. I know if a baby is born early, it's sickly. If it was mine, it would've been sickly."

Frank considered him for a long moment. "Mr. Keith," he said with mock respect. "How is it that a man so careful as yourself got caught up in this?"

"I . . ." he looked around wildly for a moment, as if

searching for someone to help him. "It was her—Nainsi. She was a witch! She tricked me and . . ." He ran a hand over his face, and his shoulders slumped with despair.

"And what?" Frank prodded.

"I already told you, I'm a careful man. I don't . . . penetrate the girls," he explained in a whisper, glancing around to make sure no one else was listening. "They just . . . They hold their legs together. It's a trick I learned from a whore years ago," he added defensively.

Gino frowned in distaste, and Frank felt his skin prickling with fury. "So you think it's all right to use the girls like that so long as you don't *penetrate* them."

"I told you, they don't mind," he insisted. "They don't have to worry about losing their jobs or getting a baby, and I get what I want, too."

Frank had to close his hands into fists to keep from striking Keith. He still needed a few more answers. "You said Nainsi tricked you," he reminded him. "How did she do that?"

"Well, she . . . See, it was like always except at the end she puts it in! Wasn't nothing I could do, either. It just happened. Then she laughs, like she did something funny," he added in amazement.

"Did she tell you the baby was yours?" Frank asked, trying to figure out what Nainsi had been trying to accomplish by taking such a risk.

"She . . . hinted," he admitted reluctantly. "When she comes in to tell me she's leaving to get married, she sort of winks and tells me she's in a family way. Says she won't know until it comes who the father is, either."

"So you told Brigit to let you know as soon as the baby was born," Frank guessed.

"I needed to be sure," he defended himself. "I can't have some little whore bringing a baby to my front door and telling my wife it's mine, now can I?"

"Is that what you thought Nainsi would do when the Ruoccos threw her out?"

Keith wiped his sleeve across his beaded forehead. "No, why would she?" he asked shakily. "She'd know it wasn't mine."

"Because she'd need money, and you're the richest man she knows."

"She'd never get a cent from me. It wasn't my kid!"

"But your wife would know it might've been, wouldn't she?" Frank said. "Is that why you killed Nainsi, Keith? So she wouldn't tell your wife what you've been up to with all the girls?"

"I didn't kill her!" he cried.

Frank remembered when he'd first questioned Brigit. He'd been sure there was something she hadn't wanted to tell him in front of Keith. "But you did know the Ruoccos thought her husband wasn't the father. Brigit told you that, too, didn't she? You knew they were going to throw her and the baby out."

"What if I did? It was nothing to do with me!" he insisted.

"It was everything to do with you if you thought she was going to talk to your wife. So you went over to the Ruoccos' place, sneaked up the back stairs, and killed her."

"I didn't! I wasn't anywhere near there that night!"

"Where were you then?"

"Here, right here! After Brigit came to tell me, I stayed until about eleven-thirty. Ask her. She was here, too."

"Where did you go then?"

"Home to bed. My wife will tell you."

"I'm sure she will," Frank said. "Officer Donatelli, take him to Headquarters and lock him up for the night."

"*What?*" Keith roared in outrage. "You can't lock me up!"

"Don't annoy me, Keith," Frank warned. "It's all I can do to keep from smashing your face in right now."

"But I didn't do anything!"

"You've done enough to deserve a night in the lockup," Frank told him pleasantly. "If Brigit and your wife vouch for you, I'll think about letting you go."

"You can't ask my wife!" he cried desperately. "She'll want to know why you're asking. You can't tell her!"

"Would you rather go to prison for murder?"

"What about the Ruocco boys?" Gino asked.

"We'll have to catch up with them later," Frank said.

"Don't tell her! Please, don't tell her!" Keith pleaded as Gino grabbed him by the collar and started hustling him down the sidewalk.

Frank ignored him. He was already climbing the steps back up to the dance house. The music was blaring again, and Frank stood in the doorway, watching the couples spinning by. He wondered what his mother would say if she saw the way these men held the girls so obscenely close. And the steps they did, so suggestive. The fellow guarding the door watched him glumly, probably expecting the worst, but this time he knew better than to challenge Frank's entrance into the hall.

When he'd circled the room twice and looked at every woman there, he had to conclude that Brigit had escaped. Seeing them carrying Keith out would've frightened her, of course. She had probably run out some back entrance as soon as they left. Well, he knew where she lived and where she worked. He'd find her soon enough. And the longer it took to check Keith's alibi, the longer he'd have to stay in jail. That suited Frank just fine.

FRANK HAD A PRETTY GOOD IDEA OF WHAT MRS. KEITH would be like, so he found himself speechless early the next morning when the woman who opened the front door acknowledged she was indeed Richard Keith's wife. Mrs. Keith was a wisp of a woman, her face pale and drawn, and her eyes sunken and shadowed. She'd once been pretty. The evidence was still present, even though suffering had etched deep lines across her beauty.

"Is my husband dead?" she asked raggedly when Frank had identified himself.

"Oh, no," he hastily assured her. "He's fine." But even still, she looked as though she might faint as her thin shoulders sagged in a sigh of relief.

"Are you all right, Mrs. Keith?" he asked, instinctively reaching to catch her in case she fell.

She closed her eyes and took a deep breath. "Yes, I'm . . . I'll be fine," she said. When she opened her eyes, he saw resignation there along with the pain that he realized must be constant. "Do you know where he is? He didn't come home last night."

"Yes, he's . . . he's helping us with an investigation," Frank said, not really lying. "Can I come in for a minute? I'd like to explain what happened with your husband, and you look like you need to sit down."

"Oh, yes. Thank you," she said and moved aside to allow him to enter.

The Keith home was modest but well tended. The parlor where she led Frank had the comfortable look of a room where a family gathered to enjoy each other's company. She took a seat near the fireplace where a coal fire burned on the grate, even though the day was mild. He realized she had a shawl wrapped around her shoulders, too, as if she was unable to get warm.

Frank took the chair she offered.

"You're certain my husband is all right?" she asked anxiously. "He's never been away from home all night before. He's late sometimes, when he has to work, but he always comes home by midnight. I've been terrified for him."

Nainsi had been killed in the wee hours of the morning, according to Maria's account of her waking up when Joe came home. Mrs. Keith had just confirmed her husband's alibi. He wouldn't even have to question her, thank God. He didn't relish the idea of causing this woman any more pain. "He's in perfect health, I promise. He'll explain everything when he gets home," Frank said, figuring that would be his small revenge on Keith. Let him come up with a believable story for this poor woman. He'd thought Keith was afraid of a harridan who would make his life miserable. Instead he'd been trying to protect a woman who had already suffered enough. Frank didn't feel any more kindly toward Keith, of course. The man was adding to her pain, even if she didn't know it. "We needed his help just a bit longer, so he asked if I would come and let you know not to worry."

"Will he be late for work? He mustn't lose his job," she asked.

Frank had seen the photograph of Mr. and Mrs. Keith and their two children on the mantel. "I'll speak to his employer as well. We're sorry to have caused you distress, Mrs. Keith."

"I'm very grateful that you came to tell me. If anything

happened to him . . ." She bit her lip and managed not to weep.

Now Frank really did want to smash Keith's face in. Unfortunately, he'd only be hurting this woman if he did.

FRANK STOPPED AT THE FACTORY NEXT, BUT BRIGIT hadn't come in to work that morning. The owner was ranting about his foreman not showing up, but Frank was able to calm him with a story about Keith being in an accident. The lie was like gall in his throat, but he thought about Mrs. Keith and the children and swallowed it down.

"I need to talk to one of your other girls," Frank added at the end of his explanation. Not waiting for permission, he strode down the center aisle to where Nainsi's other friends sat. He found the one he remembered being so talkative the last time he'd been here. He took her by the arm and jerked her out of her chair.

"I didn't do nothing!" she protested as Frank roughly conducted her to the back of the room.

"What happened to Brigit last night?" he asked softly, so no one would overhear.

The girl's eyes grew large. "She disappeared! We was all at the dance house like always, and then she and Mr. Keith was both just gone. We thought . . ."

"Well, don't think it anymore. I put Keith in jail. Brigit must've gotten scared and run. Where would she go?"

The girl shrugged. "Home, I guess. She didn't come to none of us, and she's got no place else."

He was just about to let her go when he remembered one more thing. "When did you first meet Antonio?"

She looked at him in surprise at this sudden change of

subject. "I don't know. Right before they got married, I guess. She was talking about him for so long, we all thought she made him up. Then she just shows up with him one night and says they're getting married."

He did let her go then, and she scurried back to her seat, casting an apprehensive glance at the owner before putting her head down and starting up her sewing machine again.

With a weary sigh, Frank started back downtown to the tenement where Brigit lived. He didn't want to let Keith go if there was any chance he might've killed Nainsi, so he wanted to hear what Brigit had to say before he cleared him completely.

The building was still as dark and dreary as he remembered. He wasn't sure which flat was Brigit's, so he had to knock on a few doors before a plump young woman holding a screaming baby directed him to the third floor. According to the neighbor, Brigit lived with her mother and several younger brothers. Frank knew they'd rely on her meager income to keep food on the table and a roof over their heads. She wouldn't have missed work without a good reason.

Even before he reached the landing, he could hear the sobs. Someone was crying as if her heart would break. Frank pounded on the door, and the weeping ceased abruptly.

"Who's there?" a female voice called hoarsely.

"Police," he replied in his official voice. "Open the door or I'll break it down."

He heard a little cry of distress, but after a moment, the lock turned and the door opened a crack. Frank pushed it wide, sending Brigit stumbling back into the room.

"What do you want?" she asked fearfully. "Where's Dickie?"

"Who's Dickie?"

"Richard . . . Mr. Keith," she corrected herself. Her eyes were swollen nearly shut, her face blotchy and tear-streaked. "You took him, and he didn't come back. What did you do to him?"

"He's in jail."

She cried out in dismay. "Why? He didn't do anything!"

"I'll be the judge of that, and this time you'll tell me the truth."

"I never lied!"

"Oh, I think you did, Brigit. What happened the night you found out that Nainsi had her baby?"

"What do you mean?" She seemed to be trembling. That was good. Terrified people seldom had the wit to make things up.

"What did you do after Mrs. O'Hara told you Nainsi's baby was born?"

"I . . . I went out."

"To the dance house where I saw you last night."

She nodded, relieved. "That's right. To see my friends."

"Maybe you went to see *Dickie*," he suggested.

She swallowed. "No, I . . . I didn't know he'd be there, but . . . but he was."

"I said I wanted the truth," he reminded her, taking a step closer.

Her breath caught in her throat. "He goes there a lot!" she admitted quickly. "He wanted to know when the baby was born, so I went there to find him."

"What did you tell him?" Frank asked, keeping his voice even and icy cold.

"Just that it had been born, and it was a boy."

"*What else?*"

She laid a hand on her heart, as if to quiet it. Frank figured it was pounding like a trip-hammer. "That . . . that they were all mad at Nainsi, because they didn't think Antonio was the father."

"What did Dickie say to that?" Frank asked, the contempt in his voice thick.

"Nothing!" she claimed. "He just . . . he just wanted to know, that's all."

"Why would he even care about a thing like that?" Frank asked, watching her face carefully.

"I don't know! Because she worked for him, I guess," she tried. "He was just . . . interested."

"Oh, he was interested all right. He wanted to know how long it had been since he'd slept with her until her baby came. He wanted to know if it was his."

"No!" she cried fiercely. "It couldn't have been his!"

"Why not?" Frank asked with interest.

"Because he doesn't—" She caught herself, too embarrassed to speak of such things to a stranger.

"I know he doesn't," Frank assured her. "He's usually real careful, but not with Nainsi. He had a little slip with Nainsi, you see. That's why he wanted to know when her baby was born, so he'd know if it was his."

"He didn't love her," Brigit insisted. "He didn't love any of them!"

"Does he love *you*?" Frank asked curiously.

"Yes, he does!" Her swollen eyes glowed with pride. "He's going to marry me, too."

Frank couldn't help the wave of pity he felt for her. "Don't you know he's already married?"

"His wife's real sick, though," she informed him. "She's going to die, and then we'll be married."

This was all very interesting, but not getting him any

closer to solving Nainsi's murder. Frank gave himself a little shake. "Congratulations," he said sarcastically. "Meantime, tell me the rest of what happened the night the baby was born."

"Nothing happened!"

He raised his eyebrows skeptically. "Does that mean you spoke to him, and then you all went straight home to bed?"

"No, we . . . we just . . . We danced a little. Dickie wasn't real happy that night. He kept staring off at nothing, like he was thinking about something real hard. I know he was thinking about *her.*"

"Nainsi?"

"No, his wife," she corrected him testily. "Why would he think about Nainsi?"

"Because he was afraid she'd just had his baby, and the Ruoccos were going to throw her out, and she was going to end up on his doorstep asking for money."

Brigit didn't know whether to believe him or not, but she was thoroughly frightened. "Even Nainsi wouldn't be that stupid!"

"Wouldn't she? Well, it doesn't matter now because she's dead. What I want to know is how long did Dickie stay with you?"

"As long as he always does. He has to be home by midnight, so he left a little before. He checks his pocket watch all the time to make sure he's not late. He doesn't want to worry her. She's sick, like I said."

"He's very considerate."

"Yes, he is."

Frank figured Brigit missed the irony. Well, at least he'd established Keith's alibi for the entire night. Too bad. He would've liked to see a man like that sit down in Old

Sparky, New York's new electric chair. He'd just have to hope there was a special place in hell for people like Dickie Keith.

Frank was just about to tell Brigit to get herself cleaned up and off to her job when they heard a scream. Frank ducked out onto the landing, looking up and down to see if he could tell from what direction it had come.

"Murder!" someone was screaming from above. "Help, somebody! It's murder!"

II

FRANK SET OFF UP THE STAIRS, TAKING THEM TWO AT a time. By the time he reached the top floor, people had started emerging from their flats, eyes wide with curiosity and fear. A middle-aged woman stood in front of a half-opened door wailing in terror. Then he saw which door it was, and he groaned.

Frank showed his badge, and the woman pointed. "All that blood! She's dead, ain't she?"

He pushed the door open all the way and peered in. The first thing he saw was the sprays of blood all over the wall. The metallic smell filled his nostrils. Mrs. O'Hara sat in the same chair she'd occupied when he'd called on her a few days ago. The ties she'd been sewing were still spread on the table, only now the woman was slumped over them. Her dark blood had stained them, pooled on the tabletop, and spilled onto the floor.

He stepped back and pulled the door closed behind him. When he turned, he saw a sea of horrified faces staring at him, waiting for him to make sense of it. Brigit had followed him up the stairs. She stood on the landing, her tear-blotched face now a ghostly white.

"Somebody go find a beat cop," he said, using the tone that demanded obedience. No one moved, so Frank pointed at a young man. "You!" he said sharply. The fellow turned tail and fairly flew down the steps.

"Ain't you gonna help her?" the woman who had been screaming demanded desperately.

"No one can help her now. Are you the one who found her?"

The woman's eyes were unfocused. She was probably in shock. "We go to the market every Friday, but she didn't come down, so I come up to get her," she said in wonder. "When she didn't answer, I opened the door . . ." She swayed, and one of the other women caught her before she fell. Several others hurried to get her into a neighboring flat.

"Why'd anybody want to kill Mrs. O'Hara?" Brigit asked Frank.

Frank could think of a lot of reasons, and those reasons pointed to several people in particular. He was beginning to think things might finally be falling into place.

THE MEDICAL EXAMINER HAD BEEN LOOKING AROUND the room and at the body for much longer than Frank's patience would permit.

"How long does it take to figure out somebody cut her throat?" he asked with annoyance.

Dr. Haynes gave him a jaundiced look. "Not long, since they told me that before I even left my office," he said, matching Frank's tone. "I thought you'd like to know how it happened, too, or am I wasting my time?"

"All right, you win. How did it happen?" Frank asked wearily.

"Looks like she was sitting here at the table, working on these . . . ties, are they?"

"Yeah, that's right."

"Somebody came up behind her. Probably, he grabbed her by the hair. See how it's all sticking up on top there, like somebody pulled it?"

Frank nodded.

"He pulled her head back." The doc pretended to be grabbing himself by the hair on his head with his left hand and pulling it back. "Then he sliced her throat from behind." He made as if he were holding a knife and drawing it across his throat from left to right.

"Doesn't look like she put up much of a fight," Frank observed.

"He probably snuck up behind her and took her by surprise. Maybe the door was open, and he just walked in. Or maybe it was somebody she knew who'd come to call, and she never expected him to grab her from behind and cut her throat."

"Not many people expect that."

"It's a messy way to kill someone," the doc added, pointing at the blood sprayed on the wall in front of where Mrs. O'Hara had been sitting.

"So he would've had blood all over him?" Frank asked.

"Not likely, doing it from behind like that. The blood would shoot out in front. He'd get some on his hand and maybe his sleeve, but that's about all. When he let her go, she was still alive for a minute or two. She'd be sitting up, bleeding on everything, and then she slumped down on the table when she died. Killer would've been long gone by the time the blood started dripping onto the floor, so he didn't step in it, either."

"Any idea when she was killed?"

"Not today," doc said. "She's in full rigor mortis, so anywhere from twelve to twenty-four hours ago."

"That would make it sometime between mid-morning yesterday to late last night."

"You might find somebody who saw her yesterday to help narrow down the time, although it won't help much if nobody saw the actual killer."

Frank didn't want to think about that possibility. "Why do you think there's blood on that towel?" Frank asked, pointing at a piece of rag lying on the floor near the body. "Did the killer wipe his hands?"

The Doc picked it up and looked at it. "No, the smear is too neat. I didn't find the murder weapon. Looks like the killer used this to wipe the knife off and took it with him." He glanced around the shabby room. "Why'd somebody want to kill her? There's nothing here worth stealing, and what could she do to make somebody that mad at her?"

"Did you see the stories about the Italians who supposedly kidnapped an Irish girl and killed her to get her baby?"

"Yes, the Ruoccos were supposed to have done it, but I don't believe it for a minute. I've eaten at their place for years, and I know every one of them."

"This woman was the Irish girl's mother."

"The one who wanted to get the baby back?"

Frank nodded. Doc Haynes snorted in disgust. "She took on the Black Hand and Tammany Hall. She's lucky they just cut her throat."

"Detective Sergeant?" a voice called from the doorway.

Frank looked up to see Gino Donatelli. "What is it?"

"We've been questioning all the neighbors," he reported. "Some people outside remember a woman asking where Mrs. O'Hara lived yesterday."

"A woman?" Frank echoed in surprise, instantly thinking of what Ugo Ruocco had said about Patrizia. Putting a pillow over someone's face was one thing, but slitting someone's throat . . .

"Yes, sir, a woman. Mrs. Murdock here, she was the one who sent her up to this flat."

Frank hurried to the door, and he saw a woman standing on the landing, a baby on her hip. She was the one who had directed him to Brigit's flat earlier. The child looked at him gravely, his thumb stuck securely in his mouth. "Do you remember what time it was you talked to this woman?" he asked.

Mrs. Murdock shrugged. "I didn't think about it at the time. We hadn't had dinner yet, so it was morning. Not real early, though."

"Did you see her leave?"

"No, didn't see her anymore after that at all."

"Can you tell me what she looked like?" Frank asked, reaching into his coat pocket for a pad and pencil to jot down some notes.

"She doesn't have to describe her," Donatelli said grimly. "She recognized the woman."

"You know her?" Frank asked, unable to believe his luck.

Mrs. Murdock nodded.

"You're positive?" Frank prodded.

"I should be," Mrs. Murdock said. "She delivered this baby. It was the midwife, Mrs. Brandt."

SARAH WAS LOOKING AT THE COLD HAM AND STALE bread in her larder and wondering if she dared hope Mrs. Ellsworth would drop in with something more appealing for supper when someone rang the doorbell. Hastily, she sliced off a bit of the ham and popped it into her mouth. If this was a delivery call, she wouldn't get any supper at all.

She heard the girls running to answer the bell, so she quickly took a few more bites before making her way to the foyer. Before she arrived, however, she'd already heard the familiar voice and knew she wouldn't be going on a call.

Frank Malloy was teasing the girls, and Aggie and Maeve were responding gleefully.

"Malloy," she said in greeting, but when he looked up at her, she saw instantly that he was furious. She tried to remember what she might have done to merit such a response, but she couldn't think of anything.

"Is Mrs. Ellsworth here?" he asked gruffly.

"No, she's not," she answered, confused by the question.

"Girls," he said, his tone switching instantly back to pleasantness, "why don't you go next door and pay her a little visit. I need to speak to Mrs. Brandt alone."

Sensing his anger, the girls sobered, and Maeve hastily shoved Aggie into her jacket and ushered her out the front door. At the last second, she hesitated, looking back at Sarah. "What if she isn't home?"

"Then take a little walk," Sarah said, forcing a smile before

Malloy closed the door behind her. "Whatever is the matter?" she demanded anxiously when it clicked shut.

"What were you doing down on Howard Street yesterday?" he demanded gruffly.

So that was it! She'd known he wouldn't approve, but this reaction was way out of proportion to her offense. "I went to see Mrs. O'Hara, as you must have figured out," she explained.

"What in God's name for?"

She'd seen him this angry, but never at her. "I thought . . . that is, I wanted to be sure she understood everything she'd need to know to take care of the baby." She hated sounding defensive. It was a perfectly legitimate concern. He didn't have to know she was also trying to convince Mrs. O'Hara to give up the idea of claiming the child.

"That's a pretty story, but I know you too well, Sarah. And you're a terrible liar."

"I'll have you know I'm an excellent liar!" she claimed, earning a derisive glare.

"Why did you really go down there? No, wait, let me guess. You thought you could convince her to stop trying to get the baby away from the Ruoccos."

"Why would I do a thing like that?" she asked, aware that he was right: she was a terrible liar.

"Because you're a meddling do-gooder who can't mind her own business," he informed her, running a hand through his hair in exasperation.

"Somebody has to put a stop to this," she argued. "Mrs. O'Hara can't keep the baby healthy in that place, even if Tammany Hall does give her the money they promised. And if she stops fighting for the baby, Tammany will back off and the riots will stop."

"I doubt Tammany would have even *let* her change her mind. They had too much at stake, and they couldn't let the Italians win, no matter what she wanted."

"Well, she refused to even consider it." Sarah said with a sigh. "So no harm done."

This seemed to make Malloy even angrier. "Oh, harm was done, all right. A *lot* of harm was done, because Mrs. O'Hara is dead."

"Dead!" Sarah cried, covering her mouth. Tears stung her eyes. "How could that happen? I just saw her—"

"Yesterday. Yeah, I know. That's why I'm here. A lot of people were only too happy to tell us they saw you going to visit the murder victim. Near as we can figure, you were the last visitor she had."

"Good heavens!" She looked into Malloy's dark eyes and saw the rage boiling there. "You don't think *I* killed her, do you?"

"No, but I should lock you up on suspicion just the same. At least I'd know you were safe. What if you'd been there when the killer came?" He was shouting now. "It could've been *your* blood splattered all over that kitchen along with hers!"

Sarah cried out in protest, tears filling her eyes as the truth of it washed over her in a sickening wave. Then Malloy's strong arms were around her, holding her with a desperate strength as she wept against his chest. His familiar scent enveloped her, and his hands moved across her back, comforting and caressing at the same time.

"Don't cry," he begged after a long moment. "I didn't mean to make you cry."

She gave a watery laugh at that and raised her head. She found that he was close, dangerously close, so she pulled a safer distance away. He released her with obvious reluctance, and they stood staring at each other for an awkward moment—each wanting the same thing but certain the price the other would have to pay was too high.

Sarah broke the strained silence, swiping away her tears. "I'm sorry, Malloy. I had no idea."

For a second, he looked as if he wasn't sure what to do with his hands. Then he ran one over his face, as if to clear his thoughts. "I shouldn't have yelled," he admitted. "It wasn't your fault. Are you all right?"

"I will be." She pulled a handkerchief out of her pocket and dabbed at her eyes, wondering how badly her face was blotched. "I could use a cup of tea."

"I'll make it for you," he offered almost gratefully and led her into the kitchen.

True to his word, he made Sarah sit down while he put the kettle on. She was always amazed at how comfortable he was at domestic tasks. He sat down opposite her at the table while they waited for the water to boil.

"You said there was blood . . . splattered blood," Sarah recalled with distaste. "I guess she wasn't smothered then."

"Someone cut her throat," he said baldly.

She winced, knowing his bluntness was her reprimand. "How awful."

"It was fast, at least." He briefly described what Doc Haynes thought had happened.

This time Sarah shivered. "But who would want to kill her?"

"That's pretty easy to figure out. Somebody who wanted her to stop trying to get the baby so the trouble would be over."

"But you said Tammany wouldn't back down."

"They were trying to get the baby back for Mrs. O'Hara. If she's dead, there's nobody to fight for. If they did get the baby from the Ruoccos, what would they do with it?"

"Oh," Sarah said in dismay, realizing that suspicion would fall squarely on the Ruoccos. "Could Ugo have sent one of his men to do it?"

"Maybe, just like he might've sent one to kill Nainsi, but it doesn't seem likely. Yesterday, he was trying to convince me that Patrizia Ruocco was the killer."

"Mrs. Ruocco?" she echoed in amazement.

"They don't get along. It started back when Mrs. Ruocco and her family came over from Italy. Her husband, who was Ugo's brother, couldn't get into the country because he was sick, so they sent him back to Italy. She stayed here with the kids, and he died alone. Ugo never forgave her."

"And you think he's accusing her of murder to get even? But that was so long ago. What makes you think that's the reason?" Sarah asked.

"Donatelli says Italians are like that."

Sarah blinked in surprise. "You don't believe she did it, do you?"

"She could've killed Nainsi," he pointed out. "She had a good reason."

"I guess she did, but the others had the same reason," she argued. "It could just as easily have been one of them, and she seems too sensible to take a chance like that."

The water was boiling, so Malloy got up and poured it over the leaves in the pot to steep.

"Do you think the same person who killed Nainsi killed her mother?" Sarah asked.

"That would make it nice and neat, but it might be more

than we can hope for." He paused. "I've got to ask you some questions about your visit with Mrs. O'Hara."

"Of course," Sarah said, touched that he would be reluctant to bring up an unpleasant memory.

He sat down again. "Do you know what time you were there?"

"I don't know exactly, but I went there right after I left you yesterday morning."

"Oh, yes, right after I told you to go straight home," he remembered with annoyance.

She smiled sweetly, refusing to be baited.

"How long were you there?"

"Not long. Half an hour at most. Then I went straight home."

"Finally," he muttered. "What did you talk about?"

"I told her all the things she'd need to know to take care of the baby. I thought . . . I admit it, I thought that if she knew how difficult it would be, she might reconsider and let Maria have him. She'll have a terrible time trying to keep him fed with goat's milk from bottles. She'll never be able to keep the bottles clean and getting the milk will be a constant struggle . . . Oh, listen to me, talking like she's still alive. Anyway, I tried to make her see that the poor little fellow wouldn't have much of a chance living with her."

"Didn't she believe you?"

"I think she did, but she didn't care. She must have thought anything was better than letting the Ruoccos have him. She reminded me that one of them had killed Nainsi. In her place, I would probably feel the same way."

"And now one of them has killed her."

"You don't know that for sure," Sarah argued.

"Two of the Ruocco boys left the restaurant last night. We'd stationed some men to watch the place, in case the Irish made another visit, and one of them followed them to a dance house."

"They were going dancing when a mob might attack the restaurant at any minute?" she asked incredulously.

"We thought that was funny, too, and when we went to the dance house, they weren't there. We never did find them, either."

"So they could've gone to Mrs. O'Hara's," Sarah mused.

"It would be a logical solution to their problems. If they killed her, she wouldn't be around to cause any more trouble and keep demanding they give her the baby. No mobs would try to burn their house down, and nobody would want to take the baby away anymore."

"Poor Mrs. O'Hara. I wonder if she had any idea she was in danger."

"Tammany probably promised to protect her on top of everything else."

Frank got up and poured a cup of tea. Then he reached into a cupboard and pulled out the bottle of whisky that he knew she kept for medicinal purposes and splashed a bit into the cup. He set it down in front of her and took his seat again.

She looked askance at the spiked tea.

"You need it," he said. "A little sugar will cut the taste."

She obediently put a spoonful of sugar in and stirred. On second thought, she added another. "If only we'd found the killer," she said.

"Finding the killer wouldn't have solved much," Frank pointed out. "Mrs. O'Hara might still be alive, but she'd still want the baby, and somebody the Ruoccos love would be in jail. Tammany would probably still be trying to get the baby and sending mobs down to Little Italy."

"Why would they take a chance by killing Mrs. O'Hara, though? Yes, it might stop the mob attacks, but it wouldn't stop you from trying to find out who killed Nainsi. That's the real danger to their family."

"And now I've got an even bigger reason to find the killer. The penny press will probably be full of stories about the Black Hand cutting people's throats, stirring up even more trouble."

"I didn't think of that!" Sarah said in dismay. "The Irish might even march down to Little Italy again to get revenge for Mrs. O'Hara!"

Malloy winced and rubbed his forehead. "I hope to God nobody else thinks of that."

Sarah picked up her cup and took a sip. The whisky fumes cleared her nose and burned her throat, but she forced down a swallow. After a moment, she could feel the warmth settling in her stomach. "If two of the Ruocco boys went to kill Mrs. O'Hara last night, then one of them must have killed Nainsi, too."

"Maybe."

"What do you mean?"

"I mean they might've killed Mrs. O'Hara to protect someone else in the family."

"Like their mother," Sarah guessed.

"Just because Ugo hates her doesn't mean he isn't right about her. But first, I've got to figure out which two of the boys went out last might."

"If they were protecting their mother, I'd pick Joe as one of them. He's the oldest, so it would be his duty."

"Antonio has the biggest stake in this, so he was probably the other one."

"But he's so young. I don't think I'd trust him, although Lorenzo seems too levelheaded to do something so rash."

"Lorenzo is protective of Maria and the baby, though. You said he stood up for them to Ugo before Joe did."

"Now that you mention it, he's taken an unusual interest in the baby," Sarah remembered. "He even sat up with Maria all that first night when the baby was screaming because the milk didn't agree with him. Even most new fathers wouldn't do that."

"I know I wouldn't have," Malloy agreed.

"And Mrs. Ruocco really wants to keep the baby now, too. She's determined Maria will have him."

"If Mrs. Ruocco wants the baby, then Lorenzo probably decided it belongs with them. Maybe he figured killing Mrs. O'Hara was somehow good for the family. Italians are crazy when it comes to their families. And if he thought his mother had killed Nainsi . . ."

"I still can't see him cutting someone's throat," Sarah said. "Antonio is the only one who had a real reason to kill Nainsi in the first place, but wasn't he out getting drunk the night she died?"

"According to Maria, Nainsi was still alive when he and Joe got home. She said Joe went straight to bed and didn't get up again. If she's not lying to protect her husband, then—"

"That leaves Antonio, but he just doesn't seem like the type either," Sarah argued.

"When you're drunk and angry, bad things happen," Frank said grimly.

Sadly, she knew that was true. "But why would Antonio even think of killing her? His mother was going to throw her out."

"Why would any of them? It still doesn't make sense. I'm missing something."

Sarah sighed, wishing she could help. "What are you going to do now?"

"I'm going to get Antonio and take him to the station for questioning."

Sarah winced. She knew the techniques the police sometimes used to get a confession. "He's just a boy. If he was drunk, he might not even remember he did it."

"That's a myth. If you're too drunk to remember, you're too drunk to do it."

"What if he really didn't do it?"

"Then at least he'll tell me which of them went out last night to kill Mrs. O'Hara. Once I know that, maybe everything else will start to make sense."

"And you'll have someone to lock up," Sarah noted. "That should make Theodore happy."

Malloy just grunted. "Finish your tea. I'll go next door and tell the girls they can come home again."

He went out the back door. Sarah took a few more sips of the tea. She could feel the warmth seeping into her bones now. The horror of Mrs. O'Hara's death receded a bit, and Sarah began to understand the benefits of a strong drink.

Soon she heard Aggie's footsteps clamoring up the back porch steps and then she pushed the door open and raced into the room. Her face alight with joy, she charged straight for Sarah, but when she reached the table, her step faltered, and her smile vanished. She stopped dead in her tracks and gazed around wildly, her eyes wide with sudden fear.

"Aggie, what's wrong?" Sarah asked in alarm.

Aggie looked straight at the tea cup, sitting half full on the table, and sniffed the air. Sarah realized she must smell the whisky, although she wouldn't have thought the odor that strong. Then Aggie looked around again, and this time saw the whisky bottle still sitting where Malloy had left it. She pointed at it and screamed.

"Aggie, what's wrong?" Sarah cried, jumping to her feet and snatching the child up into her arms.

Aggie started to cling to her, but then she pulled back abruptly and started screaming again. Sarah realized she must smell the whisky on her breath. Maeve came running in.

"What's happening?" the girl cried, seeing Aggie struggling in Sarah's arms.

"She saw the whisky and started screaming," Sarah said, setting Aggie down before she dropped her. The child ran to Maeve, buried her face in her skirts and started to sob.

By then Malloy was through the door, demanding to know what was going on.

"Something about the whisky frightened her. She smelled it on me and went crazy." Sarah explained. "It's all right, Aggie. Nothing is going to hurt you."

Sarah quickly took the bottle and put it out of sight. She'd get rid of it as soon as possible. Instinct demanded that she try to comfort the girl, but she knew going closer to her would only make things worse.

"Maeve, take her upstairs and try to calm her down."

Maeve picked her up and carried her out of the room.

"She just started screaming when she saw the bottle?" Malloy asked.

"She smelled it first, in the teacup, I guess," Sarah said. "It literally stopped her in her tracks. Then she saw the bottle and screamed. I picked her up, and she must've smelled it on me, too, and she started fighting to get away."

"Did anything ever scare her like that before?"

"Never. Oh, Malloy, do you think . . . ? Whatever frightened her enough to make her mute, it must have had something to do with whisky."

"When you're drunk, bad things happen," he reminded her grimly.

"But if she can't tell us what it was, how can we ever make it right?" Sarah asked in desperation.

Malloy had no answer for that.

B<small>Y THE TIME</small> M<small>ALLOY ROUNDED UP</small> D<small>ONATELLI AND A</small> few other officers to accompany him, it was well into the supper hour. Mama's Restaurant wasn't as crowded as he'd expected, though. The regular patrons still hadn't returned after the trouble the other night.

Frank and Gino went in the front door. All eyes turned toward them, and conversation ceased. Joe was serving a couple of old men, and when he saw who'd come in, he shouted something in Italian about *polizia*.

A few seconds later, the kitchen door flew open, and Patrizia Ruocco came storming out, her face twisted in fury. Behind her were Antonio and Lorenzo. Valentina stopped in the doorway, not wanting to miss anything but not wanting to enter the fray, either.

"Get out my house!" Mrs. Ruocco cried furiously. "You have no right!"

"We aren't planning to stay," Frank informed her.

Valentina made a squeal of surprise when the two other officers shoved her aside as they came into the room from the kitchen. They went straight for Antonio, and each grabbed an arm.

"What you do?" Mrs. Ruocco screamed. "Let him go!"

"We want to ask him a few questions," Frank said.

"Nobody's going to hurt him, Mrs. Ruocco," Gino assured her. "If he tells us the truth, he'll be home by bedtime."

Antonio's face had gone pale, and although his first reaction had been to resist, he quickly realized that would be foolish. "Joe," he pleaded helplessly. "Do something!"

"You can't just take him to jail," Lorenzo argued. "He hasn't done anything wrong."

"Then he doesn't have anything to worry about, and he isn't going to jail. Like I said, we just want to ask him a few questions." Frank nodded to the officers, who began hustling Antonio toward the front door.

"Giuseppe!" Mrs. Ruocco cried desperately.

"I'll go with him," Joe said at last. "I can answer your questions better than he can anyway!"

"You stay here and serve your customers," Frank advised. "If we want you later, we'll come and get you."

With that, he and Gino followed Antonio and the two officers out into the street. Mrs. Ruocco was screaming at her other two sons in Italian as Gino closed the door behind them.

"She wants them to follow us, make sure we don't hurt Antonio," Gino translated.

"Pretty soon she'll think of sending for Ugo, too," Frank said. "Let's get the boy to Headquarters before that happens."

12

FRANK LEFT ANTONIO ALONE IN ONE OF THE INTERROgation rooms for a good half hour to soften him up while he and Gino ate some sausage sandwiches they got from a street vendor. As Frank had known, the time spent sitting in the dismal room, imagining God knew what, had made the boy desperately afraid.

He gazed at Frank and Gino with terrified eyes as they came into the room and closed the door behind them. Gino stood with his back against the door, his arms crossed forbiddingly, just as Frank had instructed. With any luck, he'd keep his mouth shut, too.

"I guess you know why we brought you in tonight," Frank said mildly, pulling up a chair across the table from where Antonio sat.

"Something about Nainsi," he said, his voice thin with fear. "But I already told you everything I know."

"Where did you go last night?"

"Last night?" he echoed in confusion.

"Yeah, you remember last night, don't you? Where did you go?"

"I . . . we went out."

"Who's we?"

"Me and . . . Joe," he said, certain he shouldn't implicate Joe but too afraid to lie.

"Where did you go?" Frank asked, his voice still only mildly interested.

"We . . . It wasn't my idea," he defended himself.

"It was Joe's idea, then?"

"Well, no, not . . . not exactly."

"Your mama's?" Frank tried.

"Oh, no, she didn't like it at all! She said we should stay, in case another mob showed up. She said I shouldn't go out anymore after what happened with Nainsi, either, but . . ."

"But what?"

"But we didn't think the Irish would come again so soon, and if they did . . ."

"Yes?"

"The police are guarding the place," he said plaintively. "Joe said they'd run off the Irish if they came, just like they did before. They don't need us there to do that."

"So you decided to leave your family alone and unprotected," Frank said, the criticism thick in his voice.

"I already told you, it wasn't my idea! Maria is the one who said we should go in the first place."

Maria? Frank hadn't even considered her a suspect. She *was* desperate to keep the baby, though, so it made sense.

"Are you saying it was Maria's idea for you to go to Mrs. O'Hara's?"

"Mrs. O'Hara?" he echoed stupidly. "You mean Nainsi's mother? Why would we go to her place?"

"I can think of at least one reason," Frank said. "To kill her."

"*Kill her?*" he squeaked. "What're you talking about?"

"I'm talking about how you and Joe went out last night and murdered Mrs. O'Hara so she wouldn't be able to stir up any more trouble for your family."

Antonio gaped at him. "We never . . . We didn't go anywhere near her place last night!"

"Where did you go then?"

"To a . . . a dance house. I know it don't look good for us to do that, but we did, I swear it!"

"You will, will you?" Frank asked with interest. "Because a cop followed you to the dance house, but when I got there, you were gone."

"But we were there all night, until midnight!" he claimed frantically. "Lots of people were there. They'll tell you!"

"*I* was there, too, Antonio, but I didn't see you or Joe. Now tell me where you really went."

"I told you! We . . . Oh, wait! I remember now," he said, his shoulders sagging with relief. "We went to the one on Broadway first, but we didn't stay. Joe saw someone he didn't like, and he said we should leave. We went down to Broome Street then. Ask them there! They'll tell you!"

He gave Donatelli a silent order, and he slipped out to send someone to the dance house on Broome Street to see if anyone remembered seeing the Ruocco brothers.

Frank turned back to Antonio. The boy was sweating, and his eyes were still wild with fright.

"Let me get this straight," Frank began, still keeping his voice neutral. "Maria sent her own husband out to a dance house?"

Antonio licked his lips. He'd lied about that, and now he was trying to figure out how to tell a better lie.

"The truth, Antonio. Don't make me angry."

The boy swallowed loudly. "She didn't say to go to a dance house," he admitted.

"What did she say?"

"She said I was making her nervous. She . . . she told Joe to take me someplace out of her sight."

"What were you doing to make her nervous?"

"Nothing! She's just . . . Mama says she's worried about the baby. She yells at everybody for every little thing. Even when Mama said Joe and I should stay home, in case something happened, Maria didn't listen to her. She started screaming at Joe, so we left. I was glad to get away from her." He looked it, too.

"Why go to a dance house then? You could've gone to Ugo's saloon."

Antonio winced. "I didn't want him telling me again how stupid I was for marrying Nainsi. Anyway, Joe said we'd have fun at a dance house."

"Just like you used to, before you married Nainsi," Frank suggested.

"Yeah, that's right. The girls are real friendly, and they think I'm handsome. They don't care how close you hold them, either."

"Were you looking for another girl who'd let you under her skirt like Nainsi did?" Frank inquired.

Antonio had the grace to blush. "No girl's going to trick me like that again!"

"So you're going to take a vow of celibacy and become a priest, Antonio?"

"No! I'm just . . . I'm going to be careful. I'm going to marry a good girl, like Joe did."

"I don't suppose Joe met Maria in a dance house."

"No! Maria would never go to a place like that."

"How *did* Joe meet her?" Frank asked curiously.

"Mama found her. She knows Maria's family, and she thought Maria would be a good wife for Joe."

"Is she going to find a wife for you and Lorenzo, too?"

"Yeah! She . . . Well, Lorenzo says he doesn't want a wife, but when I'm older, she'll find me one."

"Does Lorenzo intend to take holy orders?" Frank asked with interest.

"No, he . . . he just doesn't want to get married, that's all."

"Doesn't want to settle down, I suppose. Is he having too much fun being single?"

"I . . . I guess so," Antonio admitted, uncomfortable with discussing his brother.

Frank remembered that Lorenzo had taken Antonio to the dance houses in the first place. "How did you meet Nainsi?"

Antonio blinked at the sudden change of subject. "I don't know. I just saw her and asked her to dance."

"Did someone introduce you?"

He frowned at Frank's ignorance. "That's not what happens in those places. The girls, they just come up and start talking to you. You take your pick of them."

"Why did you pick Nainsi?"

"I told you, she came up and started talking to me. When the music started up, we just started dancing."

"When was this?"

"I don't remember!"

"What month?" Frank prodded.

"I told you before, it was August, right after Valentina's birthday."

"How long was it before she let you under her skirt?"

Antonio hesitated, and a flush crawled up his neck.

"Was it that first night? The first time you met her?" Frank inquired.

"No! I mean . . ."

"What do you mean?"

He swallowed hard again. "She didn't let me really do it that time."

"But she teased you, didn't she? Let you kiss her and touch her. And she didn't make you wait very long, did she?"

The flush had turned his face red by now. "No, not long," he admitted sadly.

"She couldn't wait long because she already knew about the baby," Frank said. "She needed a husband real quick, somebody who didn't know much and wouldn't ask a lot of questions."

"She said she loved me," Antonio lamented. "She said she never let any boy do it before."

"Of course she did, and you believed her because you're young and stupid. I guess you were scared when she told you about the baby, too."

Antonio winced in shame. "I didn't know what to do, so I went to Joe. He said I should do the right thing and marry her. Maria did, too."

"Maria knew about Nainsi and the baby?" Frank asked in surprise.

"Maria knows everything that happens in our house," Antonio said. "Nobody can keep a secret from her."

Frank considered this information. Nainsi could've tricked Antonio, but Joe and Maria should have been more suspicious. He wondered why they'd encouraged a marriage like that. That was something to ask them, however.

"Where did you and Joe go last night after you left the dance house at midnight?"

"Home. Where else would we go?"

"I suppose everyone was asleep when you got there," Frank said.

"Maria was up with the baby. And Lorenzo."

"Lorenzo was up with the baby?" Frank asked in amazement.

"He . . . he feels sorry for Maria. He tries to help her."

Something stirred in Frank's memory. Sarah had remarked on how unnaturally helpful Lorenzo had been with the baby.

Antonio cleared his throat. "Is Mrs. O'Hara really dead?"

"Yes, she is," Frank assured him. "And if you know anything about it, you'd better tell me now."

"I don't, I swear. I just . . . Are you sure somebody killed her? Maybe it was an accident or something."

"People don't get their throats cut by accident," Frank said.

"Somebody cut her throat?" Antonio asked, horrified. He instinctively lifted a hand to his own throat. "Who would do a thing like that?"

"I sort of thought you and Joe did it," Frank said, and the boy's eyes widened. "Somebody took her by the hair, pulled her head back, and sliced her ear to ear," Frank explained, demonstrating on himself the way the medical examiner had done for him. "Her blood squirted all over the wall and—"

He stopped because Antonio had gone pale, clapped both hands over his mouth, and started retching.

Frank jumped to his feet and backed away as the boy vomited on the floor. With a weary sigh, he opened the door and left. He'd send someone down to clean up the mess, and then he'd let Antonio go. If one of the Ruoccos had killed Mrs. O'Hara, Antonio wasn't the one, and he still didn't know who was.

SARAH HAD DISPOSED OF THE WHISKY BOTTLE, THOR-
oughly cleaned the cup, and aired out the kitchen. Then she'd cleaned her teeth with baking soda paste and rinsed her mouth with salt water. When Maeve assured her all trace of the odor was gone, she brought Aggie down, and they had a cold supper. Aggie kept looking around, as if still searching for the bottle, but her terror seemed to have dissipated.

Maeve got the child ready for bed, and Sarah went up to tuck her in as usual. Aggie lay under the covers, clutching her beloved doll. Her eyes were wary as Sarah approached, and Sarah tried a reassuring smile.

"I'm sorry you were scared this afternoon," she said, sitting down on the bed beside the girl. "I threw the whisky— that bad stuff that scared you—away, and we won't have any in the house anymore, I promise."

She leaned down and kissed Aggie's soft forehead. "I would never have had it here if I knew you didn't like it. I love you, and I don't want you to ever be scared, Aggie. Do you believe that?"

Aggie nodded.

Sarah smiled with relief, and Aggie smiled back. Sarah swooped in and tickled her, making her giggle and breaking the tension of the moment. After a few playful minutes, Sarah kissed her again. "Time to go to sleep now, sweetheart."

Aggie pretended to pout, and Sarah tickled her again, making the pout vanish. On impulse, Sarah said the words she'd been practicing for weeks, ever since she'd overheard Aggie speaking to Malloy's son Brian when she thought no one could hear. "I was wondering if I could call you by a different name," she began hesitantly.

Aggie frowned in confusion.

Sarah took a deep breath and continued. "I know Aggie isn't your real name. It's the one they gave you at the mission. I've been thinking about giving you a better one. I've always liked the name Catherine. It's a pretty name, don't you think?"

Aggie's confusion faded into amazement, and she nodded.

"Would it be all right if I called you Catherine instead of Aggie?"

The girl's face lit up, and she nodded vigorously.

"Thank you, Catherine," Sarah said in relief, taking the girl in her arms and giving her a hug. "Thank you for everything."

FRANK WAS SITTING AT HIS DESK AT HEADQUARTERS, still trying to make sense of what he'd learned from Antonio, when Gino returned.

"The guy at the dance house door remembered the Ruoccos from last night," he reported. "He knows them both. I also saw a few girls they danced with, and from all accounts they stayed until closing."

"I figured," Frank sighed.

"They still could've gone over to Mrs. O'Hara's and killed her after that," Gino tried.

"Except that Antonio would've fainted if they did. He didn't have anything to do with killing the old woman."

"Then maybe Joe went by himself."

"They were together all night, and he said they went home after that. He said Maria and Lorenzo were up with the baby when they got home, so we can check on that—if we can trust them to tell the truth."

"Lorenzo was up with the baby?" Gino echoed. "Why would he do that?"

"Antonio says he feels sorry for Maria."

"I feel sorry for her, too, but I'd never sit up with a screaming baby."

"Neither would I. I'm starting to think Lorenzo might have more than a passing interest in that baby."

"What do you mean?"

"Well, we know that Lorenzo and Antonio used to go to the dance houses together starting in August, so there's a good chance Lorenzo used to go without him before that. We know that somebody knocked Nainsi up several months before Antonio met her. I found out tonight that Nainsi seduced Antonio just a few days after she met him. She already knew about the baby by then, and she must've decided the first time she met Antonio that he was the one she was going to trick into marrying her. But why would she pick him, out of all the men she could meet at the dance houses?"

Gino considered. "Because he's young and innocent. He

probably wouldn't know he wasn't her first lover, and he'd feel guilty enough to go along with her scheme."

"Or maybe because he was her lover's brother, and she wanted revenge or something, because her lover refused to marry her."

"You think Lorenzo is the father?"

"Somebody is, and it would explain why she chose Antonio," Frank said.

"Sounds pretty far-fetched. How could she know she'd even meet Lorenzo's brother?"

"She probably couldn't, but she did. We also know she tried to trick at least one other fellow into thinking he might be the father."

"Keith," Gino remembered.

"Yes, why else would Nainsi make sure he did her proper? She already knew about the baby, so she must've been trying to make Keith think he was the father."

"But he's married."

"Yeah, but he'd have to give her money to keep her from going to his wife. The wife's pretty sickly, so he would've paid to protect her."

Gino nodded. "She was looking for somebody to support her if she couldn't find a husband."

"That's what I'm guessing. By the time she met Antonio, she must've been pretty desperate."

"So the question is, why did she pick Antonio? If Lorenzo was the baby's father, why didn't she just try to get him to marry her?"

"Maybe she did, and he refused. Antonio says Lorenzo doesn't want to get married at all."

"Is he going to become a priest or something?" Gino asked in disgust.

"That's what I asked," Frank said with a grin. "Apparently, he just isn't ready to settle down. So if he was the baby's father, he didn't want to be stuck with it or her."

"And when Lorenzo showed up at the dance house with his little brother in tow, she latched onto him."

"It's a nice theory," Frank agreed. "It still doesn't tell us who killed Mrs. O'Hara and Nainsi, though."

"But it gives Lorenzo a pretty good reason to do it," Gino pointed out. "When his mother figured out that Antonio wasn't the baby's father, she was going to throw Nainsi and the baby out. Lorenzo didn't have any use for Nainsi, but maybe he wanted to keep his son."

Frank nodded his approval at Gino's reasoning. "He must've figured once the girl was dead, Maria would take care of the baby and everything would be fine. Then Mrs. O'Hara starts fighting to get the baby away from them."

"So he has to kill her, too. Did our men notice anybody else leaving the Ruoccos' house last night?"

"We only had two men on the place last night, so one could go for help if a mob showed up. When one went off to follow Joe and Antonio, the other might've missed Lorenzo leaving." Frank frowned. "Now we're back to having to get information from the Ruocco family. They're going to lie to protect him, even if he did go out and kill Mrs. O'Hara."

Gino swore. "So what can we do?"

"There's still one person in the Ruocco house we haven't questioned yet who would probably tell us the truth."

"Mrs. Ruocco?"

"No, she'd lie for sure. I'm talking about Valentina."

Gino reared back in horror. "You can't bring a girl into the police station to question her. She'd be ruined!"

"I know, I know. Everyone would assume she'd been

raped, and nobody would ever marry her. We can't go to her house, either, because her mother would never let us talk to her at all. So I need you to figure out how we can question her with nobody finding out."

Gino's distress made Frank smile grimly.

"See," he told the younger man. "I told you this job wasn't fun."

SARAH GAPED AT MALLOY ACROSS HER KITCHEN TABLE. "You want me to kidnap Valentina Ruocco?"

"Not *kidnap* her," he said impatiently. "Just help me get her away from her house to someplace where I can question her."

Sarah was hoping that this early Saturday morning visit from Malloy was only a bad dream, and she'd wake up any second. Unfortunately, she knew it wasn't.

"She's the only one I can be sure will tell the truth," Malloy argued. "You know her family won't let me talk to her if I go there. If I take her into Headquarters, her life will be ruined, and Ugo Ruocco would probably take his revenge in a very messy way. Think about Nainsi, Sarah. We need to find out who killed her, but we need to protect Valentina, too."

"They won't let me back into their house, either," Sarah reminded him. "Not after I tried to convince them to help find Nainsi's killer . . . Oh, no, I just realized . . ."

"Realized what?"

Sarah groaned and covered her face with both hands. "That was probably why someone killed Mrs. O'Hara. It's all my fault!"

"They would've thought of it sooner or later," Malloy

said, as if that settled it. "And it's nobody's fault Mrs. O'Hara is dead except the person who killed her. If you want to find out who that was and punish him, then I have to talk to Valentina."

Sarah groaned again. "What do you need me to do?"

SARAH AND MALLOY SAT IN THE DANK ROOM IN THE basement of Our Lady of Pompeii Catholic Church. Sarah was certain God would strike them both dead for using the church as the location for their plot. At best He would be very angry, and if a priest or anyone else found them hiding here . . .

"Shhh," Malloy said, rising to his feet and putting a finger to his lips. They could both hear the sound of footsteps and a young girl's voice asking a question. Malloy moved toward the door and opened it just as the footsteps came up beside it. In the next instant, Valentina Ruocco stumbled through it, followed by Gino Donatelli. Malloy closed the door quickly behind them.

Valentina looked startled and then confused. "What are you doing here?" she asked Sarah and then turned to Malloy. "And you?" She whirled on Gino. "You lied to me! My mother isn't sick at all!" Gino had summoned her from the line at the confessional upstairs on that pretext.

"No, she isn't," Malloy confirmed. "We needed to ask you a few questions, Valentina. We need your help to figure out who killed Nainsi."

"I don't care who killed Nainsi," she said petulantly. "I'm glad she's gone. I wish her mother wasn't dead, though. I wanted her to take that awful baby away. He cries all night long!"

"Just sit down and answer a few questions, and we'll let you go back and to confession," Malloy said wearily.

She glared at Gino again. "I thought it was funny that they'd send you," she said venomously. "Wait till I tell my *Zio* Ugo what you did. He'll kill you!"

Gino flinched slightly, but he managed an apologetic grin.

"Valentina," Sarah said quickly. "I know you're upset, but if you'd like for your life to get back to normal, the best thing you can do is help Mr. Malloy and Officer Donatelli by answering their questions."

Valentina frowned. "Why are *you* here?"

Sarah smiled sadly. "To chaperone."

She straightened as a new idea occurred to her. "I could start screaming," she informed them haughtily.

"Then people would want to know why you left the line at the confessional booth and went off alone with me," Gino said.

Valentina rolled her eyes, but she plunked down in the chair Malloy had vacated. "What do you want to know?" she asked with a sigh of defeat.

"Tell me what happened last night, after you closed the restaurant."

Plainly, she thought this a silly request. "We cleaned up like we always do, even though we hardly had any customers. We went upstairs. Maria started picking on Antonio. She's so mean since that baby came. She yells at everybody."

"What do you mean, picking on him?"

"She didn't like the way he was cracking his knuckles, and then she said he was breathing too loud. Everything we do makes her nervous. I think she's going crazy. So she starts yelling at him and tells Joe to take him out someplace away from her."

"So he did?"

"Not until they had a big fight with Mama. She said they shouldn't leave us to be killed in our beds by the Irish. She tried to make them feel guilty, but then they went out anyway, because Maria wanted them gone."

"What about Lorenzo?"

"What about him?" she asked, pretending to be bored.

"Did he go out, too?"

"Lorenzo?" she scoffed. "All he ever does is sit with Maria and moon over that stupid baby."

"Did he leave the house at all yesterday?"

"How would I know? I don't pay any attention to him."

"Valentina," Gino said in warning.

She glared at him, but she said, "I didn't see him go anyplace. He was cleaning the kitchen, or helping Maria all day. Oh, I almost forgot, he did go to the market with Mama in the morning."

Since Mrs. O'Hara was still alive then, Sarah knew that wasn't any help.

"What about the rest of the family?" Malloy asked. "Did any of them go out during the afternoon?"

"No, how could they? We have to serve lunch and get ready for dinner, and since Maria doesn't help us anymore, we all have a lot more work to do. It isn't fair!"

"What does Maria do now?" Malloy asked.

Valentina made a sour face. "She takes care of the *baby,*" she said bitterly. "She hardly even comes downstairs except to fix his bottles. I don't see why she's got to be with him all the time like that."

"Babies need a lot of care, Valentina," Sarah said. Malloy shot her a look, and she bit her lip in contrition.

"Just one more thing, Valentina, and then you can go,"

Malloy said. "Did you hear Joe and Antonio come home last night?"

"No. They come home late, after I'm asleep. Can I go now?" she asked irritably.

Malloy nodded, and she got up and started for the door.

"Valentina," he said, stopping her before she could open it. "The night Nainsi died, Joe made a lot of noise when he came in. Did you hear Nainsi yell out to him to be quiet?"

She gave it a moment's thought. "No, I didn't hear anything until that baby started crying the next morning and wouldn't stop, and I went into Nainsi's room . . ." She shuddered. *"Can I go?"* she whined.

"Yes," Malloy said, and Gino opened the door for her.

She fairly ran out.

"That wasn't much help," Gino observed, closing the door behind her.

"No, it wasn't," Malloy agreed. "According to her, none of the Ruoccos could've killed Mrs. O'Hara."

"Unless Joe snuck out again after he brought Antonio home."

"If he did—or if anyone did—no one would ever admit it," Sarah pointed out.

"So we're back to *Zio* Ugo and his men," Gino sighed.

"We're missing something. We've got to be," Malloy insisted. "Let's go over it all again."

"Ahem," Sarah said meaningfully. "Could we find a place where we'll be welcome if someone were to see us?"

"I guess we *should* leave," Gino allowed. He opened the door and looked out into the hallway. "Nobody out there. Mrs. Brandt, you go first."

Sarah stole down the hallway and out the door into the alley where Gino had admitted them earlier. After glancing around to make sure no one had paid attention to her somewhat hasty escape, she slowed her pace and walked down to the street corner, where Malloy and Gino soon joined her.

"There's a coffeehouse on the corner," Gino pointed out.

The three of them adjourned there. When they'd ordered coffee, Malloy gave Sarah one of his looks. "How do you always manage to get mixed up in these things?"

Sarah feigned shock. "If I remember correctly, you came to my house and *begged* me to do this."

"I don't mean . . . Oh, never mind. All right, what do we know about Nainsi?"

"She met Antonio at a dance house and tricked him into thinking he was the father of her baby," Gino supplied helpfully.

"But we know he wasn't because the baby was started in June, and he didn't even meet her until August," Malloy said.

"And she was already at least two months gone by then, maybe more," Sarah added.

"But her friends say she was seeing an Italian man months before that," Malloy said. "A *rich* Italian man."

"Uncle Ugo?" Gino offered with a grin.

"A girl like Nainsi wouldn't fall in love with Ugo no matter how much money he had," Sarah assured them. "Do you have any idea who the man could have been?"

"We were considering Lorenzo," Malloy told her, watching for her reaction.

"Lorenzo?" she echoed in surprise, trying to see him through Nainsi's eyes. "What made you think of him?"

"We know he took Antonio out to the dance houses because Mrs. Ruocco wouldn't let him go alone. That probably means he had been going to them himself before that. He could've met Nainsi and seduced her."

"Antonio said Mrs. Ruocco wants to find him a wife, but Lorenzo doesn't want to get married," Gino said.

"He especially wouldn't want to marry an Irish girl he met at a dance house," Sarah guessed. "His mother would never stand for it!"

"He could've eloped with her, like Antonio did, but maybe he's not as noble as Antonio," Malloy said.

"Or maybe he just didn't want to," Sarah surmised. "But we're getting way ahead of ourselves. What makes you think Lorenzo even knew Nainsi, much less fathered her child?"

"Didn't you say that Lorenzo was the one who stood up for Maria when she wanted to keep the baby?" Malloy asked.

"Yes, I did. He's been very supportive. He even sits up with her when the baby cries at night."

"You just heard Valentina say he spends a lot of time with the baby, and Antonio said the same thing. Why would a bachelor take such an interest in someone else's bastard?"

"Oh, my," Sarah said, as the pieces started to fall into place. "You're right. Lorenzo even mentioned that he didn't approve of Antonio's marriage. Of course he wouldn't want his baby brother saddled with a girl like that."

"He wouldn't like having Nainsi living under his roof, either," Gino said.

"But she wasn't going to be living under his roof anymore," Malloy reminded them. "Mrs. Ruocco was going to throw her out."

Something deep in Sarah's memory stirred. "Nainsi wasn't worried about getting thrown out, though," she recalled. "She was almost smug when Mrs. Ruocco threatened her. If Lorenzo was the baby's father, then all she had to do was tell

Mrs. Ruocco the truth. She wouldn't throw her grandson out, no matter which of her sons was the father."

"Lorenzo couldn't have that," Malloy said. "So he killed her."

"And then he fell in love with his son," Sarah realized. "I've seen it happen many times. That's why he stood up to Ugo when he wanted them to get rid of the baby."

Gino had been listening to them with great interest. "This is a really good theory," he said. "So how do we prove it?"

13

THIS SILENCED ALL OF THEM. SARAH SAW THE DISCOUR-
agement in Malloy's dark eyes and the hopelessness in Gino's.

"We'll have to bring him in," Malloy said finally, but
without much enthusiasm.

"All he has to do is keep his mouth shut, though," Gino
reminded them. "We can't prove a thing without a confession . . . or witnesses."

"His family won't turn on him, even if they know he did
it," Sarah said. "And I'm sure he wouldn't have wanted any
of them to know. Nainsi's death was silent in the darkness,
and no one saw the killer going into Mrs. O'Hara's flat. He
surely would've waited until the family was asleep—and Joe
and Antonio were out—before he left for her place."

Malloy was rubbing his chin. "But Mrs. O'Hara was

working on her ties when she died. If it was late at night, she would've been in bed."

"Maybe not," Sarah said. "Piecework doesn't pay very much, so the only way to earn more is to make more. People sometimes work all night."

"In the dark?" Malloy asked.

"Was there a lamp on the table?"

"Yes, but it was empty."

"Then she might have been burning it, and it went dry after she died."

"Or it might have been empty, and she died when it was still daylight," Malloy argued back.

"Either way, there's still no reason Lorenzo couldn't have done it," Gino pointed out. "Even if Valentina didn't see him leave the house all day, he could have. He wouldn't have been gone long."

"Then let's go bring him in," Malloy said wearily. He laid money on the table for the coffee and rose from his seat.

Sarah gathered her things and preceded the men out into the street.

"Thank you for all your help, Mrs. Brandt," Malloy said formally, because Gino was there.

"I don't think I helped much," she demurred.

"Yes, you did," Gino assured her. "We wouldn't have dared talk to Valentina without you."

"And when Mrs. Ruocco finds out I helped you waylay her daughter, I'll probably never deliver another baby in Little Italy again," she predicted with a rueful smile.

"I don't think it'll be that serious," Malloy said. "Can I convince you to go home now?"

"Yes, you can. I'll be happy to spend the rest of the day with Catherine."

"Who?" Malloy said in surprise.

Sarah couldn't help smiling. "I asked if I could start calling her Catherine, and she said I could."

Malloy grinned back, the sort of sentimental smile she seldom saw, which made Gino ask, "Who's Catherine?"

Malloy sobered instantly. "I'll tell you later. Find Mrs. Brandt a cab so she can be on her way."

"Will you send me word about what happens with Lorenzo?" she asked.

"I'll be sure you find out," Gino promised, earning a frown from Malloy.

All too quickly, they put her in a cab and left her to imagine what would happen next. Whatever it was would only bring more heartache to the Ruocco family.

THIS TIME FRANK AND GINO DECIDED TO TRY A DIFFERent approach to convincing Lorenzo to come to Headquarters for questioning. A deciding factor was that Ugo Ruocco had increased the number of men he had guarding the street outside since they'd taken Antonio in for questioning, and Frank didn't think they'd just stand by while he and Gino marched Lorenzo out the front door. He pulled in a couple of officers from another precinct and instructed them carefully in what their part would be.

Saturday had brought more customers to the restaurant for lunch. Perhaps they thought that with Mrs. O'Hara dead, there would be no more trouble. Frank and Gino waited until the crowd had thinned down, and then sent two officers in, dressed as ordinary working men. Frank and Gino waited out of sight around the corner with the police wagon. A beat cop was idly strolling down the street in front of Mama's

Restaurant, and within minutes the front door flew open, and Joe started hustling one of the disguised policemen out, convinced he was nothing more than an unruly customer. They were both shouting, and the cop was throwing punches that Joe managed to duck. Seconds later, the other officer emerged, grappling with Lorenzo. Instantly, the uniformed beat cop started pounding his locust club and shouting for help.

That was the cue for the wagon driver to slap his team into motion. The Black Maria went hurtling around the corner just as other uniformed cops emerged from their hiding places to assist in calming the melee.

Ugo's men had immediately moved in to help the Ruocco boys, but the police quickly discouraged them by grabbing every man they saw and throwing him into the paddy wagon. Joe and Lorenzo were the first inside, in spite of their vocal and violent protests that they'd just been protecting their property. The two unruly customers followed, mostly to make sure the Ruoccos didn't escape, and by then most everyone else had fled. The wagon rumbled away, and Frank and Gino met it at Headquarters when it pulled up to disgorge its passengers.

By then Joe and Lorenzo were furious and ready to take on the entire police force, until they emerged and saw Frank's smiling face.

"Good afternoon, fellows," he greeted them. "So glad you could make it."

Lorenzo gave him a murderous glare. "You! After what you did to Valentina, I should cut your throat!"

"Like you did to Mrs. O'Hara?" Frank inquired mildly.

Lorenzo had no answer for that.

"Bring them inside, boys," Frank said, and the officers escorted them none too gently up the front stairs.

Joe noticed the two "customers" walking away. "What about them?" he asked in outrage. "They started a fight in our place!"

"They're cops," Gino informed them. "We needed a way to get the two of you down here without having to wade through Ugo's men."

Frank and Gino were roundly cursed in two languages, so Frank let the boys cool their heels for over an hour down in separate interrogation rooms. He could have let Joe go, of course, but he didn't, reasoning that he might need to verify something Lorenzo said . . . or didn't say. Besides, he felt ornery.

When Frank and Gino finally joined Lorenzo downstairs, he had regained control of his temper. In fact, he looked entirely too cool for Frank's taste. Sitting in the dingy room hadn't panicked him like it had Antonio. He simply looked disgusted.

Frank took a seat opposite him while Gino manned the door. "We know why Nainsi died, Lorenzo. We know everything."

"Then why am I here?" he asked. "Why is my brother here? Why haven't you arrested the killer?"

"Tell me, Lorenzo, why did you defend Maria against Ugo when she wanted to keep the baby?"

The question puzzled him. "Because she wanted him."

"Because *she* wanted him?" Frank asked. "Or because *you* did?"

"Why would I want him?"

Frank nodded sagely. "That's a good question. Why

would a man even care what happens to a little bastard some whore delivered on his doorstep?"

Lorenzo shifted uneasily in his seat. He didn't like Frank's choice of words, but he didn't protest.

"That's what Nainsi was, wasn't she? A whore?"

The word pained him, and Lorenzo didn't want to agree. "She was foolish. Young and foolish."

"Young, but not too foolish. She got herself a husband, didn't she? A man to take care of her and her baby when the real father wouldn't."

Lorenzo refused to respond. Frank could see the muscles in his jaw working.

"Why do you think the real father wouldn't marry her, Lorenzo?"

"I don't know," he said through gritted teeth.

"Let's think about it then. Maybe the real father was the kind of man who likes to take advantage of foolish young girls. He likes to use them for his pleasure and then move on to another one. Maybe he's the kind of man who wouldn't care that he has a son somewhere whose name he doesn't even know."

Anger flickered across Lorenzo's face. "Maybe he is."

"What would you think of a man like that, Lorenzo? A man who'd turn his back on a girl after he put a baby in her belly? A man who'd turn his back on his own child?"

"He is not a man," Lorenzo decreed.

"But you didn't want Antonio to marry Nainsi, did you? Even when everybody thought the baby was his, you didn't approve. Why is that?"

"That girl, anyone can see she's a liar. Antonio would never . . . He's too young to know what to do. She would have to show him, and how would she know what to do if she hadn't been with another man already?"

"So you didn't think the baby was his right from the beginning?" Frank guessed.

"I didn't know, but I knew she wasn't a nice girl for Antonio."

"Or maybe you knew because she'd been with you already."

Lorenzo actually reared back in shock. "Who told you this?" he demanded.

"We figured it out," Frank said with some satisfaction. "Nainsi was bragging to her friends about her Italian lover for months. When she married Antonio, they all thought he was the one she'd been seeing, but we know he didn't even start going to the dance houses until August."

His expression was almost comical. "And you think I was this Italian man?"

"A young man like you, who could blame you for going to dance houses? For wanting to spend time with girls who aren't too virtuous before you have to settle down with a wife of your own? But wait, you don't want a wife of your own, do you?" Frank said, pretending to just remember that fact. "Antonio said your mama wants to get you a wife like she did for Joe, but you don't want to get married at all."

Lorenzo blanched, but he managed to hold his temper. "I never saw Nainsi before Antonio brought her to our house," Lorenzo insisted.

Frank slapped his hand down on the table, making Lorenzo jump. "Don't bother lying, Lorenzo," he said fiercely. "We know you're the one who took Antonio to the dance house where he met Nainsi. We know you'd been going there for a long time. We know you got Nainsi pregnant and refused to marry her. We know you were angry when she tricked your little brother into taking responsibility for your mistake, and we know you killed her so she wouldn't tell your mother the truth."

Stunned, Lorenzo stared at Frank for a long moment, as if trying to comprehend everything he'd just heard—or figure some way to deny it.

And then he started to laugh.

SARAH GROANED WHEN SHE HEARD SOMEONE KNOCKING on her door. She and Maeve had been practicing calling Aggie by her new name and pretending to forget to make her laugh. Sarah didn't want to stop. She wanted this joyous time to last forever. Maeve went downstairs to answer the door, but when she called up, Sarah knew she'd be leaving.

As she and Catherine came down the stairs, she was surprised to see Antonio Ruocco waiting in the foyer. She knew a moment of apprehension, thinking he might have come to berate her for her part in questioning Valentina this morning, but then she saw the desperate look on his face.

"Mrs. Brandt, Maria needs for you to come right away. The baby is sick."

Sarah might have thought it was a trick to lure her someplace where Ugo Ruocco could take revenge, but Antonio was too innocent to lie so well.

"What's wrong with him?"

"He won't stop crying," Antonio reported in dismay. "And his bowels are running, and Mama says he's too hot."

"Antonio, I want to help Maria, but I think your family must be very angry with me right now."

"Because of Valentina," he said, nodding his head.

"Yes, and because of my last visit there, too. Maybe Maria doesn't know about Valentina, but I'm sure your mother—"

"She knows. We all know. Valentina tells everyone who will listen, and then the police took Joe and Lorenzo away in a wagon today, too. We're all very angry, but Maria doesn't care. She says you are the only one who knows how make the baby well."

"But I doubt your mother would even let me in the house," Sarah protested.

"She's the one who told me to come. She's afraid of what will happen to Maria if the baby dies. Maria loves him so much . . . Too much, I think," he added sadly.

Sarah remembered what Valentina had said about Maria's state of mind. She must already be near the breaking point, and with the baby sick . . . Sarah could at least provide reassurance and support to ease the strain Maria was under. If Mrs. Ruocco would let her in, that is.

"Girls, I'm sorry, but I have to go with Mr. Ruocco."

Their obvious disappointment broke her heart, and she promised to return in time to tuck Catherine into bed. Then she checked her medical bag to make sure she had the proper remedies. Satisfied, she set out with Antonio.

When they arrived at the restaurant, they found the shades closed and the restaurant dark. They'd be hard pressed to serve dinner with the two older boys still at police headquarters. Antonio took her inside and led her to the interior stairs, calling out to let his mother know they'd arrived.

When they reached the second floor, Sarah could hear the baby crying from the floor above. She hurried past Antonio, snatching her medical bag from him. She found Maria and

Mrs. Ruocco in the parlor. Mrs. Ruocco was rocking the baby while Maria paced. She ran to meet Sarah.

"He's dying," Maria cried, nearly hysterical. She looked as if she hadn't slept in days. "You must save him!"

Sarah hazarded a glance at Mrs. Ruocco, who glared back. Her gaze could have cut glass, but Sarah managed not to flinch. "I'm sorry for what happened with Valentina, Mrs. Ruocco, but the police said they were going to question her no matter what. I thought at least I could make sure nothing improper happened."

Mrs. Ruocco rose from the chair and strode toward her. As she passed, she handed Sarah the baby and kept going. Plainly, she wasn't willing to forgive or even to remain in the same room with her. But at least she hadn't thrown her out.

"What's wrong with him?" Maria pleaded. "Will he die?"

Sarah quickly felt the baby's head and limbs. He was slightly warm, but that could just be because he'd been crying for so long. He did seem to be uncomfortable. He was pulling his knees to his chest, and the cry was distinctively one of pain. "Can I see one of his dirty diapers?"

Maria ran to fetch one, and Sarah laid the baby down on the couch and unwrapped him from his blanket to examine him, poking and prodding. When she'd finished and examined the diaper, she knew as much as it was possible to know about a patient who couldn't even tell you where it hurt.

"Is he eating?" Sarah asked over the baby's cries.

"Not since early this morning. He was fussy all morning after that and wouldn't nap. Then he started crying and wouldn't stop no matter what I did. Is it the milk again?"

That would have been Sarah's first guess. "Goat's milk rarely disagrees with a baby, but you can never be sure if what you get at the market is really goat's milk or how fresh it is or what else they might have mixed with it," Sarah explained. "Keeping the bottles clean is another problem, although I'm sure you've been doing a good job of that."

"Oh, yes, I boil them every time," Maria assured her, wringing her hands. The circles under her eyes were so dark, they almost looked like bruises, and her normally glowing complexion was chalky.

"Have you thought about finding a wet nurse for him?" Sarah asked, picking up the baby again and instinctively trying to rock him to soothe his cries.

Maria's expression changed from despair to terror. "I want to take care of him myself!"

"Of course you do, but perhaps one of the women in the neighborhood would sell you some breast milk. Even if it was only for a few weeks, until he's stronger. Then we can try the goat's milk again."

Maria looked too overwhelmed to even begin to consider such a prospect. Sarah decided to speak to Mrs. Ruocco about it, even if Mrs. Ruocco wouldn't speak to her. But first things first.

She opened her medical bag with her free hand and found the bottle she wanted. Using an eye dropper, she placed a drop on the baby's tongue. He made a face at the taste, then started to cry again.

"What did you give him?"

"Paregoric," Sarah said. "To stop the diarrhea." She didn't explain that paregoric was a tincture of opium, because she knew that would frighten Maria. Sarah hated giving it to him, but it was the only way she knew to treat the diarrhea quickly. If she didn't, the baby would die of dehydration.

"Please sit down, Maria. Pacing the floor won't help, and you're just exhausting yourself."

Maria sat, but she didn't relax. Her haunted eyes watched every step as Sarah walked the baby back and forth until the drug took hold and his cries quieted and finally ceased.

Instantly, Maria was on her feet. "Is he . . . ?"

"Sleeping," Sarah said. "Now we need to talk."

FRANK COULDN'T REMEMBER EVER HAVING A SUSPECT start laughing in the middle of an interrogation—at least not one in his right mind.

"What's so funny?" Frank growled.

Lorenzo wiped a tear from his eye and fought to get himself under control again. "You are. You think I did those things. I have never been to a dance house in my life."

Frank felt the anger roiling in his chest. "Liar," he snapped. "Antonio told us all about it."

"Maybe, but he didn't tell you *I* took him to the dance house," Lorenzo assured him, still grinning. "And he didn't tell you I knew Nainsi, because I didn't. I never even saw her before Antonio brought her to our house after he married her."

Frank wouldn't call him a liar again. He knew when someone was telling the truth, and Lorenzo had the confidence of that behind his words. But Antonio *had* said . . . He'd said that his *brother* took him to the dance house! That's it. He'd said his *brother,* and they'd assumed he meant his *bachelor* brother, Lorenzo.

Frank leaned back in his chair, sizing him up. "Are you saying Joe was the one who took Antonio to the dance houses?" he asked with interest.

Lorenzo sobered instantly. "I'm not saying anything except that it wasn't me."

Frank nodded sagely. "I see that. But my theory is still right. An Italian man got Nainsi pregnant, and then she tricked his brother into marrying her."

Lorenzo flushed. "Joe would never do a thing like that."

"Why not?" Frank asked curiously.

"Because . . . he's married," Lorenzo said uncertainly.

Frank nodded thoughtfully. "Yes, he is. He's married to Maria, but that didn't stop him from going to dance houses with Antonio, did it? And it didn't stop him from going to them by himself before that, either."

Lorenzo's jaw tightened. "I don't know anything about it. I only know my brother wouldn't do what you say."

"I guess he wouldn't kill Nainsi either, because he wouldn't care if she told his mother—and Maria—the truth about the baby."

Frank watched Lorenzo putting the pieces together in his mind. Frank had been certain the killer would have kept his secret from the rest of the family, no matter who the killer was. If Lorenzo wasn't the killer, he wouldn't have known, but now he had to face the truth.

"Joe couldn't kill anyone," he said, but without much conviction.

"Were you awake when Joe and Antonio got home from the dance house the night Mrs. O'Hara was killed?"

"Night before last?" he asked.

Frank nodded.

"Yeah, I . . . I was awake. The baby was crying and woke me up. I saw my brothers come home."

"I don't suppose you noticed if either one of them had any blood on him?"

Lorenzo just glared back.

"Or if Joe went out again later?"

He crossed his arms over his chest in silent refusal to reply. "Are you going to lock me up?"

Frank considered it. "No, I don't think so. I think I'll let you go home, Lorenzo. For now."

"And Joe?"

Frank smiled. "No, I'm going to keep Joe for a while longer."

"WILL THE MEDICINE MAKE HIM BETTER?" MARIA ASKED when Sarah had put the baby down in his cradle.

"It should stop the diarrhea. Then we have to figure out what caused it and keep it from happening again."

"I'll make sure the milk is from a goat," Maria promised fervently. "I will keep the bottles clean and boil them. I will do everything you say."

Sarah's heart ached for her. Maria was like a string that had been stretched too tightly, and Sarah feared the slightest little thing could make her snap. "Do you have any wine up here?" she asked conversationally.

"Wine? What for?"

"I want you to drink some. You need to calm down and rest, Maria. You must take care of yourself, or you won't be any help to the baby."

Maria absently brushed back a stray tendril of hair. "That is what Lorenzo says."

"He's right. Maria, I can't promise you that the baby will get better. I warned you from the beginning that babies sometimes don't do well when they're fed from a bottle."

"But I'll be very careful!"

"I know you will, but sometimes even that isn't enough.

I still think it would be a good idea to find a woman to give him milk, to make sure he does as well as he can."

She could actually feel Maria's resistance to the idea of involving another woman in the care of the baby she'd come to love as her own. "Just tell me what to do to make him better," she pleaded.

Sarah took Maria into the parlor and made her sit down on the sofa. Then she found some paper and a pencil and sat down beside her to write down instructions so Maria wouldn't forget them. Maria sat perfectly still with her hands folded in her lap, but even so, the very air around her seemed to vibrate with tension. Mrs. Ellsworth would have said she was wound tighter than an eight-day clock.

"I'm adding some instructions for you, too, Maria," Sarah said. "I want you to drink a glass of wine with each meal and one at bedtime."

Maria managed a small smile. "I will be drunk. I'll drop the baby."

"I've seen women in your condition before, Maria," Sarah said very seriously. "If you don't get some rest and some relief, you'll collapse. Then the family will have to take care of you *and* the baby. I know you don't want to put a burden like that on them. They're already short-handed without you helping in the restaurant."

Tears formed in Maria's dark eyes. "I didn't want it to be like this. I thought having the baby would be so . . . so happy."

Sarah took one of her hands. "When a baby is born, the father gives out cigars and drinks toasts and celebrates. That's because he doesn't have to walk the floor all night with a screaming infant."

Maria wiped a tear with her free hand. "I never thought of that."

"And you also never expected Nainsi to die or mobs of angry men to come beating at your door or Mrs. O'Hara to be murdered or your husband to be dragged off to jail," Sarah reminded her gently. "Any one of those things would be difficult to bear, and you're bearing all of them, in addition to taking care of a demanding infant. You need to get some help."

"Lorenzo helps," she said defensively.

Sarah remembered their theory about Lorenzo's unusual concern for the baby. "That's strange, isn't it? For a man to take such an interest in a baby, I mean."

"Lorenzo is a good man."

Sarah didn't wince. "He must be to give up his evenings out to stay with you and the baby."

Maria looked puzzled. "Lorenzo doesn't go out in the evenings."

Sarah had already opened her mouth to contradict her when she realized that Maria would know Lorenzo's habits far better than she. "But I thought . . . I mean, he's a bachelor and . . ." She hesitated, trying to find the right way to frame her question so it wouldn't seem she knew more than she should. "I know Antonio met Nainsi at a dance house. I guess I just assumed that he and Lorenzo went out together."

Maria shook her head. "Not Lorenzo. He doesn't approve of places like that."

"Oh," Sarah said lamely, wondering if Malloy had found out this valuable piece of information yet. She realized that everything they had concluded about Lorenzo having seduced Nainsi might be wrong.

And if he hadn't seduced Nainsi, then he wasn't the

baby's father. But if he wasn't, why was he so interested in the baby's welfare?

"Are you finished with the instructions?" Maria asked.

"Uh, yes, I am," Sarah said. She had just begun to explain them to her when they heard someone coming in from the outside stairway.

"WHY DID YOU LET HIM GO?" GINO DEMANDED WHEN Lorenzo had left the interrogation room.

"Because he's not our killer," Frank said wearily.

"How can you be sure?"

"After you've been doing this for a while, you'll be able to tell when most people are lying. There's some who can fool you, but not many. People like the Ruoccos, who are basically honest, can't."

"He didn't tell you everything he knows, though," Gino pointed out quite correctly.

"No, but he wasn't going to say anything else voluntarily, and I didn't see any point in roughing him up. If I need to ask him more questions, I know where to find him. He's not going anywhere. Now let's see what brother Joe has to say for himself." Frank pushed himself out of the chair.

"Did Joe do it, then?" Gino asked hesitantly.

"That's what we're going to find out."

"But if Lorenzo didn't, it has to be Joe, doesn't it?"

Frank couldn't help smiling. "Don't forget Mrs. Ruocco. Ugo is sure she did it."

"But she's a female," the young man said dismissively.

Frank just shook his head in dismay.

Gino followed him next door to the room where Joe

waited. He wasn't as calm as Lorenzo had been or as panicked as Antonio. He did, however, look guilty as hell.

"We just had a nice little visit with your brother," Frank reported, taking a seat opposite Joe.

"Did you lock him up?" Joe asked with concern.

"No, we let him go home."

"Then you know we didn't cause any trouble. Those two men came into our place and started fighting. We had to throw them out before they broke something or hurt somebody."

"I told you, Joe. Those men are cops. We sent them in there to get you outside so we could bring you into the station for questioning."

Joe frowned. He didn't know what to make of it. "But we didn't do anything wrong," he insisted again.

"Someone did, though," Frank pointed out. "Or Nainsi and her mother would still be alive."

His confusion cleared instantly. "Why are you asking me about this? I already told you, I don't know who killed Nainsi, and I don't know who killed Mrs. O'Hara, either."

"Where were you the other night, Joe?"

"I . . . I was out with Antonio," he admitted reluctantly.

"Oh, yes, at a dance house," Frank remembered. "At least that's what Antonio said. That's kind of funny, isn't it? A married man going to dance houses?"

"I went along to make sure he didn't get into trouble," he said defensively.

"Oh, that's right," Frank said. "Antonio said Maria ordered him out of the house because he was making her nervous."

Joe nodded gratefully. "That's right. She's been very nervous since the baby came. She . . . Mama says she's tired."

"Joe, I found out some disturbing news about you."

He stiffened. "What?"

"It's about those dance houses," Frank said as if he regretted having to bring up the subject. "We found out that even though you're a married man, you were the one who started taking Antonio to them in the first place."

Joe rubbed his hand over his face. "I . . . Well, we couldn't let him go alone, could we? He's too young. He might get into trouble."

"So your mama decided you should go with him?" Frank asked skeptically.

"Oh, no . . . I mean, it was my duty. I'm the oldest son."

"You're also the married son," Frank reminded him. "Wouldn't it make more sense for Lorenzo to go with him?"

Joe made a helpless gesture, as if he were trying to snatch the correct response out of the air. "Lorenzo doesn't like to go to places like that," he finally said.

"So you decided you'd do your duty to help your innocent little brother go out and meet girls who are no better than they should be and get him drunk and see how many of these girls he could poke."

"*No!*" Joe protested, although Frank knew he had described the situation accurately.

"Are you saying that's not what happened?"

"Antonio is just a boy," Joe tried. "He . . . he wants to have a good time."

"What about you, Joe? Do you want to have a good time, too?"

"I . . . I guess."

"What does Maria think about that?"

Joe felt on firmer ground here. "She knows her place. She doesn't tell me what to do."

"So she didn't mind when you went out to the dance houses by yourself, either," Frank said.

"By myself?" he echoed, as if he didn't know what Frank was talking about.

"Yeah, you remember. You used to go out to the dance houses long before Antonio decided he wanted to start going along. That's where you met Nainsi, wasn't it?"

"I . . . I never met Nainsi there," he said, but even Gino could see he was lying. The color was seeping from his face and his eyes were starting to look a little desperate.

"That's not what her friends told us," Frank lied. "They said she was seeing you way back in the spring."

"They didn't know that," Joe insisted.

Frank frowned thoughtfully. "Why not?"

"Because . . . because they couldn't," he replied lamely.

"Now let me get this straight. Are you saying they didn't know that you were seeing her?"

"Yes . . . No . . . I mean, I wasn't seeing her at all." Joe was starting to sweat.

"But you were, Joe. Don't lie to us. You were seeing her on the sly. You told her not to tell her friends, but she did. She couldn't help bragging about the rich Italian man she was going to marry."

"But I'm not rich!" Joe pointed out.

"Nainsi thought you were. She also thought you were single, so when she turned up pregnant, she was sure you'd marry her."

"You're wrong!" Joe tried.

"About what, Joe? Are you telling me Nainsi knew you were married?"

"No!"

"So you lied to her."

"No! I didn't lie. I . . . I didn't even know her," he said, but with less conviction than before.

Frank slapped the table as he had with Lorenzo. Joe yelped in surprise.

"Stop lying, Joe. You're making me angry. You knew Nainsi, didn't you?"

"I . . . Yes, I did, but I never—"

"And you seduced her with a promise of marriage." Frank was almost shouting.

"I never promised her anything!"

"And when she threatened to cause trouble, you took your little brother so she could get her hooks into him."

"No, I didn't—"

"Yes, you did, Joe. You took your little brother and gave him to your mistress—"

"No!"

"And you let him think your bastard was his—"

"Stop!" He clapped his hands over his ears, but Frank grabbed his arms and forced them away.

"And you let him marry her, but it was all lies, Joe. You ruined your brother's life with your lies!"

"No, no! It wasn't me! It was all Maria's idea!"

14

Maria jumped up to go see who had come in, and Sarah followed, stopping in the doorway. Maria had found Lorenzo in the hall, and Sarah felt a frisson of alarm. Why was he here?

"Lorenzo," Maria said with what sounded like relief. "You are back."

"They let me go," he said simply. "The baby?"

As if he'd given the fatal pluck to the taut string holding Maria together, she gave an incoherent cry, threw herself against his chest and began to sob. His arms came around her instantly, holding her to him. His hands moved gently over her back, both comforting and caressing, and Sarah watched mesmerized as his face contorted with what looked like pain.

She remembered yesterday, when she had sobbed against

Malloy's chest. His hands had moved on her the way Lorenzo's moved on Maria—tenderly, possessively. Had his face been like that, too, twisted with the agony of a desire he could not fulfill? Suddenly, Lorenzo's interest in helping Maria with the baby was crystal clear.

Sarah must have gasped aloud because Lorenzo's eyes flew open, and he saw her standing in the doorway. Rage replaced whatever emotions he had been feeling.

"What's *she* doing here?" he demanded, disentangling himself from Maria and setting her away from him discreetly.

"Maria sent for me," Sarah defended herself. "The baby was sick."

"How dare you show your face here after what you've done?" His own face was scarlet, but whether from anger only or because he felt shame at what she'd seen, she couldn't tell.

Maria was scrubbing the tears from her face with the back of her hand and trying to catch her breath. "Mama gave permission," she informed him. "The baby is sick. What else could I do?"

"You could send for a doctor," Lorenzo said impatiently.

"A doctor wouldn't care if he lived or died," Maria argued.

"And *she* would?" he challenged, gesturing dismissively at Sarah.

"Yes."

Her confidence set him aback, but he didn't contradict her. Sarah could see the inner battle between pride and honor and his feelings for his brother's wife. Maria won. He glanced around. "Where is the baby?"

"Sleeping," Maria said. "She gave him some medicine."

He glared at Sarah, as if he resented the fact that she'd helped. "Then she can leave now."

Sarah was only too happy to oblige. Why had Malloy let him go? He must have discovered that Lorenzo wasn't Nainsi's lover. "I just need to give Maria the medicine and some instructions for the next few days."

"Good," he said, reaching into his pocket. He pulled out some money. "Here, this is for your medicine . . . and for your time." He thrust it into her hand, then headed down the hall toward the interior stairway.

He'd intended to make her feel inferior, and he'd succeeded in making her furious.

"He is upset," Maria said apologetically. "There was a fight in the restaurant, and he was taken by the police this afternoon."

Sarah didn't think that justified his being rude to her, but then she remembered Joe had been taken with him. "I wonder if your husband came back with him." How odd Maria hadn't even asked about him.

Maria shrugged, as if she didn't care. "Did Lorenzo give you enough money for the medicine?" she asked.

Sarah looked down at her palm. "Yes, more than enough."

"Then tell me what I must do."

"WHAT DO YOU MEAN, IT WAS MARIA'S IDEA?" FRANK asked, glaring intently at Joe.

Joe's gaze flitted wildly around the room, as if he were desperately trying to find a way to escape. Frank slapped the table again to get his attention.

"*Joe!* What was Maria's idea?"

"She said . . . she said we couldn't let the baby go."

Frank stared at him incredulously. "You told her the baby was yours?"

"I had to! I didn't know what else to do!"

Frank could think of a lot of options, none of which involved telling his wife he'd gotten a girl pregnant, but it was too late to point any of them out to Joe. Frank glanced at Gino. The young man's jaw was hanging open, so Frank gave him a glare, silently warning him to shut his mouth and keep it shut.

"Let me make sure I understand," Frank said, letting his voice express only curiosity now. "You met Nainsi at a dance house and got her pregnant."

"I didn't mean to, but . . . She wouldn't leave me alone."

"Are you saying *she* came after *you*?" Frank asked skeptically.

Joe had the grace to look ashamed. "She liked me. She wanted to get married. I told her she was too young, but she . . . she still wanted to."

"You could've told her you were already married," Frank reminded him.

Joe's expression was pained. "She was pretty . . . and fun."

"So you didn't tell her because you wanted to keep poking her," Frank said with contempt.

"She wanted it! She told me she did," he insisted.

"Or maybe she just wanted to get a baby so you'd *have* to marry her," Frank suggested. "And then she did. What did you say when she told you, Joe?"

Joe rubbed his sleeve across his damp forehead. "I told her I couldn't get married. I told her my mother wouldn't allow me to marry an Irish girl."

"But she kept bothering you, didn't she?" Frank guessed. "Maybe she even came to the restaurant."

Joe's eyes widened in surprise that he had figured this

out. "I didn't think she knew who I was, but she found out somehow. She came by one day, and Maria saw her. I sent her away, but Maria knew. She always finds out everything. I thought she'd be mad at me, but she was only mad because I had given a baby to this girl instead of to her."

Frank thought that sounded strange, but he didn't say so. "So Maria was only worried about the baby?"

"She said it was our family. She said we couldn't let strangers raise it."

Frank resisted the urge to glance at Gino. He'd said Italians were devoted to their families, but even so, this seemed a bit much. "So you suggested that Antonio could marry the girl."

"No, no, I didn't know what to do. It was Maria. She said Antonio was too young to know anything, and we could trick him. She said he would think the baby was his, and he would marry Nainsi. Then the baby would be in our family, and we could take care of it. She said it was the right thing to do."

Just when Frank thought he was beginning to understand women a little, something like this happened. "So you're claiming it was Maria's idea for you to take Antonio to the dance house and . . . Did Nainsi know all this? Did she know you were going to trick Antonio into marrying her?"

Joe swallowed and rubbed a hand across his mouth. "I . . . Yes, she . . . I had to tell her! She had to . . . to make him think the baby was his."

Frank didn't bother to hide his disgust. "And she just went along with it?"

"She was scared . . . because of the baby. She needed to get married soon. But she . . . she didn't like it," he admitted.

"I'm sure she didn't," Frank said. "But she went along with it anyway."

Joe seemed to shrink into himself. "She said . . . she said she liked the revenge of having my baby under Maria's nose."

Now *that* was the only part of the story that sounded reasonable to Frank. "And what did Maria think about it once Nainsi was living in your house?"

"Oh, she was happy about the baby," Joe assured him hastily. "And she was nice to Nainsi. Maria is a good woman."

Nobody was that good, Frank thought. If Nainsi wanted revenge, what did Maria want? "You must've been nervous when your mother figured out Antonio wasn't the baby's father and wanted to throw Nainsi and the baby out."

"I didn't know what to do. I couldn't let her do that, but I couldn't tell her the truth, either. That's why I went to *Zio* Ugo. I thought he could help."

"But he couldn't."

"At first he just laughed at Antonio for being a fool. After Antonio passed out, I told him everything, about the baby and how we'd tricked Antonio. Then Ugo slapped me for doing such a thing to my brother and said I deserved to lose my son."

"Why didn't you just tell your mother the truth?" Frank asked reasonably.

Joe gaped at him, horrified. "I committed adultery, got another woman with child, and tricked my brother into marrying her. She would kill me!"

Frank didn't know whether he was exaggerating or not. Knowing Patrizia Ruocco, anything was possible, though. "So you killed Nainsi to save yourself."

"No! I didn't kill her! I told you that before. I was with Antonio and Ugo that night!"

"But Nainsi was still alive when you and Antonio came home."

"How do you know that?" Joe asked in surprise.

"Because you made too much noise when you came in, and she shouted at you to be quiet."

Joe frowned. "I don't remember that."

"Oh, I think you do, Joe. I think that reminded you she was lying in the room across the hall, and you went over there, and you put a pillow over her face, and you held it there while she struggled and fought, and you kept holding it there until she stopped fighting and stopped breathing and she was dead."

Joe just stared at him, completely baffled. "But I didn't even go upstairs that night."

"What do you mean, you didn't go upstairs that night?"

"I was drunk. Antonio was drunk. I got him as far as the second floor parlor sofa, and I left him there. He didn't want to sleep in the bed with Nainsi, and I didn't want to go upstairs where she was either, so I went into Lorenzo's room and got in bed with him."

"You didn't go upstairs to the third floor at all that night?" Frank asked with a frown.

"No, Lorenzo will tell you. He pushed me out of bed and made me sleep on the floor. He said I stunk of whisky."

Frank clearly remembered Maria's account. She'd said Nainsi was still alive when Joe got home, because she'd called out when he woke her up by making noise. She'd said Joe had slept beside her the rest of the night. Frank thought she'd been giving Joe an alibi.

But Joe didn't need one.

* * *

Sarah had finished her explanations and answered all of Maria's questions. As eager as she was to escape the Ruocco house, she hated leaving Maria alone. The poor woman seemed as fragile as glass.

"You have to promise to take care of yourself, Maria," Sarah said.

"I will," Maria replied, but the promise held no conviction.

"I mean it. Remember what I said about you getting sick. You have to eat three good meals a day and sleep as much as you can."

"I will be fine. The baby will be fine," Maria said, although her words sounded more like a plea than an assurance.

Sarah sighed in defeat. Not knowing what else to do, she began to close up her medical bag. Malloy should know what she'd learned about Lorenzo not going to the dance houses and about his true feelings for Maria. She wasn't sure of the significance, but she knew he needed all the information about the family that he could get. If he'd decided Lorenzo wasn't the killer—and he must have if he'd let Lorenzo go—then who else was left?

"The baby should sleep for a while," Sarah said when she was ready to leave, "because of the paregoric."

"But I'll wake him if he sleeps too long, like you said," she promised earnestly.

Sarah patted her shoulder. "I know you'll take good care of him, Maria. Have you decided on a name for him yet?" she asked in an effort to be more positive.

Maria smiled, but it wasn't a happy smile. "Yes," she said. "I am going to name him Joseph."

"Joseph," Sarah echoed uncertainly. "After . . . after Jesus' father," she tried.

"The Virgin Mother's husband," Maria corrected her. "No, that is not why."

Maria was still smiling, her face twisted into a expression that made Sarah's skin crawl. She'd seen that smile on her face before, but when? Then she remembered. It was the last time they'd been talking about a name for the baby. What had she said then? Sarah couldn't remember.

"After your husband then?" Sarah guessed.

"Yes, but not Giuseppe. The baby is American. He needs an American name."

Sarah thought Maria was asking for trouble. "Will Mrs. Ruocco let you name the baby after Joe?"

"She has nothing to say about it. He is my baby."

Sarah was sure Mrs. Ruocco would have plenty to say about it, but she decided not to mention that to Maria. In fact, she decided not to say anything else of importance to Maria at all. She looked so odd, and her eyes suddenly seemed over-bright. Just like they had before, the last time she'd been asking about the baby's name. What *had* Maria said then? Something about the baby's father.

That she should name the baby after his father!

Sarah's blood seemed to stop in her veins. But Joe couldn't be the baby's father, could he?

"Mrs. Brandt, why are you looking at me like that?" Maria asked, although she didn't seem too concerned.

If Joe was the baby's father, how would Maria know? Maybe Nainsi had told her, or maybe Joe had confessed. It didn't really matter, but that's why she was going to name the baby after him, as some sort of revenge. "I just . . . I should be going now. I've probably over-stayed my welcome." She needed to tell Malloy about Joe right away.

"I'm going to have the priest baptize him," Maria was saying.

"I'm sure that will be very nice," Sarah said inanely, moving toward the doorway. If Joe was the baby's father, he had an excellent reason for wanting Nainsi dead. "I really should be going. You know what to do for the baby. Just follow my instructions."

"Do you think Joe should be his godfather?" Maria asked, following her.

Out in the hallway, Sarah tried to decide which route to take. If she went down the inside stairs, she might meet the other Ruoccos. The outside stairs would be quicker, and she could escape unnoticed.

"I'm sure it doesn't matter what I think," Sarah said, forcing a polite smile. "That's something the family will have to decide."

"No, *I* am the one to decide, Mrs. Brandt," Maria said in a tone Sarah had never heard her use before. "No one will tell me what to do with my baby."

Sarah looked at her in surprise. Her dark eyes fairly glittered, and Sarah realized she'd been right to be worried about her. She looked as if the bonds holding her tethered to reality were quickly fraying. "Of course not," Sarah assured her quickly. "You were very generous to insist on keeping him, and you have every right to make these decisions."

"No one will tell me what to do with my baby," Maria repeated meaningfully. "Not even you."

Now Sarah began to feel alarm. If Maria decided to ignore her instructions . . . "I'm only trying to help you,

Maria, but if you don't trust my advice, please consult another nurse or a doctor. I won't be offended."

"I won't give him to another woman," she said. "I'm his mother now."

For a moment, Sarah didn't know what she was talking about, and then she recalled Maria's objection to finding a wet nurse. "I never meant you should give him to another woman," Sarah assured her. "I was just—" She caught herself. Maria wasn't thinking rationally, so reasoning with her was a waste of time. "I know you'll do what's best for him," she said instead. "I must go now."

Sarah chose the outside stairs. She had to find Malloy and figure out what to do before Maria had a complete breakdown. Maria followed her, seeing her out like a good hostess. Ordinarily, Sarah would have told her to send for her if she needed anything, but she didn't think Maria would appreciate such an offer.

Sarah opened the door and looked over her shoulder at Maria. "Good-bye," she said and quickly stepped into the stairwell. Only when she'd taken the first step did Maria's expression register: pure, molten hatred.

Shocked, Sarah turned back just in time to see Maria lunging toward her. Sarah threw herself against the wall and out of the way just as Maria's body would have slammed into hers. Someone screamed as Maria's momentum carried her headlong down the steps.

Instinctively, Sarah reached out to catch her, but she was too late. Maria's body tumbled and twisted and struck the first landing with a sickening thud. The landing slowed her impetus, and Maria's body slid down only a few more steps and stopped.

Somewhere, Sarah's mind realized that Maria had tried to

kill her, but she would deal with that later. Now, she hurried down to the landing to see if she could help. As if from a great distance, she heard people shouting, and as she reached Maria's crumpled form, someone started running up the stairs from below.

LEAVING JOE ALONE, FRANK TOOK GINO INTO THE ROOM where they'd questioned Lorenzo earlier.

"He's gotta be lying," Gino said. "He was Nainsi's lover, and the girl was going to tell his mother the baby was his so Mrs. Ruocco wouldn't throw her out."

"He does have a good reason for wanting her dead, but why would he make up a story about sleeping in Lorenzo's room?"

"Because he knows his brother will lie for him."

"He wife would lie for him, too," Frank pointed out. "In fact, she already did. She told us he was with her all night and couldn't have killed Nainsi. Why would he tell us a different story?"

Gino frowned as he concentrated on getting it right. "I don't know. It doesn't make sense. He only needs one alibi."

"That's right. He only needs one, and if he didn't kill Nainsi, then one of the stories is true," Frank informed him. "We need to figure out which one."

"How can we?"

"It's not hard. Which story did we hear first?"

"The one Maria told us."

"And what does her story prove?"

Gino thought about it for a minute. "That Nainsi was alive when Antonio and Joe came home from Ugo's place. That Joe was nearby, close enough to slip over and smother her if he wanted to."

"Maria said he never got up the rest of the night, though," Frank reminded him.

"If she was asleep, how could she be sure?" Gino asked reasonably. He was starting to catch on.

"Right, so she could be lying about that part, at least. Now, if Joe's telling the truth, what does that prove?"

"That he wasn't even near Nainsi from the time they left for Ugo's until after she was killed."

"But why didn't he just tell us Nainsi was alive when he came home, and he was in bed with his wife all night, if that's the truth?"

"Because . . ." Gino's face brightened with understanding. "Because it's *not* the truth. He told us what he really did that night."

"Then why did Maria lie?"

He thought for another minute. "To protect her husband."

Frank shook his head. "Donatelli, people sometimes lie to protect other people, but most of the time they lie to protect themselves."

LORENZO CAME RACING UP THE STEPS, TAKING THEM two and three at a time, until he reached Maria's crumpled body.

"What happened?" he demanded of Sarah.

"She fell," Sarah said quite truthfully. "I tried to catch her, but . . ."

He wasn't listening. "Maria, can you hear me?"

Antonio and Mrs. Ruocco were close behind him, both yelling questions.

"Maria fell down the stairs," Lorenzo said, his voice both angry and anguished.

Maria groaned.

"Maria, can you hear me?" he asked again, taking her hand.

"Get her inside," Mrs. Ruocco cried.

"Be careful," Sarah warned. "She might have broken bones."

"Antonio, go get doctor," Mrs. Ruocco said, sending the boy racing back down the stairs.

Lorenzo kept trying to get Maria to respond, and finally her eyes fluttered open. "What . . . ?"

"You fell down the stairs," Lorenzo said. "Where are you hurt?"

"Everywhere," she murmured.

Sarah descended the few remaining stairs to the landing. "Let me check her over before you move her." She knelt, and Maria's dazed eyes focused on her. Sarah saw a flicker of fear. "It's all right," Sarah said reassuringly. "Let me know if anything hurts."

Quickly, she felt Maria's limbs and discovered a badly wrenched knee and an apparently broken arm. Lorenzo lifted her as gently as he could, carried her into Mrs. Ruocco's bedroom on the second floor and laid her on the bed. She was moaning softly and cradling her broken arm. Was Sarah the only one who saw the adoration shining naked in Lorenzo's eyes as he gazed down at her?

"What you do on steps?" Mrs. Ruocco asked, oblivious of her son's devotion to his brother's wife. "You never look, you only hurry, hurry!"

"Is she all right?" Valentina asked from the bedroom doorway.

No one answered her. Lorenzo just stared at Maria helplessly while Mrs. Ruocco continued to berate her for being so careless as to nearly kill herself.

"Valentina, would you get a nightdress for Maria and bring it down?" Sarah asked.

For once the girl obeyed without complaint, probably grateful for something to take her away. Sarah began removing Maria's shoes.

"Lorenzo, would you step out?" Sarah asked. "We need to get her undressed so the doctor can examine her."

"Will she be all right?" he asked, his desperation painful to behold. He'd apparently forgotten his animosity toward Sarah.

"We won't know for certain until she's been examined," Sarah said, taking him by the arm and directing him to the door.

"She pushed me."

Everyone looked toward where Maria lay on the bed. She was staring at Sarah with the same loathing as when she'd lunged for her on the stairs.

"She pushed me down the stairs," Maria said deliberately, pointing at Sarah with her good arm.

Lorenzo and Mrs. Ruocco turned to Sarah in horror, but before anyone could speak, they heard someone calling from downstairs. To Sarah's great relief, it was Frank Malloy.

"SHE TRIED TO *KILL* YOU?" MALLOY FAIRLY SHOUTED AT Sarah. They were sitting at one of the tables down in the empty restaurant. Sarah had told him everything that had happened from the time she arrived at the Ruocco house earlier in the day until he'd come storming in a little while before.

"She's not in her right mind, Malloy," Sarah pointed out.

"Crazy or not, you'd be just as dead!" he pointed out right back.

"Well, she didn't kill me, so there's no sense in getting upset now."

Malloy looked like he might explode, but he managed to swallow down his frustration. After a few moments of struggle, he asked, "Is she going to live?"

"She didn't seem to be too seriously hurt, but she might have internal injuries that don't show up right away."

The doctor had arrived and was with her.

"Why would she try to kill *you*, though?" Malloy asked.

"I've been trying to figure that out, too."

"Did you say anything about knowing who killed Nainsi?"

"No! When she as much as told me Joe was the baby's father, I was pretty sure he must have done it, but I didn't say a word. I was only trying to get away from her so I could tell you what I'd found out."

Malloy rubbed both hands over his face. "All right, let's go see what she has to say for herself."

"The doctor probably isn't finished with her yet."

"Good, then she won't be expecting us."

DONATELLI WAS IN THE SECOND FLOOR PARLOR WITH Lorenzo, Antonio, and Valentina. They all looked up when Frank and Sarah appeared.

"The doc is still in there," Donatelli reported.

"Maria said she pushed her down the stairs," Lorenzo informed Frank angrily, pointing at Sarah.

"Use your head, Lorenzo," Frank said irritably. "Why would Mrs. Brandt do a thing like that?"

"Why would Maria say it if it wasn't true?" Lorenzo challenged right back.

"I don't know. Let's go find out," Frank suggested and went across the hall to the closed bedroom door.

"You can't go in there!" Lorenzo protested, but Frank pushed the door open without knocking.

Mrs. Ruocco cried out in protest, and the doctor looked up in surprise. He was tying off the wrapping around Maria's broken arm. Maria glared at him but didn't say a word.

"What you come in here for?" Mrs. Ruocco demanded. "Get out!"

"I need to ask Maria a few questions first," Frank said.

"She is hurt!" Mrs. Ruocco reminded him.

"How bad?" Frank asked the doctor.

"Broken arm and lots of bumps and bruises. She'll recover."

"Good, then I guess she can talk," Frank replied coldly, stepping into the room. Sarah came in behind him, and the others crowded around the open doorway.

"I think I'll step out and leave you to your business," the doctor said, hastily gathering up his medical supplies and stuffing them into his bag. "I'll be downstairs if you need me." He worked his way through the gathering in the doorway and disappeared.

When he was gone, Frank said, "Maria, you said Mrs. Brandt pushed you down the stairs. Can you tell me why she did a thing like that?"

Fear flickered in Maria's eyes as she stared at Sarah. "She . . . she said she would take the baby away."

Mrs. Ruocco made an outraged noise, but Sarah said, "You know that isn't true, Maria. I suggested you find a nurse for him, that's all."

"If she wanted to take the baby away from you," Frank said, "why would that make her push you down the stairs?"

Maria looked around nervously, as if trying to find an ally. "I . . . I don't know. She just did."

"That's funny, because Mrs. Brandt says *you* tried to push *her,* but she managed to duck out of the way," Frank said. "If you were afraid she wanted to take the baby away, that would give *you* a good reason to want to hurt *her,* not the other way around."

"She hates me," Maria tried. "She doesn't want me to have the baby."

"And you'd do anything to keep him, wouldn't you?" Frank asked. "You'd even kill someone."

"No!" Maria insisted, and Mrs. Ruocco gasped in shock.

"What are you saying?" Lorenzo cried from the hallway outside. "Leave her alone!" He started into the room, but Donatelli grabbed him and held him back.

"Do you want to know how much Maria wanted to keep the baby?" Frank asked of everyone present. "I'll tell you."

"Don't listen to him!" Maria begged. "He's lying!"

"It's too late, Maria," Frank said with a trace of sympathy. "Joe told us everything."

"No, he's lying. It isn't true!"

"What is not true?" Patrizia Ruocco demanded, her dark eyes narrowed in suspicion at her daughter-in-law.

"That Joe is the baby's real father," Frank said.

Maria cried out in anguish, and Sarah watched the blood drain from Mrs. Ruocco's face.

"That can't be true," Lorenzo insisted furiously. "Joe wouldn't do that!"

"He admitted it to me today," Frank said. "Nainsi didn't know he was married, and she came looking for him here at the restaurant. Maria saw her, didn't you, Maria?"

Maria didn't reply. Her face looked as if it were carved from stone.

"And when Maria found out, she wanted the baby for herself, so she made the plan to trick Antonio into believing the baby was his."

Antonio made a strangled sound in his throat, and Lorenzo roared in outrage.

"Liar!" Maria cried.

"You can ask Joe," Frank told Mrs. Ruocco, although he could see she was beginning to believe him. The story simply explained too much. "He's the one who told me all of this. It was a good plan, too, but then you figured out Antonio couldn't be the baby's father, Mrs. Ruocco. You were going to put Nainsi and her baby out. To keep that from happening, Nainsi would've told you the baby was Joe's. Maria couldn't let you find out the truth, couldn't let you know what kind of a man Joe was, and what kind of a woman *she* was, what the two of them had done to Antonio. So she killed Nainsi."

"Maria?" Mrs. Ruocco pleaded, wanting her to deny it but knowing it was true.

"I didn't! Mama, don't listen to them!"

"And then, when Mrs. O'Hara wanted the baby, Maria had to kill her, too. How did you manage to sneak out of the house without anybody seeing you, Maria?"

Maria pressed her lips into a bloodless line, but Valentina said, "I know!"

Everyone turned to where she stood in the hallway behind her brothers.

"I saw her! We were all downstairs for lunch, even though hardly anybody came that day. I went upstairs because Mama was yelling at me, and I got tired of it. When I got upstairs, I heard the baby crying. I called for Maria, but she didn't answer, so I started looking for her because I didn't know how to make him stop. Then she came in from the outside stairs. She said she'd been to the privy, but . . . she looked so strange and . . . I didn't think of it before, but she had her hat on! Why would she wear her hat out to the privy?"

Everyone turned back to Maria, who hissed something at Valentina in Italian.

"I don't suppose you noticed if she had blood on her," Frank said quite casually. "There wouldn't have been much, though, because she cut Mrs. O'Hara's throat from behind. Did you use one of the knives from the kitchen downstairs, Maria?"

Mrs. Ruocco caught her breath, and Frank looked at her sharply.

"You know something," he said. "What is it?"

She wasn't looking at Frank, though. She was looking at Maria with horror in her eyes. "I could not find knife at lunch," she said.

"That's right!" Valentina remembered with satisfaction. "It was your favorite knife, the one you keep really sharp. That's why you were yelling at me. You said I lost it, and I told you I didn't do it!"

Her mother didn't spare her a glance. She kept staring at Maria. "I look and look. Then I find at dinner. You kill with my knife, then put it back in my kitchen!"

Maria's face had gone white, and two red spots burned in her cheeks. Her eyes were wild as she looked around frantically for someone to help her. "I didn't have any other choice! Nainsi wouldn't have been a good mother! If she didn't marry Antonio, she would've abandoned the baby. Lorenzo, tell them! I had to protect the baby!"

But Lorenzo had nothing to say. Like everyone else, he was staring at her in horror. Donatelli wasn't even restraining him anymore.

"Mama!" she cried desperately. "He's your grandson! I couldn't let that woman have him!"

"What woman?" Mrs. Ruocco asked bitterly. "Nainsi? Mrs. O'Hara?"

Maria clutched at the bedcovers with her good hand. "It was all Joe's fault! He was unfaithful to me. He got that girl in trouble! He arranged for Antonio to meet her!"

"Giuseppe kill no one," Mrs. Ruocco reminded her. She turned to Frank. "You will take her away?"

"No!" Maria screamed. "You can't let them put me in jail!!"

"If the doctor says she can be moved, I'll send for a matron and an ambulance right away," Frank told the woman.

"Mama, don't do this!" Maria begged. "I was only trying to protect the family!"

Mrs. Ruocco refused to even look at her. "I not you Mama," she said and walked out of the room. Valentina and Antonio followed her, but Lorenzo stood there, still staring at Maria in disbelief.

"What will happen to her?" he asked Frank.

Frank didn't want to mention Old Sparky, so he simply said, "That'll be up to the judge."

"What about the baby?" Lorenzo asked.

"The baby is mine!" Maria cried furiously. "Bring him to me! I have to take him with me!"

"You can't take the baby to jail," Sarah said with more kindness than Frank would have shown.

Maria gave a primal howl and started sobbing hysterically.

"Officer Donatelli, would you go and ask the doctor to come back up?" Sarah asked.

No sooner had he gone than Sarah heard the baby wailing upstairs. "Lorenzo, Joe is the baby's father, so he's really your nephew. Why don't you go get him and take him to your mother, where he belongs?"

Lorenzo took one last look at the woman he'd come to love, the woman who had betrayed them all. Then he turned away.

15

Roosevelt looked very pleased with himself when Frank entered his office.

"Good work, Detective Sergeant," he said. "Solving the Italian murder, I mean. Sad situation, of course, but at least no one can say we tried to hide the truth to protect anyone."

"No, sir," Frank agreed grimly.

"Even Tammany Hall seems satisfied. Of course, they're always satisfied if they come out looking as if they really tried to help the working man—whether they really did or not."

Frank had no reply to that, so he offered none. He wasn't sure why Roosevelt had summoned him. Surely, he wanted more than to tell him he was pleased with the outcome of the Ruocco case. As he waited uneasily, he realized Roosevelt seemed a bit uneasy, too.

Finally, the Commissioner cleared his throat. "I . . . uh . . . I had a letter from Mrs. Brandt."

Frank shouldn't have been surprised. They'd agreed she would contact Roosevelt. "Did you?"

"Yes, and I understand from her that you have uncovered some new information about her husband's death." He made it sound like an accusation.

Frank resisted the instinctive urge to be defensive. "Yes, I found a witness and . . . and some other interesting facts that weren't known when Dr. Brandt was killed."

"After all this time?" Roosevelt asked skeptically. "It's been three years, hasn't it?"

"Almost four," Frank admitted.

Roosevelt peered at him intently through his spectacles "And this witness suddenly came forward after *almost four years?*"

"He heard I was asking around about the case," Frank lied. He'd actually hunted the boy down after hearing about him from an informant. He wasn't even sure if he could find him again.

"What about this new information? Where did it come from?"

Frank wanted to grind his teeth, but he forced himself to admit the truth. "Felix Decker gave it to me."

"Are you saying he had information about who killed Dr. Brandt and he didn't use it at the time to find the killer?" Roosevelt demanded in outrage.

"He didn't think it had anything to do with Dr. Brandt's murder. The officers who investigated believed Dr. Brandt had been killed by someone trying to rob him."

"But you don't?" Another accusation.

"Dr. Brandt wasn't robbed," Frank said as respectfully as

he could manage. "And the witness heard him arguing with his killer. When I heard that and saw what Mr. Decker had found out, I started thinking Dr. Brandt had been killed by somebody he knew and not by some petty criminal."

Roosevelt removed his spectacles and rubbed his eyes before carefully replacing the glasses. "Mrs. Brandt has asked me to reopen the case and assign you to work it," he said without expression.

That was what Frank had asked her to do, of course. He'd been hoping for it, in fact. He couldn't tell how Roosevelt felt about it, though, so he waited.

"I don't have many men on the force that I can rely on, Detective Sergeant. You've proven yourself to be one of those few. I can't spare you to spend all your time on a four-year-old case," he said.

"I understand, sir," Frank said, not bothering to hide his disappointment. He should have expected this.

"But," Roosevelt added thoughtfully, "Mrs. Brandt is an old friend, and she deserves to know the truth, if that's possible."

Frank waited again, holding his breath.

"I'll give you permission to investigate it so long as it doesn't interfere with your regular work. I'll inform Chief Conlin," he added, naming the chief of police.

"Thank you, sir," Frank said. He should have felt gratitude, but he didn't really know whether to be grateful or not. What if he never found Tom Brandt's killer? And what if he found out things about Brandt that would hurt Sarah?

"I think you're on a fool's errand, Mr. Malloy," Roosevelt warned, "but I wish you luck, for Mrs. Brandt's sake."

Frank knew he'd need much more than luck.

* * *

Sᴀʀᴀʜ ᴡᴀs ʟᴀᴛᴇ. Sʜᴇ'ᴅ ʜᴀᴅ ᴀ ᴅᴇʟɪᴠᴇʀʏ ᴀɴᴅ ʜᴀᴅɴ'ᴛ gotten Malloy's message until she had gotten home. He'd sent a note, asking her to meet him at a coffee shop near her house.

Why hadn't he simply come to her front door as he usually did?

Her concern had made her even more flustered about being late. What if he hadn't waited for her? How would she find him? And how long would she have to wait to find out what was so sensitive that he didn't want to discuss it at her house?

When she entered the shop, she didn't see him at first. He was back in a corner, reading a newspaper. She drew a calming breath and let it out in a sigh of relief. As if he'd sensed her presence, he looked up and caught her eye, but he didn't smile.

With growing apprehension, she hurried over to his table. He laid the paper aside, rose, and held her chair for her.

"What's wrong?" she demanded as he seated her.

"Nothing's wrong," he assured her and signaled the waitress to bring her some coffee before sitting back down himself.

"Then why did you want to meet me here instead of coming to my house?"

"Can't I invite you out for coffee without you suspecting something's wrong?" he asked with a smile that looked forced.

"Apparently not," she replied tartly as the waitress brought her coffee.

When the girl was gone, she said, "Have you heard anything about what's going to happen to Maria?"

He seemed relieved by the question. "She confessed, and she's a female, so they probably won't execute her."

"I went to see her," Sarah admitted.

He frowned in disapproval. "After she tried to kill you?"

"I was curious," Sarah said, defending herself. "I needed to know why she did it."

"Why she tried to kill you, or why she killed Nainsi?"

"Neither. I wanted to know why she came up with the plan to have Nainsi marry Antonio in the first place. Most women wouldn't want anything to do with their husband's mistress and bastard child."

"You said yourself she's not in her right mind," Malloy reminded her.

"She's not now," Sarah reported sadly. "She has a bundle of rags that she carries around the jail with her. She thinks it's her baby, Joseph."

Malloy winced. "Then I don't suppose you got any answers from her."

"Oh yes, I did. She was only too happy to explain her reasoning to me. She feels justified in everything she did, and she wants the family to understand her reasons. They certainly don't want to hear about it, especially from me, but she didn't seem to realize that."

"So did she want the baby for herself, and plan to kill Nainsi all along?"

"No, not at all. She did want the baby, of course. She thought Joe owed it to her because he refused to fulfill his husbandly obligations to her. That's why she figured out the plan to get the baby into the family by marrying Nainsi off to Antonio. She apparently thought Nainsi would get bored with being a wife and mother and run away, though. Maria might even have planned to encourage her to do just that, but we'll never know."

"And that would leave the baby for Maria to raise."

"Exactly. She'd have Joe's baby, which is all she ever wanted. And Antonio wouldn't be stuck with a wife he didn't want anymore. I gather he might have even been able to get an annulment if she abandoned him, but I'm not sure Maria cared about Antonio's future. She'd have the baby, and that's all she cared about. She thought it was a perfect plan."

"Have you heard how the Ruoccos are getting along with the baby?" he asked.

"Not firsthand, of course," Sarah admitted. "I did hear that they got a woman in the neighborhood to nurse him, though, so he should be fine."

"If they can keep Valentina away from him," he remarked slyly.

That seemed to end their conversation about the Ruocco family. Sarah sipped her coffee to extend the silence, giving Malloy a chance to say what he'd called her here to say. When he didn't, she said, "Why did you really ask me to meet you here, Malloy? And don't tell me any fairy tales this time."

He fiddled with his cup for a few seconds, as if looking for an answer there. Finally, he said, "Roosevelt gave me permission to work on your husband's case."

This wasn't what she'd been expecting. "I wrote to him . . ."

"I know. He told me. I have to keep doing my regular work, of course, but he said he'd clear it with Conlin to let me work on it when I can find time."

"Oh." It wasn't what she'd wanted, not exactly, but it

was more than they'd had before. "What are you going to do next?"

"I'll go back to the families again, and this time I'll have the authority I need to question them." They had discovered that Tom was treating some mentally ill women just before he was murdered, and Malloy believed that had given someone a motive to kill him.

"I told you before that I'll help in any way I can," she reminded him.

He managed a smile at that. "Have I ever mentioned how much I hate having you involved in my investigations?"

"I'm serious, Malloy. You know I can go places that you can't and talk to people who won't speak with you. I can even ask my family for help if necessary."

Did he flinch slightly? She was sure he had. He was probably remembering her mother's involvement in one of their earlier investigations. "Do you think your family would be interested in helping solve your husband's murder?" he asked.

She'd never thought of that. "It doesn't matter if they are or not. They'll help me if I ask them," she said with certainty.

That seemed to satisfy him. "I won't need them, though," he said. "And I won't need your help, either. It's too dangerous for you to be involved."

"But, I—"

"No," he said sharply. "How many times have you gotten yourself into danger when you were just an innocent bystander? Just a few days ago, Maria Ruocco tried to push you down a flight of stairs! You're too close to this case, so you're not going to help. No arguments."

"All right," she said, although she really didn't mean it.

He fiddled with his cup again. He wasn't telling her

everything. He was trying to protect her, but she didn't need protection. She needed the truth.

"What is it, Malloy? What aren't you saying?"

He sighed and looked up again, meeting her eyes with a directness that made her want to turn way. "These women who were your husband's patients might not have anything to do with your husband's death," he said.

She nodded her understanding.

"And even if one of them does, I might not be able to prove it. I'll do everything I can, legal or not, but it might not be enough."

"I know," she said, although she hadn't let herself admit it before.

"And if I figure out who did it, but I can't prove it, you'll have to live with it. Can you do that?"

She didn't want to hear this, and she certainly didn't want to think about it. Knowing someone had murdered Tom and had been walking around free all this time was maddening. Knowing who it was and that he would still never be punished would be so much worse. "I don't know if I could live with it or not," she admitted.

He nodded once. "That's what I thought."

She stared at him uncertainly. "Does that mean you aren't going to try?"

"No," he said. "It just means that if I find him, but I can't prove it, he'll still pay."

"Malloy!" she said in alarm. "You can't . . . You can't do something like that, not after the way you've worked this past year to build a new reputation for yourself. Everyone comes to you now when they have a difficult case or one that requires discretion. They know you're trustworthy and honorable. You're just the kind of man Theodore wants on his modern police force."

The smile he gave her was full of bitterness and regret. "It won't always be Theodore's police force. He's an ambitious man. He won't be satisfied here long, and when he's gone, his reforms will go with him."

"But things could never go back to the way they were before," she argued.

"No, they'll be worse. A lot worse. And so will I."

"No, you won't!" she protested, reaching out and laying her hand on his. "You were never that kind of man before, and you never will be."

He looked down at where her hand rested on his and gently pulled his free. "I'm the kind of man I have to be, Sarah. I have Brian to think about, and if it's a choice between my honor and my son, I'll choose my son. I have to."

He reached in his pocket and pulled out some money, laying it on the table for their coffee.

"I'll let you know if I find out anything about your husband's murder," he said, rising from the table. "Good-bye, Sarah."

As she watched him walk away, his image blurred. Only then did she realize she was crying. She dashed the tears away angrily. How dare he try to make her think less of him? How dare he pretend to be something he wasn't?

And how dare he think that any of that would matter to her? She would, she supposed, simply have to convince him otherwise.

Author's Note

WRITING THIS BOOK BROUGHT BACK A LOT OF WONDERFUL memories of visits with my Italian great-aunts, aunts, uncles, and hordes of cousins. I think I was channeling them all to help me create Patrizia Ruocco and her family. I hope you enjoyed this installment in the Gaslight series. Please drop me a line and I will be happy to put you on my e-mail list. I'll keep you posted on places where I'll be autographing, and I'll also send reminders when I have a new book coming out. You may contact me through my Web site, victoriathompson.com.